Credits

This book is not sponsored, endorsed by, or otherwise affiliated with any companies or the products featured in this book. This is not an official publication.

- Editor in Chief – Bill Gill, AKA "Pojo"
- Creative Director & Graphic Design – Jon Anderson
- Publisher – Bob Baker
- Contributors – Scott Gerhardt, Vijay Seixas, DeQuan Watson, Nick Moore, Israel Quiroz, Chris Schroeder, Augustine Choy, Phil McKinney, Christine M. Joseph, and Adam Forristal.

Can't Get Enough Yu-Gi-Oh? Neither Can We!

Here are some facts about the Yu-Gi-Phenomenon in Japan:

- Yu-Gi-Oh was Created by Kazuki Takahashi in 1996
- It has generated more than $2 billion in sales
- More than seven million Yu-Gi-Oh video games have been sold
- 23 million comic books sold
- And three billion trading cards have been purchased.

And now its impact is being felt around the rest of the world. In the U.S.: the anime (cartoon) is #1, The Video Games are selling phenomenally, and the Collectible Cards are the rage!

Now it's our turn to deliver more info that the fans want!

If you are like me ... you want to know how it all started. Yu-Gi-Oh started as a manga (a comic book). But the comic has not been released in the U.S. (Probably because it is too violent for American kids, and might ruin its popular wholesome image).

Did you know that in the U.S. that the first series of cartoons from Japan have not aired ... and may not be shown at all? (Probably for the exact same reason as stated above).

If you want to know what happened during Season 1 from Japan ... we've got you covered. If you want to know what happened in those comic books ... we've got you covered. You want Bios? You've got 'em'

We've also assembled a great staff to tackle the extremely popular collectible card game too. You'll find Top 10 Lists from the current cards on the market. We've got a handful of Killer Decks for you. And if you are short on cash, we teach you how to make some cheap decks too.

The Yu-Gi-Oh can be confusing at times, so we've got answers to a lot of questions to help you out. We've also got a complete list of cards to help you build decks too!

Remember, if you want to stay current on events in the Yu-Gi-Oh world, hit www.pojo.com. Enough of my rapping ... Dive in and enjoy!

Pojo

Table of Contents

Contents

LET'S GET INTO THIS!

Character BIO's

— By Mika Matsumoto

The Yu-Gi-Oh series is filled with heroes & villains. If you are new to the characters, let us introduce them to you. If you watch the anime (cartoon) in the United States, then you are missing some storylines from the anime & manga (comic book). These biographies should bring you up to speed.

Character names are in English, with the original Japanese names in parentheses. If only one name is provided, that character only has a Japanese name, or the English & Japanese names are the same.

Yugi Mutou

Yugi is a freshman at Domino High School and after a rough start became friends with Joey and Tristen. He lives with his grandfather Solomon, playing all the games he has in the store he runs. Solomon gave him a priceless Egyptian game thinking that Yugi would never be able to solve it, but once solved, Yugi felt the magic of the "Millennium Puzzle" enter him and since then he has never been the same. He transforms into the invincible Game King, the spirit of a 5000 year old Egyptian pharaoh who through his games is able to change a person's destiny. A symbol of an eye appears on his forehead briefly and it glows a bright gold color. The Game King baits his opponents, sometimes playing on their own rules, but he beats them then forces them to suffer the torment of their loss.

Yugi, of course, can't beat them all. He has a rival named Seto Kaiba, who is a master of the game they play often, Duel Monsters (Magic and Wizards in Japan). But when Yugi beats Kaiba with the card he lusted after the most, "Blue Eyes White Dragon", Kaiba sets himself on a course to destroy Yugi. He also encounters the Egyptian Sha-di, who is a "messenger of justice" for all of the Egyptian graves that were pillaged by archaeologists.

Both sides of Yugi are able to speak with each other and collaborate on efforts such as defeating Maximillian Pegasus at Duelist Kingdom. Dark Yugi's secret lies in the fact that the puzzle is only one of seven millennium items that are needed to revive the power of the Pharaoh. There are several people in this quest to revive the power, but if the power falls into evil hands, it can destroy everything.

On a lighter note, Yugi is a very friendly person, sometimes too friendly. It is because of his loyalty and caring that saves his friends from troublesome situations. Yugi relies on his friends for their strength when he doesn't physically have it, just as his friends rely on him for strength of spirit.

Joey Wheeler
(Katsuya Jounouchi)

Joey is a freshman at Domino High School and is used to the reputation of always being in a bad situation, such as fighting too much. He changes a lot once he becomes friends with Yugi. A good guy at the core, Joey really cares about his friends and goes out of his way to help them. He usually takes matters into his own hands when he sees something he doesn't like. He has a soft spot for Yugi because he knows how vulnerable he can be, even though he tries to put up a good front. When he's not spending his time hanging with Yugi, he's usually with his long-time friend Tristen.

Sometimes he doesn't come to school, but don't go to his house! His father is quite a drunkard and he will throw a bottle of beer at you!

Joey seems older than his teenage years. His parents separated several years before, taking him away from his younger sister Serenity. She lives alone but has serious medical problems, which is the reason why he travels to Pegasus' Duelist Kingdom: to get money to pay for her operation.

His rival is also Seto Kaiba, but for very different reasons than Yugi. Joey's hot temper often gets him into trouble; his loss to Kaiba badly wounded his pride (that and the fact that Seto called him a "Loser" didn't sit too well either). He proves himself to be an excellent duelist once the Duelist Kingdom match ends, leaving him well prepared for the Battle City tournament Kaiba hosts.

Joey's constant goal is to prove himself as worthy a duelist to Dark Yugi, instead of having Yugi always bail him out of situations.

Tea Gardner
(Anzu Mazaki)

Tea is a freshman at Domino High School with a very upbeat and cool personality. Her most fervent dream is to travel to New York to study dance. In the meantime, she spends her time with her friends at school. Tea knows Yugi from back in grade school, so when she was saved by the

person she suspected to be Yugi, she was surprised. After the "Burger World" incident, she began to wonder about the other side of Yugi.

She can often be found with Yugi, and sometimes mistaken for Yugi's girlfriend. Yugi would like that, but perhaps Tea finds some safety in the fact they're just friends. Tea cares a LOT about her friends, and shows it on a regular basis.

At Duelist Kingdom, she meets Mai Valentine and although she rubbed Tea the wrong way at first, they became very good friends. She finally admits to liking of the Game King, but comes to the realization that both Yugi's are essentially the same and she has to accept them both for what they are.

Tristen (Hiroto Honda)

Tristen is a freshman at Domino High School and is Joey's closest friend. They've known each other for a LONG time. The two of them tease each other, make fun of each other, even beat each other up, but it's ALL out of love! Tristen and Yugi's relationship isn't as developed as Tea's and Joe's, but Tristen and Yugi do consider themselves good friends, and he would not hesitate to back Yugi up.

Solomon Mutou (Sugoroku Mutou)

Solomon is the owner of the Game Shop where Yugi lives and is an all-around expert gamer. He is Yugi's grandfather. Not much is known about Yugi's parents, but presumably he's raising Yugi. Solomon has his own mysticism. He's been to America before and has several friends there. He has connections to Egyptian artifacts, mostly games, and has friends in universities in Japan and abroad. Who knows where else Solomon has been, or what else he has gotten in his travels?

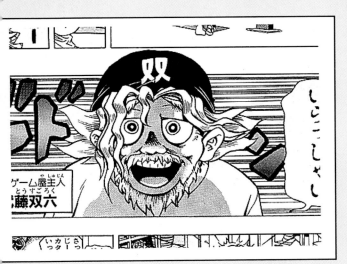

Solomon's a great player of "Duel Monsters" too. He has a special card, the "Blue Eyes White Dragon". It is claimed that it can only be used by the person whose heart it belongs to. Seto Kaiba tried to steal it from Yugi, was successful in his attempt, but in the end, the heart of the card was for Yugi's grandfather. Seto couldn't use it.

He cares a lot about Yugi, and perhaps that is why he gave him the "Millennium Puzzle ". He knew what secrets it held, and wanted Yugi to become stronger. But stronger comes at a consequence and price. .

Recent discoveries place Solomon at the site where the Egyptian games were once hidden away for centuries, trying to uncover the secrets of the Dark Game.

Ryo Bakura

Ryo is a freshman transfer student to Domino High School. Ryo is weak of body, just like Yugi. Ryo has a similar pendant to Yugi's, except it's called a "Millennium Ring."

The ring overpowered Ryo's will, taking over control of his body and mind. At first, his power took the group's spirits and turned them into little mannequins to be played on Ryo's favorite game, "Monster World". Yugi was able to defeat him (after going through a LOT of trouble because of it.) However, after the dark Ryo was defeated, they all quickly became friends. Since that time, he hasn't worn the ring.

He's considered bishonen (pretty boy), followed faithfully by all the cute girls in the school, but he's an aloof kind of guy and generally keeps to himself.

Ryo accompanies the duelist group to the Duelist Kingdom, discovering another aspect of his Millennium Ring. It is a "millennium item detector". The voice of the Ring reappears to Ryo as well, claiming that he will be with him forever. Without him realizing, the Ring takes possession of Ryo again, commanding him to do his will, which included killing Pegasus for his Millennium Eye and dueling against other contestants for their millennium items. His dark side is a collector and won't stop until he possesses all seven items to take control of its power.

After Ryo's match against Malik in a "dark vs. dark" match, Ryo loses horribly and suffers through Malik's fierce punishment. In the process, he loses possession of the Ring.

Sha-di

This Egyptian man is out for justice. He traveled from Egypt, showing up at a university exhibit of Egyptian collections. As a result, he encountered Yugi. He was surprised to see the Millennium Puzzle around the neck of Yugi as a pendant. Sha-di has this cool ability, using HIS own pendant, the ankh, to see into what he calls your "heart room", what your true self is. Most only have one room that defines who they are, what their desires are and so on. When looking into Yugi's, he discovered two rooms. Yugi's normal self, but another with the door closed, and the infamous "eye" on the front.

Sha-di is an enigmatic man and not much is known about him, but he did promise Yugi that he would return to challenge him once again. Sha-di is JUST as skilled as the Game King at playing. But Yugi is more resourceful than Sha-di is.

His relationship with Pegasus proved how deadly Sha-di

could be, by blackmailing him into using the Millennium Eye with a false promise of forever seeing his lady love. The search for the items will not be complete until Sha-di returns to challenge Yugi and in the process, revealing what fate has in store for everyone involved.

Sha-di also had a hand in Malik and Isis' discovery of their "pharaoh spirit". It was through him they began using the Rod and Torque.

Seto Kaiba

Seto is rich. Stinking filthy rich. He manages his own bank accounts, rides around in limos all the time and has an unlimited passion for "Duel Monsters". He's even arrogant enough to create the ULTIMATE gaming place, Kaiba Land! He can't live with the fact that Yugi beat him, but he realizes how Yugi changes when he starts playing. He also knows Yugi's pendant is the key. But even if you take away Yugi's pendant, he is STILL capable of transforming into the game master! His ultimate goal is to beat Yugi, using whatever means necessary.

Seto has a younger brother named Mokuba. He shares the same passion for gaming, and wants to see Yugi humiliated for messing with his brother.

Since both of their parents died, and his brother and Seto

were sent to an orphanage, Seto promised Mokuba to take care of him no matter what. Seto challenged the President of Kaiba Corporation, Gozaburo Kaiba, to a game of chess when he came to the orphanage to adopt. As a reward of the game, Seto and Mokuba became his adopted sons. However, Gozaburo treated Seto cruelly to train his successor. That's why he's so cold-hearted.

Seto is a bold guy! He took over Kaiba Corporation and

kicked his OWN father out of office! He also has a group of guys working for the Corporation called the "Big Five". They're big, bad and ugly. . .and under Seto's control. Or at least, so he thought. . .

The "Big Five" betrayed Seto to Pegasus. The original idea was that Pegasus would get rid of Seto, take over the patents for the different "battle gaming systems" that he created, and Pegasus would take over as an independent partner.

Seto's latest venture takes over all of Domino City for what he calls "Battle City", a Magic & Wizards fight anywhere in the city. The ante, however, is VERY HIGH. . . .only RARE cards accepted. He gets to fight against Yugi in an all-out battle of the god cards but the result is a surprise even to him. He also has flashes of another life during the duel and of his true connection to Yugi.

Mokuba Kaiba

Mokuba is Seto's little brother. He shares the same thing for gaming as his brother, but not to the full extent yet. In the beginning, he's an evil little boy, out to beat everyone. Mokuba is NO match for Yugi though. Not even close!

Mokuba and Seto's mother died giving birth to Mokuba. Their father died in an accident when Mokuba was 3. They were left in an orphanage by relatives when Seto was 10, Mokuba 5. Being the caring brother, he promised Mokuba that he'd take care of them both, and not to trust anyone else.

He loves his brother a lot and was extremely saddened when he lost to Yugi in the Death-T tourney. The two of them were once close, but the drive for power and gaming drove them apart.

After the Death-T tournament, his brother Seto lapsed into this comatose-like state. Mokuba, determined to get his brother back, set out to the Duelist Kingdom to defeat Pegasus. Upon meeting Yugi and crew, Kaiba's old self was revived. However, Mokuba's spirit was taken and stored in a M&W card by Pegasus.

Since Seto's restoration, Mokuba faithfully follows his brother in whatever he does.

Serenity Wheeler (Shizuka Jounouchi)

Serenity is Joey's pretty younger sister. According to Joey, Serenity moved far away from him after their parents got divorced. However, Serenity has a sickness with her eye, and requires a very modern and expensive operation to save her eyesight. Without it, she will go blind.

The video letter Serenity left basically said that she hadn't seen him in so long that she wanted to send a videotape so that he would remember her face. It ALSO said that she wanted to see her older brother's face one last time. . .

After Joey gets out of Duelist Kingdom and gets the money for the operation, Serenity makes it through just fine and is able to see once again. Once Joe is dueling again, it takes his sister's spiritual strength to help him refocus. She is her brother's stability and without her, Joe would probably be lost.

Maximillian Pegasus (Pegasus J. Crawford)

Pegasus is the main character in the "Duelist Kingdom" arc of the Yu-Gi-Oh! plot. As his name shows, he's an American. He's also a famous designer and illustrator of Duel Monsters cards. The long blond hair Pegasus has covers his left eye, his secret Millennium item, the "Millennium Eye". It has the ability to scan a person's mind, which can come in handy when playing a game such as M&W.

Pegasus has a troubled history. His father was a VERY successful businessman, so he had the life of luxury. After the loss of his long-time friend and love, Cynthia, all of that

was worth nothing. He then found himself in Egypt doing artwork, when he encountered the young and ever elusive Sha-di. Sha-di took the liberty of seeing into Pegasus and realized he was living his life in the past for this girl. He played on Pegasus' emotions and told him he would be able to see his beloved Cynthia again if he did what he was told. Believing in the impossible, Pegasus did it, and in the process, had his right eye removed and replaced with the Sen-nen Item, the Millennium Eye.

Ultimately, Pegasus paid with his life, at the hands of the evil side of Ryo Bakura.

Mai Valentine (Mai Kujaku)

First appearing in Battle #64, she becomes an unofficial addition the crew. Mai is commonly known for her use of feminine wiles to get her way, and her continuous use of her most favorite card in M&W battle: Harpy Lady.

Mai is a confident duelist, but is shaken by Joey and his tactics when the two actually battle. She gets seriously humbled when Yugi fights on behalf of Mai to get back her starchips. It's at that moment Mai understands how true Yugi and true Joey were.

Her true purpose for being in Duelist Kingdom is still unknown.

She's taking part in the Battle City tournament, putting her prized Harpies on the block. Although she is a very talented duelist, much of the battling has the undertone of the millennium items. Mai is left at the mercy of Malik's Rod when the time for her to fight him comes.

'Bandit' Keith Howard

Bandit Keith first appears during the Duelist Kingdom, fighting to defeat Pegasus. He's an American, always wearing an American flag bandanna around his head. He has a serious love for guns and anything related to them. During the duel, he uses three other duelists to fight his battles for him, then steals their star ante from them. He and Joey rub each other the wrong way and the two are set against each other from that moment. They play against each other in the final duel in Pegasus' castle, but he

loses to Joey. He had an agreement with Pegasus to be paid serious cash upon the end of the duel, but Pegasus goes back on this promise and punishes Keith for his loss. Keith doesn't appear in the Battle City saga.

Maco (Ryouta Kajiki)

Maco loves fish! He befriends Joey and the crew in Duelist Kingdom. He uses mostly water and fish creatures in his deck while playing Magic & Wizards. His father was a fisherman who met a horrible fate at sea, but he wants to follow in his footsteps and one day have a boat of his own where he can sail the seas to find him. He has a personality very similar to Joey's, which is why the two get

Manga/Anime - Character BIO's

along so well. Though Maco doesn't advance at Duelist Kingdom, he reappears for the Battle City tournament, once again fighting against Joey. The two have a mutual respect for their playing styles, never giving an inch just because they're friends.

They duel against each other, rare ante at stake, but when Maco loses to Joey, he gives him the card that reminds him of his father: The Legendary Fisherman. Maco knows that Joe will use the card keeping his father in mind.

Rex Raptor (Dinosaur Ryuzaki)

Rex is 15 years old, already a seasoned tournament player at Magic & Wizards. Known for his use of reptile cards, Rex is an intense duelist and is often at all major dueling events. Although neither Yugi or Joey play against Rex while at Duelist Kingdom, everyone sees his playing style and he's a very desired competitor. While at Battle City, he fights against Esper Roper but is unexpectedly defeated. He doesn't advance any further in either tournament.

Weevil (Insector Haga)

Weevil, age 14, is another seasoned player of Magic & Wizards. His duels tend to bring him fighting against Rex and occasionally Yugi. As his name suggests, he uses insect characters in his duels, but unlike Rex, he is a bit arrogant in his play, considering himself a high-level duelist. He plays dirty sometimes, spraying his opponents with insect spray to take their cards from them. During Battle City, Joey sets Weevil straight by beating him and proving who is the stronger duelist.

Malik

Malik is the keeper of the Millennium Rod, another Sen-nen item with tremendous power. He has a psychic ability that he shares with his sister Isis. The rod can possess a person and allows Malik to use them as puppets for his own purpose. His purpose at Battle City is to possess all of the god cards, legendary and extremely powerful cards that have their basis in ancient Egyptian legend. Malik's normal side befriends Yugi and crew under the name Nam, but they quickly find out that the fake Malik was just a puppet.

He grew up in Egypt with Isis. Their father was very strict and once when he did something wrong, his father beat him and his friend Rashid. Through Sha-di, Malik took possession of the Rod and in a moment of insanity, killed his own father. Since then the darkness inside Malik has grown uncontrollably, consuming him with the desire to destroy.

During his battles, he nearly kills Joey, possesses Tea to use her as bait and fights a devilish game against the evil that consumes Bakura.

Isis Ishtar

Isis is Malik's sister and the last qualifying person in the Battle City tournament. She gave Seto Kaiba one of the ancient god cards, Obelisk, an ancient and powerful dragon, as a test of his ability. Her ability is being able to tell the future of any event. She predicts the order of the

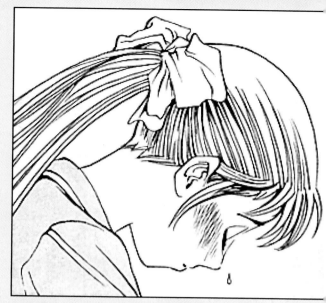

to do what she wants, considering how much he like her. Her personality is so perky, it borderlines on nauseing. She likes games, but she likes boys more. Her clos friend in the series is Tea, who enjoys her company in more guy versus girl activities. ✪

Battle City tournament, but Seto proves her wrong by changing his future. Isis loves her brother, but realizes how unsalvageable he is when the darkness consumes him. She befriends Yugi and crew, lending her strength to Joey when Malik attacks him and giving the Millennium item she wears, the Torque, to Yugi to help him in his battles.

Miho Nozaka
(Japanese anime series only)

Miho is a freshman at Domino High School. She was a creation of the author, Kazuki Takahashi, from the manga series in Volume 1 and only occurs in the first season of the anime series. She has a strange way of getting Tristen

u-Gi-Oh! : The Manga eries and Series History

— By Mika Matsumoto

you thought that Yu-Gi-Oh started t strictly as an anime series, think ain. Everything that is Yu-Gi-Oh rted out as the manga series created Kazuki Takahashi. It was released 1996 from Weekly Shonen Jump mics, slowly gaining popularity, but ceived its first chance at widespread cognition when the anime series was leased in 1998. While the anime oryline stresses the point of the battle rd game "Duel Monsters", the manga ries, like most manga, has a certain eme. In this case, much of the series nters on their friendship and loyalty rough hardship.

ur hero is Yugi Mutou, a young high school fresh-man who's a little on the k side due to his small size. He the chance of a lifetime to experi-e the power of the Millennium zle his grandfather owned. ough his grandfather doesn't eve the Egyptian treasure can easi-e solved, Yugi does it and omes the "Game King", which is literal translation of the Japanese racters in the series' title. His puzzle ne of seven "sen-nen" (which ans "millennium") items, which are

all held by individuals throughout the series.

The whole premise for the series is the use of games, which in the manga there are several. Originally, the popularly known game "Duel Monsters" was called "Magic & Wizards", but was renamed due to its popularity. Some say that the card game is based slightly on "Magic: The Gathering" and the "Pokemon" card games, but the game has come into its own as an original card game. Some of the other games it introduced were "Capsule Monster Chess"

(Capumon for short), D*D*D (Dragon, Dice & Dungeons), as well as varia-tions of commonly known card games. Bandai, the Japanese creator of a majority of the series' toys and games, released Capumon and D*D*D as separate games, but they never gained any press because they were overshadowed by "Duel Monsters".

Yu-Gi-Oh! made the quick transition from manga to video games overnight. As expected, the games became big hits in Japan. The first game, "Yu-Gi-Oh Monster Capsule: Breed & Battle" was released for Playstation in summer 1998. It took advantage of the Capumon idea from the manga series, but the simulations were poor quality and the graphics were low rate. Due to poor sales, Konami decided to try out the newer games on Game Boy, resulting in instant success. The next 2 games, "Duel Monsters" (in black & white), and "Duel Monsters 2: Dark Duel Stories" (in color), featured the battle card game. Konami anticipated the boom and added special secret codes on the REAL Duel Monsters cards for use in the video games. These codes are located in the left-hand corner of all Japanese Duel Monsters cards.

Once again, Konami decided to try with the Playstation console, releasing "Shin Duel Monsters: Fuuin Sareshi Kioku" ("New Duel Monsters: Sealed Memories") in December 1999. The much awaited 3D Fighting Card Battle Game was so popular, it sold out throughout Japan the day it was released. Diehard gamers were paying upwards of 10,000 yen for the newest video game in the Duel Monsters series. The selling price was 5800 yen.

Video games aren't the only thing that Yu-Gi-Oh offers as products. In early 1999, Bandai created a series of shitajiki (pencilboards) from the anime series. There were also special monster toys that were sold in regular supermarkets with candy, with creatures like Blue Eyes White Dragon, Holy Elf, Dark Knight Gaia and others. Typical items in Japan for animation series include stationary items, special books, and CDs.

The anime series continued with the new series, "Yu-Gi-Oh! Duel Monsters", premiering in April 2000 and continues to air on TV Tokyo. It features arcs of the series "Duelist Kingdom" and "Battle City", which both continue after volume 7 of the manga series. Since arriving in the United States, the anime continues to keep fans and players tuned in to find out what the latest is in the series.

The manga series still airs in Japan, with many devoted fans still reading along with Yugi and his friends' adventures in gaming. So far, there hasn't been any mention of translating the manga series into English, but it has been translated into French by Kana publications. It also can be found in various languages throughout Asia, including Chinese and Korean. It shouldn't be long before an English translation of this series can be found.

With that, let's go through just what has happened and is now going on in the manga series, starting from the beginning. The summaries of the manga series are filled with references to the Duel Monsters card game and ancient Egyptian lore. They are direct translations from the volumes and aren't referencing anything that exists in game form today.

Volume 1 (Battles 1-7)
Title: The Dark Puzzle
Released: 3/9/1997

The history of the game is clearly defined on the first page: "5000 years ago, long ago in the Egyptian era, there was a game where humans and kings played for the promise of eternity, where magical ceremonies could decide your fate … this was called 'the dark game'." We first meet Yugi Mutou, who after being bullied into

giving up his money, comes across his grandfather's old Egyptian puzzle. He puts it together and the power of the puzzle enters him, transforms him into a completely different person and he challenges the bully to a deadly game of cards. It is enough to save his newfound friends Joey and Tristen from further trouble. Another friend of his, Tea Gardner, finds herself in trouble at her part-time burger job, but is saved by Yugi's alternate personality, the Game King. She suspects it is Yugi, but is not certain. Tristen, in love with another student named Miho Nozaka (she appears as a regular in the first anime series), tries to give her a jigsaw puzzle gift with a special message, but an evil teacher steals it and embarrasses him. The Game King teaches her a lesson she'll never forget!

Volume 2 (Battles 8-15)
Title: The Card With Fangs
Released: 5/6/1997

Magic & Wizards is first introduced by Yugi's grandfather, Solomon. A visitor comes to the game shop, Seto Kaiba, who shows a case full of Magic & Wizards cards to everyone. The card he wants is Solomon's "Blue Eyes White Dragon" (BEWD), but he won't sell it to him. Yugi takes it to school and is duped by Kaiba, who switches the real card for a fake. This prompts the first duel of many between the two. Kaiba is surprised when the monsters in the cards become real and actually duel against each other! The fight goes back and forth until Kaiba draws the BEWD, but it refuses to

work for him and disappears. Solomon's spirit is behind the use of the card! Yugi plays his "Resurrect Dead" card to use BEWD, winning the match. A strange man from Egypt named Sha-di appears at the recent exhibit at Domino University. Yugi's puzzle is borrowed for the day to put on display, but he can't find it at the day's end. Meanwhile, Sha-di passes judgment on the grave robbers for their deeds, using the "sen-nen" items he possesses: the scales and the ankh. Sha-di, after peering into Yugi's mind and revealing the hidden room where the Game King lives, returns the millennium puzzle to Yugi's possession. But afterwards, he uses the professor as a puppet to capture his friends and challenge the Game King to a duel!

Volume 3 (Battles 16-24)
Title: Capsule Monster Chess
Released: 7/9/1997

Sha-di taps into Tea and brainwashes her, forcing her to stand on the edge of the University building! He forces the Game King out of Yugi to face his challenge and uses Joey to fight against him. Joey takes away his Millennium Puzzle, but somehow he breaks free of Sha-di's spell. Yugi and Joey are able to save Tea, revealing to Sha-di it was the power of unity that broke the spell. Everyone at Domino High School catches on the latest craze: digital pets. However, a bully is going around eating up everyone's digital pets when they face off against each other. Yugi's pet, U2, feels the power of the Puzzle and powerpunches the bully's pet. Tomoya, one of the students at Domino, is a huge collector of American comics and shares his collection of "Zombire" with Yugi and friends. Some bullies kidnap him by making Tomoya believe Yugi was kidnapped, but when Yugi finds out, he goes after them to save him. Seto Kaiba's little brother Mokuba challenges Yugi to his best game, Capsule Monster Chess. His arrogance causes him to lose against the Game King.

Volume 4 (Battles 25-33)
Title: Project Start!
Released: 9/9/1997

After playing a fighting game against a stranger, Yugi's puzzle gets stolen and Joey is forced to fight against the thief using the "sennen" power. Seto Kaiba awakens from the nightmare of the Game King's punishment, vowing to begin his "Death-T". Previously invited to the Kaiba home by Mokuba, Seto takes Joey and Yugi to Kaibaland, a multi-story gaming complex. Inside, Seto has kidnapped Yugi's grandfather, imprisoning him inside a glass cube and challenging him to a game of M&W. All watch as Seto defeats Solomon with 3 Blue Eyes White Dragon cards. Everyone appears at the "death theme park" and are forced through a series of stages: first, a laser gun challenge against military-class people which is very real; next, "Murders Mansion", where they have to solve a puzzle or they lose their hands; then, Joey fights against a monster in a pit filled with gasoline; finally, they are left in a room where cubes fall from the ceiling to crush them! Tea finds a rhythm to the drops, but just as they find a way out, Tristen's jacket gets stuck, forcing him to be left behind.

Volume 5 (Battles 34-42)
Title: Fear the Blue Eyes!
Released: 11/9/1997

Although Yugi, Joey and Tea are upset at having to leave Tristen behind, they continue to the next stage and for the first time, they see the transformation from regular Yugi to the Game King. The next challenge is against Mokuba, a rematch in Capsule Monster Chess. His brother threatens him not to fail him, so he enters with more arrogance than before. But when the Game King defeats him,

Mokuba is shocked and has to suffer through the scary holographic monsters he played with attacking him, courtesy of his brother Seto. Finally, Seto and Yugi fight playing Magic & Wizards, Yugi using his grandfather's deck and Seto with the deadly 3 Blue Eyes White Dragon cards. They fight, each losing lifepoints until Seto draws his BEWD cards, dropping Yugi down to 700 lifepoints. With just enough time, he draws the "Sealing Swords of Light" card, trapping the dragons for three turns. Yugi starts to lose hope, but his friends lend him their strength, enough to draw out the fifth card he needs to complete the destructive infinity attack fusion: Sealed Exodia. Yugi wins, Tristen is still alive, and they all learn from Mokuba that his brother was forced by his father to leave his love of games behind when he was younger, forcing him to be the harsh person he was today. Tea daydreams about the Game King; she likes him. Joey gets the chance to win one million yen, but is duped by a fake game runner.

Volume 6 (Battles 43-51)
Title: Monster Fight!
Released: 1/14/1998

A new game called "Monster Fighter" makes it way to Domino. When Yugi plays against another guy, he takes advantage of him when he loses and tries to beat him up. As his punishment, his monsters come alive

and attack him. Tea and Yugi go to the amusement park for the day, but get caught up in hostage situation with Tea in grave danger on the ferris wheel. The captor plays a deadly game with the Game King, but he manages to save Tea from the frightening number 13. Imori, one of Yugi's friends, brings over an ancient Chinese game called "Dragon Cards" but discovers it is filled with dark spirits that takes over Imori and makes Yugi play against him for his life. Yugi wins and manages to return the spirit to the box Imori brought with him. Joey attacks a yo-yo gang to save Yugi from being hurt. There's a handsome new student in the school with a dangerous secret: Ryo Bakura. He is the keeper of the "Millennium Ring", which weakens him and blocks any memory of its dark side coming forth. Everyone is invited to Ryo's house to see his game collection and they all get tricked by Ryo's dark side into playing "Monster World".

Volume 7 (Battles 52-60)
Title: Millennium Enemy
Released: 3/9/1998

Once playing "Monster World", they find out Ryo's secret side. After a low roll on the dice, Tea's spirit disappears into her game piece (which looks exactly like her) and the same slowly happens to Joey, Tristen and finally Yugi. After Yugi's spirit disappears, the Game King comes forth and fights against the "sen-nen" power of Ryo's ring. Ryo cheats into making the dice roll in his favor and the Game King catches him, so they play by the book. They have a near death roll while fighting in the castle against the main monster, Zork, but all make it out with one hit point left. From deep inside Ryo's consciousness, regular Ryo comes alive and fights to save his new friends. Becoming a character in the game,

Ryo heals the group and the Game King gives them second chance to attack Zork. It works and the crew is released from their tiny bondage. Ryo's ring falls from his neck and everyone's spirit returns to their bodies. On TV, Joey and Yugi watch the Magic & Wizards tournament with 14 year old Weevil and 15 year old Rex Raptor. Rex loses in the match against Weevil; they see the creator of the game, Maximillian Pegasus. Yugi gets a package in the mail, a glove, two stars and a videotape. They watch the tape and see that Pegasus is speaking to them as if they were actually live. He starts a duel with Yugi, who quickly realizes it's really a dark game.

Volume 8 (Battles 61-69)
Title: The Battle Begins
Released: 5/6/1998

Pegasus seems cool when the Game King begins playing against him fiercely, but when the 20 minute timer runs down to five minutes left; he makes his move using his illusionist card "Bewitching Eye". It takes over all of the cards the Game King continues to play. He then realizes that Pegasus somehow was reading his hand all along. Seconds are left on the clock but Yugi is still 100 points behind Pegasus. He loses, Pegasus reveals his secret: the Millennium Eye in his left eye socket. He punishes Yugi for the loss by taking his grandfather's spirit and trapping it in the videotape. Determined, he vows to set his grandfather free. Meanwhile, Joey also receives a videotape from his sister Serenity and discovers that she is very ill and requires a major eye operation that he can't afford. The only way is for both of them to travel to the Duelist Kingdom, to save Solomon and Serenity. They travel by boat, trading cards with other players along the way, including Mai Valentine. On the island, Pegasus greets them and

explains the rules of the Kingdom. Immediately afterward, Yugi and Weevil duel for the star ante. After a back and forth fight, Yugi uses a fierce combo to overcome Weevil and his insect cards. Thoughts of Serenity on his mind, Joey finds his first opponent: Mai. He underestimates her and soon Mai's harpies have Joey on edge.

Volume 9 (Battles 70-78)
Title: The Legendary Dragon
Released: 8/XX/1998

Mai whips Joey into shape with her Harpies, who are damaging him pretty badly. He's starting to lose hope that he'll make his way back to beat Mai. Yugi, watching on the sidelines, reminds him of something he told him a long time ago about looking for unseen things. Joey's heart thinks of his sister who needs him badly to win; it is then that he realizes something about Mai's cards and comes up with a strategy to fight back. Silently thanking Yugi, he plays his "Baby Dragon", and then prays for the card he wants, "Time Magician". Luckily it comes out in his draw, aging his Baby Dragon into a Thousand Year Dragon! It has enough attack power to take out all of Mai's Harpies. Joey gets the win. After trying to steal cooking fish, the crew makes friends with Maco, another duelist who invites them to a meal then challenges Yugi to a duel! On a 95% sea field, Yugi has limited options of play, but that 5% is all he needs. His rock creature, combined with the Moon card, pulls away the water for the tide, revealing Maco's water creatures! "Curse of Dragon" gets played and its fire blows Maco out of the water. He loses, but is a good sport about it. A mysterious duelist challenges Yugi, desperate for a win. It turns out to be Mokuba, who after trying to steal Yugi's starchips, confesses that he's at Duelist Kingdom for his

brother's sake. Pegasus is trying to take over Kaiba Corp and all of Seto's battle simulation creations. Just as Mokuba willingly gives Yugi his starchips, he's stopped by one of the Big 5, now working for Pegasus. Yugi is forced to fight a puppet master that's using Kaiba's cards, but as the Puppet Master tries to use the Blue Eyes Dragon, it disappears, signaling Kaiba's return to the land of the living. After beating him, they find out Mokuba is gone, probably to Pegasus' castle. Mai returns with Rex Raptor, looking for a fight. Joey is stopped by Rex Raptor to fight and he tells his friends he wants to do this with his own strength. They all understand, especially when they see the fierce way he attacks Rex! With his "Flame Knight" clashing against Rex's "Megasaur" and successfully destroying it, Joey's confidence is sky high!

Volume 10 (Battles 79-87)
Title: Storm Brewing in the Kingdom
Released: 10/7/1998

The close battle between Rex and Joey continues, until Joey gets blasted down to 65 lifepoints. He draws his card "Magician Clock" and fortune works in his favor, blasting Rex to zero. Tea confronts Yugi, at Mai's insistence, about her feelings for him. Having known each other since grade school, Yugi knows Tea very well, but she admits to him that she likes Yugi for him, not just his other side. A new opponent comes to fight Yugi; he antes up all of his stars against the "Dark Player Killer". The match in the duel box grows intense, Yugi trapping the Player Killer's "Card Eraser" with his "Curse of the Six-Pointed Star", but it comes to a head when the Player Killer's own monsters can't escape his conjured castle and he loses. Seto Kaiba is brought to the island to play because his brother Mokuba was kidnapped by Pegasus. Seto appears before the group and hot-headed Joey wants a piece of him. His new device, the Duel Disk, a holographic monster projector, is given a whirl but Joey is quickly knocked down to nothing by Seto, who wants to beat Pegasus with a passion. Joey beats himself up for the loss, but Tea and Mai cut into him and remind him of his goal. The Game King comes alive and promises Seto that he will defeat Pegasus, but Seto says a plain "Whatever you say…" and walks away.

Volume 11 (Battles 88-96)
Title: Neverending Duel
Released: 1/13/1999

The group is back on the train to Pegasus' castle and to get the max of 10 stars to enter. Yugi, now a legend among players for beating Seto Kaiba back at Death-T, is scoped out by Bandit Keith, an American player. He sends one of his minions to duel against Joey (so that Keith can duel against Yugi), playing on a grave field while his opponent uses a ghost deck. He keeps hearing Seto's mean words, "You're a loser!" in his head. Pulling himself together, he tries to use his "Magician Clock" again, but it fails him and he loses more lifepoints. His opponent uses very strong zombie cards to knock Joey down, but he draws the "Red Eyes Black Dragon" to destroy one of his creatures. It gets destroyed, but another card gives Joey a chance to live by switching his opponent's defense and attack scores and because of it, the zombies attack decreased down to zero. Joey wins and is up to 8 stars. Yugi and Joey play a tag team duel against the "Maze Brothers". The battle is neverending; each losing half their lifepoints by mid-match. The brothers create an elemental genie from Lightning, Wind and Water called

"Gate Guardian", but Yugi and Joey have a combo of their own by creating "Black Demon's Dragon"!

Volume 12 (Battles 97-105)
Title: Cruel Duel
Released: 3/9/1999

Hidden in Yugi's "Magical Silk Hat" was the "Black Magician". Joey plays a magic card which ups the "Black Demon's Dragon" to 4040 attack! The turn comes back to Yugi who plays his magic card, "Shift Change", transforming his "Black Magician" and melding his dragon to form "Meteor Dragon"! Joey and Yugi win, but through a trick, they find their way out of the maze the brothers created for them. Meanwhile at Pegasus's lair, Seto fought his way into the castle at gunpoint to save his brother. Pegasus reveals to him that Mokuba is jailed in a dungeon beneath. He holds on to an old picture of him and Seto, praying for his brother to remember his goodness and save him; Seto has a similar pendant around his neck. The only way to save him is to defeat Yugi. Once at the castle, the group finds Kaiba ready to challenge Yugi; he accepts and they begin their duel with the disks Seto created. After some creative moves, Yugi uses his "True Eye" magic card to reveal Seto's BEWD in hand. It isn't enough to stop Seto from fusing his 3 cards into one 4500 attack creature! With 100 points left, Yugi plays "Clibo" and the "Multiplier" magic card to eat away at the BEWD's attack points. He then plays a three-card combo of "Magic Arrow", "Fusion", and "Graveyard Mammoth", waiting until "Clibo" eats away 300 points at a time at BEWD until it dies. Kaiba regroups and plays his "Resurrect Dead" card, bringing back the BEWD. Just as Kaiba attacks, Yugi feels the Game King leave him, the pressure of defeat by Kaiba too great.

Volume 13 (Battles 106-114)
Title: The King's Fear!
Released: 5/5/1999

Everyone's in shock at Yugi's loss to Seto. Determined, Seto disappears into the castle. Short on stars, Mai gives Yugi her extras from her previous wins. Everyone enters the castle, the three contestants, Yugi, Mai and Joey ready to battle. Bandit Keith is already inside and all begin to watch the match between Pegasus and Seto for Mokuba, whose spirit is trapped inside a duel card. At the duel field, they play but shortly into the match, Pegasus stops Kaiba and tells him exactly the moves he was planning on making! He then plays the "Dark Rabbit" and forces the field to be a "Toon World", giving bonuses to any toon characters Pegasus plays. Seto fights hard, but doesn't see a way to destroy the toon cards except through traps. The last attack kills his "Sword Stalker" and makes his lifepoints zero. Pegasus' punishment traps Seto's spirit in a card as well. Yugi vows to make Pegasus pay for his actions. They are all given cards for the stepladder tournament in the castle and are taken to a banquet hall filled with food. There Yugi sees a portrait of Sha-di as well as a beautiful woman. At dinner they determine who will play against the other and they retire for the night. Tristen sneaks out to save the others in the dungeon, but is caught. The dark Bakura appears to help him. The next day, the treasure is brought forth and the order determined: Mai vs. Yugi and Joey vs. Bandit Keith!

Volume 14 (Battles 115-123)
Title: Gamble Toward Victory!
Released: 7/7/1999

Mai vs. Yugi! Mai starts early with her harpies, then comes out with "Harpy's Pet Dragon", which blasts

Yugi's monster. When he plays "Black Magician", Mai counteracts with the magic card "Temptation Shadow", destroying Black Magician and knocking Yugi down 300 life-points! The Game King realizes that his other side wasn't strong enough to fight and it takes the power of them both to defeat an opponent. Fighting for real now, he comes back to destroy the Pet Dragon, but Mai resurrects it. Yugi traps it with the "Sealing Swords", then plays one card face down. When revealed, he transforms the field into a "Chaos Field" then uses his "Demon Knight Gaia" to create "Chaos Soldier"! Her harpies destroyed, Mai is shocked by the new card, enough to surrender her cards and accept a loss. Joey gets up to play against Keith, but doesn't have his treasure card. He runs to get it but doesn't find it. Mai, after berating him, gives him her card. Bandit Keith vs. Joey! The two bite into each other early, but Keith presses him with his "Revolver Dragon". Joey plays his cards right and creates a fusion from his "Red Eyes" to create "Red Eyes Black Metal Dragon"! Using a card to steal away Keith's "Time Machine" trap card, Joey uses it against him and the combination of his "Metal Dragon" and Keith's card gives Joey the win.

Volume 15 (Battles 124-133)
Title: Soul Fight!
Released: 10/9/1999

Pegasus punishes Keith for his loss by forcing him to shoot himself in the head. Afterward, Joey gives Yugi the reins and tells him to fight Pegasus. The win will save Solomon, Seto and Mokuba's lives as well as get the treasure prize. Yugi plays hard, but Pegasus is still able to read in his mind what cards he'll play next and Yugi can feel Pegasus looking into his mind. Pegasus opens the toon world once again, where the monsters can't be attacked directly for damage. Pegasus' toons attack Yugi again and again, but in a drastic measure so that the moves can't be read, the Game King hands the play over to regular Yugi. They agree to switch up during play so that Pegasus will get confused. It works with the play of the "Magic Arrow" & "Sacred Barrier" trap card, but Pegasus comes back with his card "Sacrifice", attack and damage both zero. It eats Yugi's next monsters, absorbing its power and using it as its own. To stop the switchup, Pegasus attacks regular Yugi, leaving only the Game King to play. While his friends' spirits protect his cards from Pegasus' eye, he plays the "Clibo" combination to set up "Black Soldier" for the attack. Pegasus loses miserably, which immediately releases the spirits held captive. They learn Pegasus' deadly story from Egypt, where he got the Millennium Eye and about his lady love, Cynthia. There he met a young Sha-di who promises he will be able to see Cynthia all the time if he wore it. The secret of the seven millennium items comes to light, evil Bakura rips the eye out of Pegasus' socket and Seto's young spirit sets him free. Although they're rivals, Kaiba flies the group out of Duelist Kingdom and back to Domino.

Volume 16 (Battles 134-142)
Title: D*D*D!
Released: 12/27/1999

A new game arrives at the Black Crown called D*D*D (Dragons, Dice & Dungeons). They meet Ryuji Otogi, who becomes an immediate rival to Joey and Yugi. Knowing Yugi's game skill, Otogi has Yugi carted to a secret room in the Black Crown to play the new game, taking away his Millennium Puzzle. Otogi remembers his father's words (he is always dressed as a dark clown), telling him that he cannot lose against Solomon's grandson and if he does, he'll never forgive him. After explaining the rules of D*D*D, Yugi does his best to play, the fate of his puzzle landing on the roll of the dice. During the match, however, Otogi's father reappears as well as an unexpected visitor: Dark Bakura. His father disassembles the Millennium Puzzle before Yugi's eyes, eliciting tears. With one lifepoint of three remaining, Yugi pulls himself together while Bakura watches the game. Meanwhile, his friends have been searching around town for Yugi all day and realize he was still at the Black Crown. Otogi tries to put the puzzle together for himself, which was his father's original intention, but something on the field changes the route of the game.

Volume 17 (Battles 143-151)
Title: The Lost Card
Released: 3/8/2000

A turtle creature appears from the Dimension Dice and Yugi's player character picks it up to use it as a shield! Its shield ability is enough for Yugi to attack directly for an instant win. Otogi reluctantly admits defeat, but Yugi's more concerned with putting together his puzzle. However, sneaky Bakura stole a vital piece of the puzzle that Yugi hasn't noticed. Greed overwhelms Otogi's father, who steals the puzzle pieces and sneaks through a secret passage. Otogi, finally seeing his father's wickedness, sides with Yugi to get back his pendant. Strangely, the puzzle itself rejects Otogi's father, turning his mind into a maze. In the process, he knocks over a candle setting the entire center on fire. Joey and crew rush in to save Yugi, but he won't leave without putting his puzzle back together. The fire grows more and more out of control, but he finally does it; Joey carries him to safety. At Kaiba's home, an Egyptian visitor named Isis Ishtar comes to tell him of the connection between Magic & Wizards and Egyptian legend. She gives him a great rare card called "The God of Obelisk", one of three "god" cards. In simulations, Seto is amazed by the power of Obelisk, eager to use it in match play. Tea and Dark Yugi go out on a "date" where she is finally able to show off her dancing ability on "Super Dancer" (which closely resembles Dance Dance Revolution). Afterward, they go to the museum to see the exhibit; Yugi remembers his past life and his rival in the form of Seto Kaiba, written on the walls of an Egyptian mural. Isis appears, to further the remembrance. Kaiba officially begins his "Battle City", the quest to find all 3 god cards. Joey and Yugi register, but early on, a "Rare Hunter" stalks Joey and steals one of his best cards, beating him with Sealed Exodia!

Volume 18 (Battles 152-160)
Title: Millennium Battle!!
Released: 5/3/2000

At 8:05 a.m., duelists from all over assemble at the Domino Clock Tower to begin Battle City! Joey's already lost his "Red Eyes Black Dragon" to the Rare Hunter and he wants it back. For sake of his pride, Joey didn't tell Yugi about the loss. Fighting for him, Yugi faces Rare Hunter's Exodia set, but before it assembles he plays a magic card to seal one of the hands for a few turns. Admitting defeat, the Rare Hunter turns into a possessed zombie-like creature with another voice speaking through him, that of another Millennium item holder

named Malik. Holder of the Rod, Malik's goal is the same as Kaiba's. Joey, on the other hand, feels bad about Yugi defending him and decides not to take back the "Red Eyes" card until he becomes worthy enough to duel with Yugi; from there, they split up. Joey runs into Rex Raptor, who is fighting Esper Roper, a self-proclaimed psychic. Deciding to fight, Joey steps up but somehow is held down by Roper, who predicts all his moves. The secret really is that he has two younger brothers sneaking down from the rooftop looking at Joey's cards and telling big brother! All the fortune in the world couldn't prevent Joey's win. Kaiba is playing in his own event, gathering rare cards (the ante in this match) with his stupendously powerful Obelisk. Meanwhile, Malik releases his god card from lockdown: the Ra card! Yugi gets to play against the second rare hunter, Pandora!

Volume 19 (Battles 161-169)
Title: Magic Battle!!
Released: 7/9/2000

Pandora uses a similar set of cards as Yugi, which makes it very difficult when you feel like you're playing against yourself! They pit Black Magician versus Black Magician, baiting each other until Pandora traps Yugi's card on a thorny cross, but before Yugi could be attacked directly, his Black Magician's spirit took the blow for him, allowing him to live. In a surprise attack, Yugi unleashes "Black Magician Girl", who through another combo blows Pandora out of the water. Joey takes a ramen break, then returns to the dueling action, this time against Weevil. Weevil's been ruthless in getting his rare cards, so Joey wants to teach him a lesson on how to be a true duelist. Bakura, Solomon and Tea are watching along, while Tristen and Otogi

go to Serenity's hospital to tell her what is happening with her brother. Her operation was complete and a full success, and now, she wants to return the favor by being there for her big brother at Battle City; they leave to find Joey. Back in the fray, Joey is taking a beating from Weevil and just as he starts to lose a little hope, Tea reminds him to have courage and keep fighting! In a lucky draw, just as Weevil's "Insect Queen" grows to 6600 attack, Joey pulls out a trap card: "Bug Spray", killing the Queen and ensuring Weevil's loss.

Volume 20 (Battles 170-178)
Title: The God Comes Near
Released: 9/9/2000

Malik finally arrives in Domino at the docks, riding off toward Domino City on his motorcycle. Dark Yugi thanks his other side for his friendship, the true reason for them continuing on. The moment fades and another Malik-possessed opponent appears to challenge Yugi. After a few turns, his opponent reveals the second of three rare god cards: Saint Dragon, God of Osiris. Another powerful card, it does damage regularly to opponents and has the ability to range in attack or defense from 1000 to 6000+ points! When Osiris climbs to 9000, Yugi gets worried, but hears Kaiba's voice telling him to stand up and keep on fighting, that he didn't come this far to lose like this. He comes up with a plan to defeat the god card by resurrecting his "Buster Blader" and using the "infinite rule", Malik loses due to the lack of cards in his deck. As a result, Yugi adds the rare god card Osiris to his deck for the win. Malik arrives in Battle City; Bakura senses his arrival as well. Joey, on the other side by the zoo, runs into Maco. Like old times, the two bait each other, but agree to a friendly duel between them. Prepared to fight with his ghoulish deck is Bakura, against the rod-holder Malik!

Volume 21 (Battles 179-187)
Title: True Unity
Released: 11/7/2000

Malik makes a proposal to Bakura to work together to get all seven of the Millennium items together; Bakura is completely selfish and in response, shows Malik his knife. No deal. Joey plays against Maco with fire, but even though Maco is losing, his thoughts keep returning to his father, the reason he continues to battle. Before an entire audience, Maco loses, but does so with grace. He gives his "Legendary Fisherman" card, the one that reminds him of his father, to Joey, knowing he would fight keeping his father's memory alive. In order to befriend Yugi's crew, Malik puts aside his darker side and makes friends as Nam, just another duelist among many. In a nasty setup, two new players set up Seto and Yugi, forcing them to fight in a tag team match. They are the Light and Dark Masks, with lots of tricks up their sleeves. Seto is revived when he plays his Blue Eyes Dragon, but card by card, the Mask Brothers continue to eat away at Yugi and Seto's lifepoints. Instead of playing individually, Yugi makes a move for them to play together, unified in their efforts. Seto is surprised by Yugi's move, but equally glad at the damage.

Volume 22 (Battles 188-196)
Title: Another Person's Decision
Released: 12/27/2000

Believing only for the moment, Kaiba plays along with the "power of unity" tune, fighting with Yugi in the most real sense possible. After Kaiba loses his Blue Eyes, Yugi plays his "Magnet Valkyrion", attack 3500! It puts a dent into their opponents, but when Kaiba's turn returns, he switches up their fused character's spirits, then in a decisive move, plays his Obelisk card, utterly destroying them! Behind the mask is Malik once again, this time

threatening Yugi's friends. Malik has taken control of Joey and Tea, using them as puppets in the game of darkness. They meet in the promised place, Domino Harbor, while Seto and Mokuba come along with Yugi in the helicopter. In her possessed state, Tea gets a phone call on her mobile, but doesn't realize that it's Tristen saying they're on their way there; she merely cuts off the line. An evil Joey takes Yugi to the fighting place, an island on the water with a tremendously huge anchor in the center. They tie their arms to the anchor as part of the rules, then begin their play. Yugi decides to add Joey's Red Eyes Dragon card to his deck, in hopes that it will revive the Joey inside. Yugi gets struck by damage-causing magic cards from the start, dropping his lifepoints in more than half. The Game King steps aside to let his regular self come forward to play against his friend. Joey plays the "Exchange" card, but even though Yugi shows he has the Red Eyes card in his hand, the Joey inside refuses to take it. In an even stranger move, Yugi gives his Puzzle to Joey and although he could destroy it, he doesn't, his insides battling. The fight to the death continues, with only eleven minutes to go on the clock.

Volume 23 (Battles 197-205)
Title: Face the Fight for Friendship!!
Released: 4/9/2001

The Ghouls' guys draw Kaiba's attention from the match by grabbing Mokuba, but Kaiba quickly retaliates by cutting them with the edge of his Blue Eyes Dragon card, then giving them a right cross with his Duel Disk. All the while, Yugi is trying to evoke memories of their friendship in Joey. Although his memory comes alive, Malik's words are very suggestive. Time runs lower still when Joey plays his "Death Meteor" magic card, but Yugi counteracts with his "Ghost Mirror" deflecting the attack. Sacrificing himself for his friend's life, Yugi takes off his gear and tells Joey the fight is over, then takes the damage of the Death

Meteor all by himself! Yugi's down to zero points with one minute left on the clock. This sacrifice by Yugi releases Joey; he begs the Red Eyes Dragon to attack him to help save his friend and it does, seconds before the timer runs out. The anchor above them explodes and dragging both of them beneath the water. Joey somehow manages to find the key that was released and frees Yugi from the chains. The rest of the crew arrives, with Joey able to see his sister for the first time after her operation. Bakura edges his way into the final round, traveling with the crew to the new battleground: Domino Stadium. The lots are drawn for who goes first; the first round is Yugi versus Bakura. He plays "Dark Necrophia", one of many in Bakura's occult deck; although taking damage once, it attacks with a spirit stealer, giving Bakura back his hitpoints and taking Yugi's instead!

Volume 24 (Battles 206-214)
Title: A One-Turn Death Struggle!!
Released: 6/9/2001

Still stealing lifepoints from Yugi and spelling the word "DEATH" on the ouija board from his magic attack combo, Bakura is shocked when Yugi pulls from his deck "Saint Dragon: God of Osiris"! The fake Malik threatens Yugi that he'd be hurting his true friend Bakura if he attacks him and although regular Ryo comes through to show his pain, the Dark Bakura returns seconds before Yugi's turn is over, forcing him to use Osiris' power. One turn completed Bakura's loss at Yugi's hand. They all make sure Bakura is okay, but in the process, Tea picks up the Millennium Ring and without realizing it, the Ring ends up around her neck and Malik is watching her. It's Joey's turn to battle against the fake Malik. The battle starts fast paced with Joey playing expertly, but when he sets up a trap, the fake Malik turns the trap around on him and attacks with "Anubis' Judgment", destroying all of Joey's cards and causing him damage! More Egyptian cards attacking him,

Joey is left at 50 lifepoints, but is left to draw on the strength from the cards he won: Esper Roper's Psycho Shocker and Maco's Legendary Fisherman. When Serenity looks away from the grim scene, Joey tells her to have courage to face this darkness and watch him no matter what. Rashid (the fake Malik) remembers an incident in his past; being found by Malik's father and raised in their household; Malik being punished for his "lack of respect". Rashid felt guilty over the beating Malik suffered through and mutilated himself to face his darkness. It is what makes him so indebted to Malik.

Volume 25 (Battles 215-223)
Title: Broken Duelist
Released: 9/9/2001

Joey reveals what he now knows to be true: his opponent is not Malik. After some influential words from Malik, Rashid calls upon the third and final god card, "Ra – The Sun God Dragon"! However, the card Rashid is using is a copy and the real Ra card rebels against its usage by attacking Rashid and Joey. As Rashid is rendered useless, the darkness inside Malik explodes into life, revealing to everyone his true identity. Joey manages to get to his feet and wins by default. The next match is between Mai and Malik, a deadly matchup with Malik's even darker skills. Her friends are rooting for her, but Malik attacks her fiercely to the point where she sees her own blood drawn. Somehow Mai got her hands on the Ra card and she intends to use it! Each monster she plays, Malik takes pleasure in torturing before destroying it. Taking a step forward, Mai plays her Harpies then plays the Ra card, but Malik smirks knowingly at her use of the card. On her card, there is no text to describe the card's attack abilities, but on the one Malik has, the real one, it is written completely in an ancient Egyptian text, a spell that must be said aloud by the user. After an electrical torture session, Mai is dumbfounded when Malik

begins to chant the spell on the Ra card, revealing the dragon within the beaming ball hovering between them. Unable to fight back, Joey rushes into the match to save her, the blast of the dragon hitting Joey full force, but determined not to let Mai nor Joey die is Yugi, who comes in to take some of the attack from their shoulders.

Volume 26 (Battles 224-232)
Title: The One Choosing Darkness
Released: 11/7/2001

Ra's attack ends, letting Joey and Yugi up for a minor rest, but it doesn't save Mai from Malik's punishment for the loss, putting her inside an hourglass dripping scarabs and scorpions on her. Joey curses Malik and promises to make him pay for Mai's pain. The next match begins: Seto versus Isis! She has the ability to see into the future, predicting all of Seto's moves well before he makes them. Plainfaced through it all, Isis counters his attacks, even maintaining her composure when she realizes Seto had drawn his god card Obelisk. Convinced that he could take her down given Isis' cards already played, he follows through with playing Obelisk. Something strange happens to Kaiba; Obelisk won't attack at his command! His vision grows dark, influenced by the Millennium Rod, and he sees a vision of an Egyptian mural of his Blue Eyes Dragon. Malik speculates that his Rod holds the key to his memories, sealed deep within Seto Kaiba. Following his instincts and in a bold move, Kaiba sacrifices the god card for his Blue Eyes Dragon, destroying Isis' previous knowledge of the future. His dragon attacks fiercely and Isis, with grace, accepts her defeat. Seto returns to his computer center where Mokuba is trying to decipher the writing on the Ra card; he has an adverse reaction again, looking at the text and somehow understanding what is written. Taking a break, everyone visits Mai to see her condition; Isis shows up and reveals to them her and Malik's

history, how they came to be holders of the Millennium Items courtesy of Sha-di and particularly, the events that started Malik on the path to the dark side.

Volume 27 (Battles 233-241)
Title: The Battle Day Has Arisen!
Released: 3/9/2002

Isis gives Yugi the torque to help defeat Malik. It is the time for sleep; Yugi is settling through things with his other half, while Joey is fast asleep. Malik, on the prowl, is about to complete his task from before of killing Rashid when he sees Dark Bakura standing waiting for him. The two begin to pit dark power against dark power in the struggle for domination. They duel and with each loss of hitpoints, their bodies begin to be enveloped in darkness!! Malik plays his Ra card, using all of his power to attack Bakura. He succeeds and wins the death match. Bakura fades into nothingness and the spoils, his Millennium Ring, go to Malik. Rashid's body disappears after Malik's better side warns Isis through Tea. In sleep, Yugi ventures for the first time into his other side's dark maze room, talking about what they'll be facing. First light breaks and Seto is ready for the next play arena: Alcatraz! They enter and begin to play in elevated seats, all four of them fighting against each other. At the onset, it almost seems like Joey is the one they're trying to eliminate, but Yugi backs Joey's moves to cause damage to Kaiba and Malik. The long battle to win continues…

Volume 28 (Battles 242-250)
Title: To the Light of the Future!
Released: 5/6/2002

The battle order is determined by the losers playing each other and the same with the winners. Malik loses, followed promptly by Joey. They are then paired off to fight. To keep his promise, Joey follows bravely into the fight with Malik, despite his rules of it now being a "dark game". Malik freaks

Joey out by having spirits' hands creep from his cemetery, then in a play by Malik, one of the hands grabs a card from Joey's hand! Joey's hand gets lighter with another steal move from the cemetery, but he gets to play his "Psycho Shocker" card to cause some damage to Malik. Joey tries to avoid the use of Malik's Ra card, but can't hold him back. It attacks, everyone watching along to see if Joey can make it through. Still alive, Joey keeps reminding himself he must keep dueling; he pulls a card from his deck, "Iron Warrior", which would have been the win against Malik for him, but the attack from the Ra card topples Joey. His friends cry in horror as they try to revive their friend unsuccessfully. Mokuba hails for an emergency unit, while all of them cope with the possibility that Joey may be dead or dying. Seto tells Yugi that he can return to the duel stage once Joey comes around. Yugi, unable to continue fighting, battles the hurt inside him. He remembers his vow to become a true duelist and to challenge him when the time came. From his pocket, Yugi withdraws the Torque Isis gave him, taking a glimpse into the future. Joey, in the future Yugi sees, tells him that their Battle City isn't over yet. With that knowledge, Yugi goes ahead to continue fighting, for the sake of being a true duelist.

Volume 29 (Battles 251-259) Title: Osiris versus Obelisk!! Released: 8/7/2002

Yugi returns to the duel stage to face off against Kaiba in a battle over pride. Kaiba draws his Obelisk card early, but in a smart move, Yugi cuts him off from using it by using his magic card to seal it for 3 turns. Kaiba uses "Heavenly Voice of Submission", which makes Yugi hand over Kaiba's card of choice, namely the Osiris dragon! With no other choice, Yugi does so, but immediately plays his "Exchange" card, returning Osiris to his hand! Yugi goes ahead and plays

his three-card combo of "Jack's Knight", "Kings' Knight" and "Queen's Knight", then he sacrifices these three to play Osiris. Kaiba also sacrifices his "XYZ Dragon" to play Obelisk. At the hospital, everyone tries to awaken Joey so that he can see the two god cards facing each other, but he doesn't come around. Yugi and Kaiba, in the heat of the fight, set their god cards against each other and a massive blast of energy consumes the stadium. Malik's rod glows once again, triggering a memory for both Yugi and Kaiba. They are taken back to ancient Egypt and below their floating bodies, they see what looks like their past selves dueling, using the exact same monsters they favored: Yugi's Black Magician and Kaiba's Blue Eyes Dragon. The memory ends as the smoke clears. As if following their fates, Kaiba sacrifices his Obelisk to play the Blue Eyes he draws; Yugi follows suit by resurrecting his Black Magician. In a smart move, Kaiba uses his resurrect card to bring back Obelisk and gives Yugi some damage. Amazingly, Kaiba has one more trick up his sleeve; Obelisk disappears and he brings all three Blue Eyes Dragons to life and Yugi realizes that he doesn't have any more cards that could help in his hand.

Volume 30 (Battles 260-268) Title: The Immortal Ra! Released: 10/9/2002

Although Kaiba has his three Blue Eyes Dragons in play, Yugi gets a boost from Joey's spirit and realizes that he can play his Red Eyes Black Dragon. Yugi's barely holding Kaiba off from attacking, by reversing Kaiba's original attack with a magic card, then playing his "Six-Pointed Star" trap card. All the while, Joey amazingly awakens briefly just as his spirit wishes him well. Yugi backs down a bit, putting the Red Eyes in defense mode, but Kaiba forces all the monsters to remain attacking with his magic card. Joey awakens fully and with everyone behind him, races to the Stadium. Backed into a wall, Yugi watches as

Kaiba's dragons fuse into one "Blue Eyes Ultimate Dragon"! Kaiba's whole purpose in fighting against Yugi is to prove that he is the best and defeating him would settle everything for him, but Yugi isn't about to let him bask in his glory just yet. He transforms his Black Magician into "Black Paradeen". They fight to mid-stage for up-points, but Yugi ends up trapping Kaiba by diffusing his fusion, turning his dragon back into three. Then, from his hand, Yugi plays his magic card, spreading Black Paradeen's attack over all three dragons! The surprise loss by Kaiba shocks everyone, especially Kaiba. Reluctantly, he hands over the Obelisk card as part of the ante rules and leaves thoroughly upset. Isis tries to stop Seto from leaving, but has a hard time convincing him. It takes her vision for him to realize he must stay and give Yugi his "Devil's Sanctuary" card. So, after Yugi adds it to his deck and has a brief pep talk with Joey, the duel begins. Malik, inciting the "dark game", holds regular Yugi and regular Malik hostage, also revealing a trapped Mai. In a play similar to before, Yugi sacrifices his cards to play Osiris. But Malik knew Yugi's plan and trapped him by using Yugi's dead resurrection card to bring out his Ra! He takes Osiris' damage, but sets Yugi ablaze with Ra. Malik again plays his "Dark Magic" trap card to bring the resurrection card back into his hand. The turn is now on Yugi, nervous but hopeful that the sleeping card in his deck will give him back the match. ✪

Yu-Gi-Oh! Series 1 Episode Summaries

— By Mika Matsumoto

The first Yu-Gi-Oh series lasted 27 episodes, from 4/4/1998 to 10/10/1998. It featured events from the manga series such as the "Death-T tournament" and "Monster World", covering the first 6 volumes of the comic.

The opening theme was "Kawaita Sakebi" by the Japanese group Field of View. The closing theme was "Ashita Moshi Kimi Ga Kowaredemo" by the Japanese group Wands.

Episode 1: Fierce Battle: The Dark Game

At lunchtime, Yugi's left alone to play his games, until Joey and Tristen arrive telling him he should be more like a man when getting back what is his. Tea arrives and sets them both straight; Miho also arrives after waiting for Tea. A bully named Ushio runs into Joey and Tristen; Yugi tells the secret of the Egyptian game he carries around, but Yugi doesn't realize he took away one of the key pieces, throwing it into the river behind the school. Ushio tricks Yugi into making him be his bodyguard even though he doesn't agree, then beats up Joey and Tristen the next day. He wants payment for his services: a whopping 20,000 yen! Joey, feeling guilty, retrieves Yugi's lost piece after he put the entire puzzle together. He gives it back and Yugi puts the last piece in, a glowing eye penetrating his mind. Out comes the Game King, challenging Ushio to a deadly card game on the edge of the school building. He loses and suffers a horrible fate. Joey admits to Yugi that he's made a new friend with him.

Episode 2: Devilish Gamer: Hell's Trap

Solomon's shocked that Yugi's completed the puzzle and makes sure he's

feeling okay, given the legend. An incident happens with the police the night before, the thief gets away. Tea discourages the group from going to Burger World, the newest eating joint. Her friends are curious at her reluctance and follow her one by one. The thief strikes again, but hears on the news that the jewels he stole are fakes! What a horrible thief. Joey and

Yugi find out their friends have part-time jobs at Burger World, Tea needing the money to travel to America and study dance. Detectives are following the thief, who makes his way inside Burger World. They all look for the thief's injury to his leg. He gets trapped by his fear of eggs and the detective finds him, but they're all wrong as the real thief holds Tea captive. Fearing for Tea's life, the Game King comes alive after asking Yugi to bring a bottle of liquor and cigarettes. Playing a deadly game of fire and liquor, he loses control and believes he's ablaze. Tea comes away unscathed but curious as to who her savior was.

Episode 3:
Clash! The Strongest Monster

Kaiba's goons beat up an innocent boy for his game card. Yugi explains to the group the next day on how to play Duel Monsters, which he learned from his grandfather. There's a new student in the school: Seto Kaiba, the same of Kaiba Corporation. Seated next to Yugi, he finds out they share a liking of the game; Seto invites him and his friends to his house to see his card collection. His house is a massive complex with gardens and many stories. He has cards all over the wall, as well as trophies from the tournaments he's won. Tea reminds him about a card his grandfather showed him. They return to Solomon's shop to see the "Blue Eyes White Dragon" card. Seto offers a case filled with cards for the one Blue Eyes, but he refuses.

Kaiba tricks Yugi into letting him see the card again, but gives him a fake instead. Joey and Tristen saw the switch and confront Kaiba, but his goons get in the way. Yugi finds out, sees Joey and Tristen beat up, then asks Kaiba to return his grandfather's card. He refuses and the Game King challenges him to a match. The monsters come to life! Seto tries to use the Blue Eyes to defeat Yugi, but it disappears when he realizes his grandfather's heart is behind the card. Yugi resurrects it and revives the dragon, but Seto has a trick up his sleeve, plays and leaves in a puff of smoke.

Episode 4:
The Illusionary Rare Watch Drama

Tristen promised Miho to get her a rare watch that was on sale that day. (Miho is a minor character that Tristen thinks is cute. She never becomes a major character in the storyline). The line is out the door; Yugi holds his place in line and pays for the watch, the last one in the store. A collector comes from behind him and insists that the watch is his, threatening to beat him up. Tristen comes along and sets the guy straight. Miho

gives the watch to Tristen to safeguard, but when he goes to wash his hands, he takes it off and the collector picks his pocket for it. Yugi sees the collector, suspecting it was his fault. Tristen's driving himself insane, so Yugi follows the collector and finds out he has the watch. After being beat up, the Game King comes forth, challenging him to a timing game: grab the

watch before his hand gets sliced off in the 10 second time span. He's too slow and his hand gets cut off, losing miserably. Yugi returns the watch to Tristen, restoring his good name with Miho.

Episode 5:
Can I Lose Now? Yugi's Secret

An Egyptian exhibit is showing at the museum and the group plans to go. Since Solomon knows the exhibitors for a long time, they get nice treatment. They ask for Yugi to put his Millennium Puzzle up for exhibition for the day. He agrees and his friends are excited to see the mummies and the other items. Yugi meets an Egyptian man looking at the pharaoh's mummy, crying. He dismisses him as a cute little boy, which disturbs Yugi immensely. Everyone heads home, but Yugi stays behind to pick up his puzzle. The director, Mr. Kanekura, is confronted by the Egyptian man carrying scales and wearing an ankh as a pendant. The Egyptian man is inflicting his justice on the director for his heinous crimes against the dead. His untruths cost him his sanity. The Egyptian takes the puzzle on Kanekura's desk, leaving the office, but runs into Yugi and discovers that it belongs to him. Using his ankh, he enters Yugi's mind, revealing his secret side. The Game King tests him to find the way out of his maze; once released, the Egyptian returns Yugi's puzzle to him and tells him his name is Sha-di.

Episode 6:
No Explanations! The Fight for Deep Friendship

At Sha-di's hand, the professor falls from the second story window and ends up in the hospital. They all believe the curse of the mummy is causing this to happen. Sha-di chooses Tea to draw out the Game King and mesmerizes her into hurting Yugi, first with steel beams, then with a basketball down the stairs. Joey, Tristen and Miho discover Tea trying to choke Yugi, the spirit of Sha-di speaking through her. Yugi finds Tea standing on a ledge on the roof of the school, held by a single piece of rope. Sha-di also takes Tristen over, stopping Miho and Joey from interrupting their fight. The Game King comes alive for Sha-di to battle, first giving him a field of 9 question marks to choose the one that will release them all. He wins that game, but Joey steals Yugi's puzzle away under Sha-di's power. Yugi believes in his friend Joey, that he wouldn't do anything to hurt him. Sha-di's illusion of Joey disappears, giving Yugi only seconds to save Tea. Joey holds up the plank from beneath her, until she is touched by the ankh, releasing her from the spell. Tristen is also released from the spell, but Sha-di is long gone.

Episode 7:
Slick Trick: Digital Pet Rebellion

Digital Pets are the latest thing at Domino High School, kids taking secret breaks during class to clean after their pets. They have a connection feature where two pets can play with or against each other. A new and ugly bully arrives and he not only hits kids up for their money, but also takes people's digital pets and eats them with his own pet, Devil Monster. Tristen decides to stay at home from school to train his digital pet for Miho's sake. After the bully eats Tea's and Joey's pets, Tristen returns with his "cleaning pet" to challenge Devil Monster and cleans the monster straight away. Miho gets kidnapped to draw in Tristen; he finds her strung from two steel poles while the bully falls beaten by a whip. The boy Hayama that was bullied for his money is possessed with the desire to wreak revenge. The Game King comes alive after Tristen is knocked out and uses his digital pet, U2, to fight Hayama's possessed pet. U2 uses the dark power and is able to defeat Hayama.

Episode 8:
The Gaming Big Four Makes a Move

Kaiba is set on defeating Yugi and sends for his "big four" to bait Yugi.

While at school, Yugi gets called to the nurse's office for a surprising game of Magic & Wizards with the nurse. The innocent game turns devilish when the nurse starts playing very offensively. As a part of his loss to the nurse, she takes one of his cards. The nurse turns out to only be a puppet, led by an old man working for Seto Kaiba. Yugi goes to the local game center after school, but is tricked into entering a limo heading for the old man's place. Seto watches as Yugi plays against him with the card he took. The Game King comes out to face the old man, defeating him after several plays. He leaves Seto to deal with the loss.

Episode 9:
Explosion! The Ultimate Yo-Yo Secret Technique!

Joey is really good at yo-yo's, but there's a new yo-yo gang in town that's threatening everyone. He's heard about this gang and is determined to find out what's going on himself. When he doesn't come to school the next day, everyone is worried and goes to look for him. They find him now with the gang fighting along with them. Joey denies knowing them he continues with them, even after one of them hits Yugi. As a test for the gang, he knocks out all five members of a rival yo-yo gang, then when Tristen confronts him, he punches his best friend in the gut. They kidnap Yugi, but Joey turns around to fight and save Yugi from the gang. A yo-yo battle ensues and both Yugi and Joey are able to put the gang out of commission.

Episode 10:
The Pretty Teacher Presses Close: A Secret Mas

A popular teacher is as strict as she is beautiful and she uses it to her advantage to gain favors from the principal. One of Tea and Miho's classmates, Mayumi, has a thing for Joey but wants to get him something to tell him she likes him. They go to Yugi's grandfather for a good game to give Joey, a blank jigsaw puzzle where a message can be written. Mayumi leaves the box for Joey, who is late for class, but the teacher takes the box from him and embarrasses Mayumi in front of the class. Tea confronts the teacher and takes the heat for having something like that in class, but the teacher returns the jigsaw puzzle to Tea after giving her a job to sign up people for a school event. The whole thing was a setup, but the Game King hears her plan and forces her to a blindfolded mirror jigsaw puzzle match. For cheating, her pretty face falls apart into puzzle pieces and reveals an ugly woman.

Episode 11:
Rumored Capumon: A New Entrance

An admirer gives Miho an entire machine filled with capsules filled with game pieces and toys. One of Yugi's classmates has a major crush on Miho, but Yugi finds out that he is the one that gave her the machine. He keeps his secret, only to realize that he's obsessed with Capumon and with Miho. Yugi tries to tell him that all the

Capumon won't bring Miho to him, he tries to impress Miho, but she beats him up when he gets too insistent on being his love. Upset and troubled, he poisons the group's drinks, all with the exception of Miho and Yugi. He leaves a note for Miho, who once and for all, wants to resolve this. Yugi and Miho go to his secret hideout to confront him. He forces them to play Capumon, but Miho loses and passes out. The Game King plays for Miho and sets him up for one long blast of all his monsters, defeating him. His punishment is capture in his own capsule.

Episode 12:
The So-Called Lucky Opponent: Invincible Legend

The popular game show "Big Money Get Game" is in Joey's sights to win 1 million yen! The current champion of the show is a new student named Ryuichi at the school, but he's completely arrogant. All the students want to know what it is like to be on TV, but everyone else isn't impressed.

He has a streak of luck that is amazing, to the point of winning a free meal at a Chinese restaurant for the entire crew as well as a trip to Italy! He is summoned before Seto Kaiba and is sent to play against Yugi, but he is accosted by his pool balls as a threat. Joey gets a chance to be on TV to play against him, but the games change, this time he plays a card matching game where Joe gets electrically shocked every time he wins. Ryuichi gets challenged by the Game King, the same as Seto told him, playing with the rules of a dark game. He calls the joker, instantly losing. On TV in the next show, Ryuichi loses at electric roulette, tossed from his champion status.

Episode 13:
Aiming For The Girl Students: The Great Predictor's Fangs

A fortune teller appears on the school grounds, bringing tons of girls to him trying to find out their futures. During Joey's reading, the fortune teller's predicted earthquake comes true! Tea turns down the fortune teller's offer to read her future, preferring to "make her own future". After a prediction about Joey's life, they begin to be unsure of the fortune teller's ability. Yugi interferes with Tea's fortune session, but the fortune teller warns Yugi to be careful because something horrible might happen to him. He returns a book to the library and the cases begin to fall behind him! The Game King saves Yugi, follows him into the classroom where Tea was knocked out with chloroform. His challenge turns the fortune teller's words into trash. Tea is once again saved by the elusive Game King, but she sees a similar bruise from the Game King on Yugi's hand...

Episode 14:
Explosive Game at the Worst Date!

Tea asks Yugi if he wants to go to the special event at the amusement park. They go while Miho, Tristen and Joey are spying on them. Having lots of fun at the park, Tea's taken with thoughts of the Game King. Meanwhile, the police are scoping out a crook's activities, taking him straight to the amusement park. Tea goes up in the ferris wheel when there's an explosion. The crook forces the police to play his deadly game where the balloons they release correspond with a particular car on the wheel. The Game King comes out to play for Tea's sake and finally understands what it all means from the color wheel behind the ride and saves Tea and the other riders.

Episode 15:
Scary Woman! I Can't Transform!

Someone leaves a love letter in Yugi's locker and his friends are extremely jealous! He meets the girl from another school named Lisa. She touches Yugi's pendant and has an evil reaction from it. Instead she leaves, giving Yugi a present she made. Tea is not happy about this and has a bad feeling. Tea finds out that Yugi is sick

the next day and Lisa somehow is able to get everything before Tea does. She suspects something when she sees someone that looks like Lisa in the store. Lisa seems to be after the card Tea gave Yugi. They find out that there are three of them, but now Yugi can't transform since they stole his pendant! Kaiba, from out of nowhere, comes to play on his behalf and wins in short moves, but warns him next time he won't lose against Yugi.

Episode 16:
One-Shot Turnaround: The White Gown Crisis!

Joey reveals that he has a younger sister named Serenity who's in the hospital sick. Yugi and Joey go to visit Serenity, getting her to smile despite her physical situation. Joey is taken by Serenity's nurse, Miyuki, who patches him up after the fight he was in earlier. Miyuki is accosted by the doctor, who is forever trying to bait her, but she puts him off with an "I'm busy..." His friends realize he likes Miyuki and encourage him to speak with her, but he's shy and manages to screw it up. When he visits Serenity, she tells him the doctor yelled at her and forced

her to quit her job. Joey is upset to the point of tears about it, which sends Yugi to the doctor for a dark game of golf through the hospital. All the while, Joey runs to meet Miyuki at the train station before she disappears, but she was planning to leave the hospital all along. Yugi teaches the doctor a lesson and he suffers through the spirits of all the patients he accosted.

Episode 17:
Last Minute Match: The Invited Model

Supermodel Aileen returns to Japan to see Seto Kaiba, who has a job for her: to bait Yugi and defeat him! Even he has noted the change that happens in Yugi, so he prepares her for it. At his grandfather's shop, Yugi and Tea are talking about Aileen just as she enters the shop, signs Tea's video and leaves a shocked Tea with stars in her eyes. She wants Yugi to bring a fun game with him when Tea has her private lesson with Aileen. Aileen reveals her true purposes, locking Tea in the dance room to hold a one-leg pose until they return. She works for Kaiba and forces Yugi to play her game. The Game King plays her game after the rules are explained. Once he understands and wins, Aileen accepts her defeat and lets Tea free from her difficult pose. She returns to Kaiba and explains to him what happened and says that Yugi's stronger than Seto ever will be.

Episode 18: A Forbidden Game Held In Hand

One of his classmates is grateful for saving him from being taken advantage of by bullies. He shows Yugi an old secret at his home, a secret passage leading to a locked room. Yugi solves the puzzle on the front of the door to reveal a dragon. Inside is a sealed, legendary Chinese game. They take it back to Solomon, but he warns them not to open it since it's a dangerous game. In the "dragon blocks" holds the power to turn the stability of yin and yang inside out. Yugi's puzzle glows in warning of the power inside the box. On his way home, Ryori is attacked by the bullies who make him accidentally drop the game on the ground. Somewhere around the world, it caused an imbalance, creating a tidal wave and horrible earthquakes. Ryori steals Yugi's pendant, but in order for him to get it back, he has to play "dragon blocks". On a bad move, the spirit inside steals Yugi's spirit, but the Game King comes out to fight using the elements. They realize the danger of the game, once the evil spirit inside releases Ryori and both make sure the game is sealed and locked away once again.

Episode 19: Rebellious Fight!! Popularity Contest

All of the guys love Himeko, the most popular girl in school. Miho, despite the fact that she could be more popular, has no care for the upcoming popularity contest that

many are entering. So are Tea and Joey! Miho meets a cute guy walking down the street and that's enough for her to enter the contest. Fan clubs start for the contestants, most popular are Himeko and Miho. Himeko sends her friends to sabotage the contestants in any way possible. They switch Tea's dance music and she's immediately embarrassed forcing her to drop out. Getting ready for the swimsuit competition, Miho realizes someone destroyed her swimsuit, but by sheer luck, she finds a mermaid-type suit to replace it. The final sabotage places a drugged Miho with a ripped evening gown, courtesy of Himeko. Yugi finds a rose and knows who did it. The Game King confronts Himeko on stage and challenges her to a short game with her flowers. She loses and her punishment is instant aging and embarrassment in front of the whole school.

Episode 20: Come Out!! Last of the Strongest Trump Cards

After Mokuba tries to find out what Seto is going to do after three straight losses from the people he's sent to defeat Yugi, Kaiba goes to the grave to revive his gaming trainer for a job. A limo nearly runs Yugi over, to reveal an old man passed out in the back seat. They take him to the hospital, Tea and Yugi following them there. The old man wakes up and Yugi keeps him company by playing Duel Monsters. Kaiba appears and takes the old man with him back to Kaiba Headquarters. In the boardroom, Kaiba is ruthless, voting off one of the

old members. Meanwhile, Tea and Yugi visit an amusement center, going to a monster house. Inside, a mechanical dinosaur holds Tea captive, preparing to eat her. Behind it all is the old man and Kaiba. The Game King plays Duel Monsters against the old man. The fight goes back and forth until turns the game around and wins against the old man. The dinosaur releases Tea and Kaiba becomes maddened further by the fact that none of his men were able to beat Yugi.

Episode 21: Completion!! The Ultimate Gameland

A new student appears at the school: Ryo Bakura, the same person Miho and Yugi met during the popularity contest. He's immediately popular because of his cuteness. Bakura seems very weak, especially after touching Yugi's pendant. They all go to an arcade and find out many of the high scores on the games are from someone with the letters "KAI". The KAI belongs to Kaiba's younger brother Mokuba. While everyone is playing a racing game, a limousine appears in the game and inside is Mokuba speaking to them live. Seto appears, challenging Yugi to go to his newest creation, Kaibaland. They took Solomon hostage at Kaibaland which forces them to go. Before that, a challenger on the fighting game takes it seriously when Yugi beats him three in a row. He beats him up in quick order and steals his pendant. Joey goes after him and fights him on a narrow beam across the river. The guy slips up on a can of cola Joey opens and returns the pendant to Yugi. The next morning, all of his friends appear to help get back his grandfather from Kaiba. But Bakura, with the ring around his neck that weakens him, follows in the shadows.

Episode 22:
Broken Bound Shooting

Thousands of kids are at the grand opening of Kaibaland, super gaming center. The group is escorted by Kaiba guards to a secret location on site to watch Solomon battle against Seto at Duel Monsters. Amazingly, Seto has three of the Blue Eyes Dragon cards! The illusion disappears and the group is forced to go through Death-T, the toughest game at Kaibaland. The first stage takes them through a shooting game like laser tag, but the opponents are military using real lasers! Miho, out of sheer fear, manages to kill all three of them on her own! Next, they face an unusual puzzle that's binary, but get out just before getting smashed into pieces. Their next stage puts them in a room filled with dropping cubes!

Episode 23:
Capumon King! The Battle's Summit

Death-T continues in the room of falling cubes. Bakura is watching from the audience. Tea is able to find a rhythm to the falling blocks, but they have to use them to climb to the exit above them. Just as everyone gets out, they realize Tristen is left behind, his jacket stuck between the blocks. As the next stage draws near, Seto warns

Mokuba that he had better win against Yugi. In a bold move, Yugi reveals there's another side to him because of the puzzle's power. Joey tells them they have to continue on and can't give up, for the sake of their friends. Mokuba sets the stage up for Capumon Chess versus Yugi. In a strange move, Yugi refuses to make use of his turn, but through some skillful moves is able to defeat Mokuba. As promised, Seto forces his own brother to face the fear of his monsters until Yugi pulls him free. Meanwhile, Joey and Miho are looking through the complex for Tristen and Solomon, and with a bit of spiritual help from Bakura, find him trapped inside an hourglass filling with water. Yugi continues to the final stage with Seto.

Episode 24:
Now! Decision Time, The Miracle of Friendship

While Yugi gets ready to duel against Seto, Joey and Miho have problems of their own when they have to face off against Aileen and Ryori once again, this time playing in battle body armor that one person control like a video game. Yugi starts playing against Seto, starting off slowly. Miho finally gets an idea of what needs to be done and starts fighting seriously. Using his grandfather's deck, Yugi tries to fight but Seto draws his Blue Eyes cards. Once all three are out, his friends give him the strength to draw the fifth card he needs to created the "Sealed Exodia" set. Lending that same power back, Joey's life power increases after going down to zero, just enough to fight Aileen

again. Exodia comes out and destroys all three Blue Eyes dragons. As a punishment, Seto enters a comatose-like state. Everyone makes it out unscathed. Bakura, however, is taken over by the ring around his neck by an evil source.

Episode 25:
New Development : Attack of the Handsome Boy

Seeing Bakura again, everyone greets him, but something powerful is attacking him. The voice of the Ring calls to him, but it literally pains him. The voice tells him he wants Yugi's pendant and to defeat him; it then takes him over completely. When something happens, he doesn't remember what. Yugi and crew stop by Bakura's house to make sure he is doing okay and he reveals his Battle World game piece collection. They decide to play his game and Bakura sets up everyone's characters. In the game, they roleplay to find out information in order to beat the game. For the first time, they see the nasty creature they must beat, Zork. But when it is Zork's turn to play, Bakura plays as him and as part of the "super critical hit", he chose to steal Miho's soul and store it in her character piece. He does the same to Tristen when he goes out of turn and when Joey gets the lowest hit he could possibly get. Yugi and Tea would rather become game pieces to fight alongside their friends. The Game King comes out to play on everyone's behalf and to beat Bakura.

Episode 26: Rivals Clash – The Greatest Pinch

The game continues with everyone as game pieces and the Game King playing for them. After a few rushes against monsters, Bakura realizes Yugi caught onto the fact that he was influencing the dice by the way he tossed it. They agree to continue without influencing the dice in either direction. The group makes it through a forest and toward the castle. Once the gate lowers, they make it inside the castle only to find out it's a trap. Barely holding on, they hold up the block that nearly collapsed on them. Miho somehow solves the puzzle and saves them, but after Zork attacks, the group gets in a string of hits. It still isn't enough to beat Zork!

Episode 27: Friendship – From Legend to Legend

Bakura changes the dice for a weighed down version, but even after a critical hit, the group somehow survives with one hit point. An internal battle is waging inside Bakura with his more innocent side. Tea heals the group, while regular Bakura throws his evil side off by switching hands when he rolls the dice. Amazingly, Yugi casts a spell on Zork and from one of his wounds, the character of Bakura appears! Zork transforms into something more evil, but Bakura protects them from the attack with a magical barrier. He tells them exactly where to place their fire, in the center of Zork's heart where an evil eye appears. The fated last roll comes but Bakura cheats by reinforcing them with his dark power. They both have a critical hit of '00' but because evil Bakura cheated, his dice cracked and disappeared. Tea using her "Big Bang" casts a super spell to kill Zork once and for all. Their spirits return to their bodies; Bakura's Ring falls from his neck onto the floor. Once back to normal, Ryo shows everyone the special display case he made with all of their characters from Monster World, including one of the Game King. ✪

Yu-Gi-Oh! Series 2 Episode Summaries

— Philip McKinney (GymLeaderPhil)

Even though we list this series as Season 2, it is essentially Season 1 to many fans. The real Season 1 has not aired in the United States. The may be due to the fact that Yami-Yugi (Yugi's alter ego from his millennium puzzle) was an extremely violent character in the beginning of the series. Season 2 focuses almost entirely on the card game Duel Monsters. Duel Monsters is one of many stories in Season 1. Here's everything that happens in Season 2:

Episode 1: The Heart of the Cards

Yugi is seen playing Duel Monsters with Joey. While dueling, Seto Kaiba overhears that Yugi's grandfather has a "super-rare" card in his possession. Yugi wins and offers Joey a lesson in Duel Monsters from his Grandfather. Later at Grandpa's shop, Yugi's grandfather shows Yugi, Tea, Joey, and Tristan the rare card, Blue Eyes White Dragon. Suddenly Kaiba shows up and offers to trade or purchase the rare card. Yugi's Grandpa refuses because the card was a gift from a long time friend. Grandpa is then forced the next day into a duel with Kaiba and loses his Blue Eyes White Dragon, which Kaiba then tore into pieces when Yugi and gang arrived at Kaiba Corp. Yugi took his defeated grandfather's advice to teach Kaiba about the heart of the cards and dueled Kaiba. By believing in the cards and his Grandfather's advice, Yugi assembled all the pieces of Exodia winning the match against Kaiba and his three Blue Eyes White Dragons. With the aid of his millennium puzzle, Yugi opens Kaiba's mind and got rid of the evil thoughts that clouded his life.

Episode 2: The Gauntlet Is Thrown

Joey is shown facing Tea in a duel, clueless about how to play. At Grandpa's shop, Joey asks Yugi's Grandpa to train him in Duel Monsters. Long, hard training with Grandpa begins and moves into the living room where Yugi and Joey's other friends watch Rex Raptor battle Weevil on television. Weevil, who uses bug cards, is able to win with a trap card and was awarded Regional Champion by Maximillian Pegasus, the creator of Duel Monsters. Just then, Yugi remembers a package that came in. It is from Industrial Illusions, Maximillion Pegasus' company. Inside are a dueling glove and two star chips along with an invitation to the Duelist Kingdom and a video. Yugi popps the video into the TV. Pegasus appears and freezes everyone except Yugi with his Millennium Eye and challenges Yugi to duel in a timed match. When Yugi is about to win, the time ran out and Yugi lost. With his Millennium Eye, Pegasus takes Yugi's Grandfather soul, forcing Yugi to go to the Duelist Kingdom to win it back.

Episode 3:
Journey to the Duelist Kingdom

Joey receives a video from his sister, Serenity. It is revealed that she has an eye disease that will render her blind if she doesn't get an expensive operation. Joey decides to go to the Duelist Kingdom with Yugi to battle and win the two million dollar prize to pay for a surgery that will help Serenity. When Yugi tries to board the ship going to the Duelist Kingdom, Joey comes along. Yugi is allowed to pass, but Joey has trouble because he does not having a dueling glove and star chips. As a result, Yugi gives Joey a star chip so he can board. Tea and Tristan also board the ship hiding in a box of cargo and notice a schoolmate, Bakura, on the deck of the ship. While on the ship, Yugi and Joey meet Weevil and Rex. Weevil reveals the new rules of the tournament. Meanwhile Rex loses his room on the ship over a duel against Mai, a duelist who can predict cards. Out on the deck, Weevil asks Yugi to see the rare Exodia cards. He takes this opportunity to throw the pieces of Exodia into the ocean. Joey jumps in to try to retrieve the pieces but fails.

Episode 4:
Into the Hornet's Nest

The Duelist Kingdom cruise ship is seen docking into the Duelist Kingdom. Yugi and the gang take the ramp off, and with all the other duelists, gather in front of Pegasus' castle. Pegasus explains the new rules and those who get ten star chips will have the right to enter his castle. As the tournament starts, Yugi and the gang walk until Weevil confronts them. He leads them on a wild goose chase, right into the forest area. Yugi and Weevil proceed to duel. Weevil bets two star chips, while Yugi bets his deck and one star chip in replacement for another chip. Weevil explains about the field power bonus his monsters get being a forest field and a wasteland field. He lays down an insect monster and realizes that the wasteland area also powers up Yugi's dark type monsters. Weevil then unleashes his favored Basic Insect combo, in which Yugi activates his Mirror Force, reflecting the attack right back at Weevil destroying all his monsters in attack mode, reducing his life points to 555 with Yugi still at 1350 life points.

Episode 5:
The Ultimate Great Moth

Weevil reveals that he has an ultimate combo coming out that would eliminate Yugi, once and for all. Even though Yugi just blasted through his monsters, Weevil reveals a monster to be the Larvae Moth and sealed inside a Cocoon of Evolution. He brags that in five turns the Ultimate Great Moth will appear and do away with Yugi due to its huge field power bonus. Joey cheers on from the sidelines. Joey shouts at Yugi to get fired up. Although a figure of speech, the suggestion gives Yugi an idea. Playing the Curse of Dragon, he equips it with the Burning Land magic card before attacking the forest arena around the cocoon. With the forest burnt down, the cocoon loses its field power bonus, making it weak enough to destroy. 4 turns was enough for a Great Moth to evolve stronger though. The Great Moth in turn destroys one of Yugi's defense monsters, and Yugi takes his turn playing Magical Mist to stop The Great Moth's

poison before killing another one of his monsters. Yugi plays his Summoned Skull that has an electrical attack. The Magical Mist conducts the attack and destroys Great Moth, wiping out Weevil's Life Points.

Episode 6:
First Duel!

With Yugi's first duel over with, Joey starts looking for an opponent. Joey starts to doubt his skills, but the gang reminds him of his sister. Just then they see a kid complaining about how Mai cheats and knows the cards faced down. Mai confronts Yugi, Tai, Tristan and challenges Joey because he only has one star chip, an easy duel. Joey accepts and battled blind because Mai's tricks made him hesitate about his strategy. Mai then used a magic card to multiply her cards, but with some thinking and the help of Yugi's borrowed cards from aboard the ship, Joey catches on to Mai's tricks. Mai uses perfume on the cards and by smelling the different scents she is able to tell which card was which. Joey then regains confidence and uses the Time Wizard to transform a Baby Dragon to Thousand Dragon and to make Mai's Harpies Ladies older. Joey proceeds to destroy Mai's monsters and the rest of her Life Points with the Thousand Dragon's Flame Breath attack.

Episode # 7 - Attack from the deep

Yugi and the gang have eventually grown hungry after going through their first two duels. They didn't pack any food, and have come to the Duelist Kingdom unprepared. Joey smells something cooking off in the distance and goes to check it out. Tristan and Joey go off to eat the fish when they are caught by the top ocean duelist: Mako Tsunami. He asks who they are, and when he finds out that Yugi is one of their friends, he gladly offers the gang some food. In return, however, Mako challenges Yugi to a duel. Going on a field that is half-land, half-sea takes Yami Yugi by surprise at first. The first few monsters Yugi lays out are fish bait, due to the sea-based part of the field covering Mako's monsters. Yugi uses his last attempt to win by summoning Great Soldier of Stone in attack mode. After Mako carelessly surrounds Yugi's Rock Soldier with all of his monsters, Yugi attacks the Full Moon card he had placed on the field. This reverses the tides, dries up Mako's water monsters, and wins Yugi the duel.

Episode 8: Everything is Relative

At Pegasus' castle, a masked Mokuba makes his escape via a short cloth rope. Meanwhile, Yugi and the gang run into one of Pegasus' men hassling a duelist that had his deck and star chips stolen. Yugi vows to find whoever stole the star chips and

return them to the duelist before he gets kicked off the island via boat. The thief turns out to be Mokuba, who challenges Yugi to a duel. Yami Yugi comes out, and the entire intentions of Pegasus come up. Mokuba explains if someone representing Pegasus, or Pegasus himself defeats Yugi, Kaiba Corp. will be transferred under Pegasus' control. So Mokuba was dueling Yugi to protect Kaiba Corp. He ends up getting two of his monsters destroyed while dueling Yugi. Meanwhile, Pegasus has his henchmen try to kill Kaiba at his company, but he escapes. Mokuba then tries to steal Yugi's chips, but Yugi stops him and tries to get him to return the stolen deck and star chips. The boat has already left, and Pegasus' henchmen grab Mokuba and tell Yugi to duel a special opponent set up for him at the nearby duel ring. The opponent is a deceased Seto Kaiba.

Episode 9: Duel with a Ghoul

The henchman says that Kaiba's ghost is the one standing across from Yugi. Yugi doesn't know what to think, and goes along with the duel. "Kaiba" starts out with a Cyclops as the real Kaiba started the previous duel the two had in the first episode. Yugi shakes this off and destroys it with the Dark Magician. "Kaiba" now brings out his legendary Blue Eyes White Dragon. While this is going on, the real Kaiba tries to hack into the Duelist Kingdom's computers, working his way through to find the area in which Yugi is located. Back to the duel, Yugi plays Curse of Dragon on the defense, activating "Kaiba's" Seal Defense. "Kaiba" orders the Blue Eyes White Dragon to destroy Curse of Dragon with its White Lightning attack. The real Kaiba is using his computer terminal to hack into the Industrial Illusions mainframe to find out what is happening in Yugi's duel. Yugi managed to cover his Dark Magician in one of four hats. Confusing "Kaiba", Yugi explains

that if he guesses the wrong hat, something bad will happen to him.

Episode 10: Give up the Ghost

The real Kaiba finds the field just as a Blue Eyes White Dragon is about to attack Yugi. Yugi was able to buy some time by using the Magical Hats magic card to confuse the fake Kaiba. Just as the Blue Eyes White Dragon begins to attack, his attack points begin to lower dramatically as the real Kaiba uploads a virus. In the end, Kaiba has to run away to avoid getting caught, but he helped Yugi enough to make him win. The fake Kaiba was actually a spirit from the demon realm that possessed Kaiba in the first episode. With the help of Yugi's Millennium Puzzle, the demon was returned back to the realm and was sealed there. After the duel, Yugi and the gang see that Mokuba has disappeared again.

Episode 11: The Dueling Monkey

Yugi and company fail in their search for Mokuba. Joey finds some of Tristan's cards on the ground and notices Swamp Battleguard. Mai spots Rex Raptor. Mai makes herself visible to get his attention. Rex Raptor then challenges Mai to seek revenge for kicking him out of his room on the boat earlier. Mai said she would accept only if Rex defeats Joey in a battle, so she can get revenge. Meanwhile, Joey receives a card from

Tristan and says he doesn't need any help or pity from his friends. Then, Rex Raptor challenges Joey and he accepts but he must receive no help from his friends or else he'll be disqualified. Joey still accepts and begins the battle very overconfident and then drifts off into the unsure world. Rex calls Joey a "dueling monkey", because he has no idea what he is doing. This makes Joey really mad, and makes him want to win even more. Meanwhile, Yugi and Tristan are talking about Joey. Tristan wants Yugi to help Joey, but Yugi says that they have to believe in him. Yugi reminds Tristan about Joey's sister, and how he needs to be able to win on his own.

Episode 12:
Trial by Red Eyes

The battle between Joey vs. Rex Raptor continues. Joey defeats Rex's monsters on the field but just then, Rex Raptor sends out his strongest dragon card, the Red Eyes Black Dragon. Joey's only choice is to use time warp with the Time Wizard. The Time Wizard's wand spins and the two choices are a time machine, which will speed up time and a skull, which will hurt Joey's life points. With luck, the pointer lands on a time machine and turns the Red Eyes Black Dragon into a fossil. Joey wins and also gets the card along with his two star chips. After a long day battling the gang sets up tent for the night and Mai offers them food. Mai walks off, and Bakura makes his appearance at the camp.

The gang talks about their favorite cards, with Yugi's being the Dark Magician, Tea's being the Magician of Faith, Tristan's being Cyber Commander, Joey with Flame Swordsman, and Bakura with Change of Heart. Bakura challenges Yugi to a duel, but instead transforms to Yami Bakura and locks the gang's souls into their favorite cards and attempts to steal the Millennium Puzzle until Yami Yugi appears.

Episode 13:
Evil Spirit of the Ring

Yami Yugi and Bakura begin their duel, but Yugi realizes that this isn't Bakura at all! Its an evil spirit of some kind, that has the power of the Shadow Realm The duel starts, with Yami Yugi going with the Cyber Commander in which Tristan's soul is in. Bakura annihilates the Commander with his White Magical Hat. Joey is next, as he is the Flame Swordsman. He destroys the White Thief. As Yami Bakura sets a face down defense monster, Joey is hasty and attacks. It turns out to be a trap, and forces the players to discard their hands and draw 5 new cards from their deck. Yugi plays Dark Magician and Reborn the Monster to revive Tristan. The normal Yugi, entrapped in the Dark Magician attacks another Metamol Pot. Yami Yugi plays Saint Magician in reverse defense mode and Bakura sets another monster while activating his trap, Just Desserts, doing 500 damage to Yugi for every monster on the field. The Black Magician attacks Bakura's set monster, which is the Electric Lizard. As Bakura then plays Change of Heart, Yami Yugi switches the souls of the normal Bakura and the dark Bakura, putting Yami Bakura's soul in the Change of Heart card. The Black Magician attacks, destroys the dark Bakura, and wins the duel. After they return to the real world, they hear a scream and rush to it.

Episode 14:
The Light at the End of the Tunnel

As the gang rushes to find out who they heard screaming, they find Mai and an eliminator (like the fake Kaiba) named Panik who had taken all her star chips. Yugi vows to beat him and return Mai's chips. The duel starts, but Panik raises the odds. If Yugi beats him, Mai will get her chips back, if defeated Yugi will lose all his chips, and his life. He then plays The Castle That Spreads the Darkness in defense mode. It shields Panik's side of the field in darkness, so Yugi can't see what he's up against. Yugi tries to light up Panik's side by observing it when his monsters attack. Yugi plays Winged Dragon and fires his fireball attack. This fails, as Yugi's monster and following monsters are defeated consecutively. Yugi then starts playing mind games with Panik, calling him a coward and messing with his head. This turns out to be successful as Panik starts to lose his focus. Yugi plays Swords of Revealing Light, not only revealing Panik's monsters, but locks them in place for 3 turns. Panik plays Card-Hunting Grim Reaper, but it gets frozen by a Spell-Binding Circle.

Episode 15:
Winning Through Intimidation

Yugi plays Curse of Dragon and ends his turn. Panik plays another monster to bolster his defenses. Right now, Panik has his Chaos Shield in place also raising his defenses. Yugi starts getting confident as playing the Chaos Shield has lead to Panik's own demise. Yugi plays Dark Knight Gaia and flips over Polymerization which turns Gaia and Curse of Dragon into Gaia the Dragon Champion with the attack strength of 2600. The final turn of the Swords of Revealing Light has arrived and Yugi deals the final blow. Yugi summons Catapult Turtle and loads Dragon Knight Gaia onto its catapult. This raises Dragon Knight Gaia's attack to 3200, equal to the defense of the Castle and Chaos Shield combined. Yugi orders the launch and Gaia blows up the floatation ring of the castle. Once the Sealing Swords of Light disappear, the castle will come crashing down on Player Killer's monsters seeing as how Panik has trapped them in with the Chaos Shield. This reduces Panik's Life Points to 0. Panik tries to kill Yugi with flamethrowers but the Millennium Puzzle protects him and Yugi gives him a Mind Crush. Yugi tries to give back Mai's chips, but she refuses. After some reverse psychology from Joey, she accepts.

Episode # 16: Scars of Defeat

A helicopter lands near Yugi and the gang. It is Kaiba, ready to duel Pegasus. Joey doesn't want another player in his way of winning the money and challenges Kaiba to a duel after insulting the duelist. Kaiba accepts and they debut Kaiba's new invention: Duel Disks. Kaiba starts out with the Battle Ox and proceeds to rip through Joey's Armored Lizard and his next few monsters. Kaiba fuses two of his monsters and creates Minocentaur. This monster destroys Joey's monsters continually until Joey finally draws the Red Eyes Black Dragon. Using its Inferno Fire Blast, Red Eyes kills the Minocentaur. Kaiba smirks and ends

the duel by playing Blue Eyes White Dragon annihilating Red Eyes. Kaiba then warns Yugi how he cannot beat Pegasus. To prove a point, Kaiba tells a

story about when Pegasus was at the intercontinental championships and how he saw Pegasus duel a guy called Bandit Keith. Pegasus used his Millennium Eye to see Keith's strategy, wrote it down, and called out a kid from the crowd, who beat Keith following the instructions. Kaiba then flies to the castle, with Joey at a loss.

Episode 17: Arena of Lost Souls (Part 1)

In the morning, the troop continues their tournament journey. Unknowingly, they are being observed by three of Bandit Keith's cronies. Keith reveals his plan to get revenge on Pegasus after the intercontinental championships. Joey, having some weird feeling like they are being watched, leaves the group. As he leaves, he gets knocked out and brought to a dueling ring inside a cave. He wakes up and Keith forces him to duel one of his cronies, Bonz. Joey is forced to bet 4 star chips. Meanwhile, Yugi and company search for Joey but can't find anything and split up. As the duel starts, Bonz tries

to play a zombie card but Keith tells him to play Dark Armor Zanki, which is quickly annihilated with Joey's Axe Raider. Keith tells Bonz to keep playing non-undead monsters. Continuing, Bonz puts down Crass Clown and Earth-eating Dragon. Both destroyed by the Axe Raider and Flame Swordsman. Then, Bonz draws Call of the Haunted, which revives all the monsters killed by Joey and turns

them into the undead sub-type. Joey starts to worry about the trouble he has gotten into.

Episode 18: Arena of Lost Souls (Part 2)

With Call of the Haunted on the field, this practically makes all of Bonz's monsters invincible. If they get struck down, they just regenerate, along with a ten-percent power boost. Joey has still failed to notice that all the zombie's defense strengths are zero. Joey catches Bandit Keith off-guard when he plays Time Wizard and tries to use the Time Magic. This fails, and Joey's monsters get destroyed along with a whole chunk of his Life Points. Bonz plays King of Ghosts: Pumpking that boosts all his undead monsters. Joey is forced to continually defend. By now, Yugi and the gang show up at the duel arena ready to support Joey. Tristan gives Joey back his wallet, which reminds Joey of his sister. Joey then draws the mighty Red Eyes Black Dragon and incinerates Pumpking, stopping the growth of his monsters. Red Eyes is still no match as the pumped up Dragon Zombie destroys it. Yugi hints to Joey about one magic card in his deck that could turn the tide. As Joey defends, Bonz plays Defense Paralysis to keep Joey from defending. Joey draws the magic card Yugi told him about being Shield and Sword, switching all attack and defense points. This pumps Joey's Battle Warrior to 1000 attack, while all the undead monsters have zero attack strength allowing Joey to win the duel. When Yugi and the gang try to leave the cave, Keith's "people" close the cave up with a boulder. Keith steals all his henchmen's star chips and gets enough to go into the castle.

Episode 19: Double Trouble (Part 1)

Trapped inside the labyrinth cave, Yugi and the others follow Bakura's Millennium Ring, hoping it will lead

them to Pegasus. Yugi and friends find an alternate exit, but the door is guarded by Pegasus's Paradox Brothers. For Yugi and his group to exit the cave and the maze, they have to defeat Para and Dox in a tag team duel. Yugi chooses Joey as his partner. If they do defeat Para and Dox they will have gained enough star chips to enter Pegasus' castle as well as exiting the cave. Para and Dox also play a riddle with Yugi and Joey about which door to choose. The catch is one is telling the truth, one is lying. Yugi has his doubts. This duel ring has several different rules. First of all, the monsters on the board move like chess pieces, moving only a maximum of their monster level. The Labyrinth Bros start first, laying Labyrinth Wall in attack mode. This turns the duel ring into a maze. Yugi sends in Beaver Warrior, which is annihilated by the Wall Shadow. As the turns progress, Joey and Yugi pile their forces up. Joey sets a card and plays Axe Raider close to him. Dox summons a Labyrinth Tank and sends it seven spaces forward. Yugi sends his Celtic Guardian into the maze and as the Wall Shadow is about to attack, Joey activates Kunai with Chain.

Episode 20: Double Trouble (Part 2)

At the beginning of this episode, Kaiba runs into Kimo, Pegasus' guard that captured Mokuba earlier, and takes him hostage to get him into Pegasus' castle. Meanwhile, at the Labyrinth Bros. tag team duel, Joey

consolidates their forces by sending Flame Swordsman into the fray. Yugi summons the Dark Magician. The brothers counter by playing Labyrinth Change splitting up the forces. Joey's Axe Raider runs into a Landmine Spider and pays dearly. While Para and Dox wait for the three guardians, laying them in defense mode as they get them, they send out Dungeon Worm. The Worm annihilates the Celtic Guardian. Yugi plays Magical Silk Hats hiding the Black Magician and Flame Swordsman. As the brothers play Monster Tamer, increasing Dungeon Worm's attack, they choose to attack one of the hats, and fail. Joey releases the Flame Swordsman, plays Salamandra and destroys the Worm. Unfortunately, Para and Dox have bought themselves enough time to assemble Sanga, Kazejin, Suijin, which the sacrifice to summon the Gate Guardian. Para orders the Gate Guardian to attack the Flame Swordsman with its Thunder Clapse attack...

Episode 21: Double Trouble (Part 3)

As the Thunder Clapse attack converges on the Flame Swordsman, Yugi activates his Mirror Force card reflecting the attack right back at the Gate Guardian. Para and Dox, however, use the Gate Guardian's attack nullifying ability to negate the attack. Not known to Para and Dox the attack still hits and annihilates their Monster Tamer. Joey tries to attack with the Swordsman and fails, which allows Para and Dox to attack with the water elemental part of the Gate Guardian, destroying the Flame Swordsman. This, however, leaves a trail of water leading back to the Gate Guardian and with this, Yugi plays Summoned Skull and attacks with Lightning Strike. This channels through the water stream and destroys the water elemental part of the Gate Guardian. Gate Guardian tried to negate it, but Yugi activated Spell-Binding Circle.

Yugi and Joey take advantage of this delay. Joey plays his Red Eyes Black Dragon and Yugi activates his set Polymerization to combine Demon Summon and Red Eyes to form Black Skull Dragon. The Labyrinth Bros. then tell them that the maze is a no-flying zone, meaning the Dragon can't move. Dox plays the Force magic card, which drains half of Joey's and Yugi's Life Points and gives its power to the Gate Guardian's attack strength. Yugi moves his Dark Magician to the end of the maze and plays Reborn the Monster to revive Suijin, the water elemental. Gate Guardian tries to attack the Dark Magician, but Yugi uses the attack negation ability of Suijin. Joey then plays Mimicking Illusionist, copying the Force magic card, decreasing Para and Dox's Life Points by half, and transferring it to the Black Skull Dragon now with attack and defense strengths 4000/2500. Gate Guardian annihilates Suijin, and Yugi just laughs. Yugi activates Monster Replace. This switches the position of the Black Skull Dragon and Black Magician allowing the Black Skull Dragon to destroy it with its Molten Fireball attack. Yugi and Joey win the duel. Meanwhile, Kaiba finds Mokuba but is confronted by Pegasus. In the maze, Yugi tricks the Labyrinth Bros. into telling them the right door to exit the maze. Pegasus uses the Millennium Eye to trap Mokuba's soul in a card...

Episode 22: Face off (Part 1)

For Kaiba to get entrance to the castle to face Pegasus, Pegasus says he must defeat Yugi for five star chips. As Yugi and the gang make it out of the dungeon, Yugi and Tea have flashbacks of how they met and so on. This goes on for about half the episode. As Yugi is about to enter the castle, he sees Kaiba standing in his way. Kaiba explains how he's changed, and Yugi accepts the duel. As they duel with Kaiba's Duel Disks, Bandit Keith gets a front row seat.

Yugi beats Kaiba's Gargoyle Powered with his Curse of Dragon, but it was a setup as Kaiba plays a powered up Vengeful Swordstalker. Yugi counters with Monster Replace, which swaps the Curse of Dragon with the Dark Magician and destroys the Swordstalker. Kaiba then sets a card with La Jinn: Mystical Genie of the Lamp. Dark Magician attacks, but Kaiba activates his Magic Lamp trap. This redirects the attack to the Curse of Dragon. Kaiba grins, as Yugi has no idea about Kaiba's plan to fuse all three Blue Eyes White Dragons into the ultimate creature...

Episode 23: Face off (Part 2)

This episode continues following the duel between Kaiba and Yugi. Kaiba plays De-Spell to remove the Sealing Swords of Light in Yugi's hand. Yugi is curious about Kaiba's hand so he plays Eye of Truth, revealing Kaiba's hand. Yugi is shocked to see a Blue Eyes, and the fact Kaiba hadn't played

it. Yugi plays the Magic Boxes in combination with his Dark Magician and destroys the Magic Lamp. Yugi destroys La Jinn and ends his turn. Kaiba sets a card and leaves out Sagi: The Dark Clown. Yugi blindly attacks Sagi with Gaia: The Fierce Knight and Kaiba activates his trap. The trap is Crush Card Virus. This infects Yugi's deck destroying any card with 1500 or more attack points in Yugi's deck. Yugi defends until he plays Griffol in combination with Unicorn's Horn, which destroys Kaiba's monster. Kaiba finally has all three Blue Eyes in his hand, so he summons one and destroys the Griffol with its White Lightning. Kaiba then draws the Polymerization he needs and fuses all three Blue Eyes. This creates the most powerful monster known in Duel Monsters to this point, the Blue Eyes Ultimate Dragon. Yugi knows he can't give up and how everything rests on this last card.

Episode 24: Face off (Part 3)

Yugi plays Kuribo in attack, and when Kaiba starts to make fun of it, the hologram gets "mad". Anyway, Yugi also plays Multiply with Kuribo strengthening his defenses. Kaiba continues to attack, but the Kuribo keep multiplying. Yugi then has his next combo in store for Kaiba. He uses Living Arrow with Polymerization and the Mammoth Graveyard to fuse it with the Blue Eyes Ultimate Dragon, which will reduce Blue Eyes Ultimate Dragons' power by 1200 every turn. Kaiba just blindly attacks the Kuribo to no avail, as the Blue Eyes Ultimate Dragon continues to decay. Yugi summons Celtic Guardian and destroys one of the Blue Eyes' heads. Kaiba moves backward to the edge of the roof. If Kaiba loses all his Life Points, he will fall. Kaiba then plays Reborn the Monster. This revives one of the normal Blue Eyes and focuses on the last turn. Yugi has a choice. Yami Yugi decides to deliver the finishing attack

that would cause Kaiba's Life Points to drop to zero, but normal Yugi decides not to take that risk, and he regains control and stops the attack. Kaiba attacks with Blue Eyes and wins. He gloats and enters the castle. Meanwhile, Yugi is frozen and won't respond to anybody.

Episode 25: Shining Friendship

At the beginning of this episode, Yugi is well near paralyzed to the fact that he almost lost control of his other side when dueling Kaiba. He won't respond to his friends much less Mai's offer to lend him 6 of her star chips. Mai challenges Yugi to duel for his remaining star chips, but since Yugi won't respond, Tea steps in his place. As the duel begins, Mai is beating Tea into the ground with her Harpy Ladies. Tea plays a few wimpy monsters and powers them up slightly. Halfway through the duel Mai goes into her taunting about friendship and Tea gets ticked off. She plays Shining Friendship and starts getting some combo ideas. With the quick thinking of Tea and her Magician of Faith she powers up her Shining Friendship card to insane amounts, and wipes out Mai's Harpies. Mai is about to flip over Harpy's Feather Sweep but decides not to. She hands the star chips over to Tea. Yugi can finally enter the castle.

Episode 26:
Champion V Creator

As Yugi and the gang make their way into Pegasus' castle, they see Bandit Keith and hear about Kaiba and Pegasus dueling soon. Kaiba offers Pegasus to duel with the Duel Disks but Pegasus refuses and acts dumb. He makes the stakes a little higher, saying if they would duel via the duel disks, Mokuba would make Pegasus' moves for him. Kaiba declines, and they proceed to duel on a normal duel ring. Pegasus, at the beginning, is toying around with Kaiba, as he mocks Kaiba's Rude Kaiser and Kaiba's grim look. As Kaiba motions to slap down his Blue Eyes White Dragon, Pegasus activates a trap called Prediction. If Pegasus guessed the card Kaiba was about to play was over 2000 attack power or lower than 2000, Pegasus gets the card. Pegasus guesses high, and steals Kaiba's Blue Eyes. Kaiba puts his Kaiser into defense and sets his Virus combo up. Pegasus knows this and readies his move. Pegasus plays Dark Energy, tripling Sagi's attack points, making him an illegal sacrifice for the Crush Card Virus. Kaiba now starts to worry, as Pegasus' Millennium Eye allows him to see his hand.

Episode #27:
Champion V Creator
(Part 2)

The episode picks up halfway through the Kaiba/Pegasus duel. Pegasus starts ranting about toons and the types of cartoons he watched as a child. Then, Pegasus plays Toon World, which turns his monsters into toons. Pegasus attacks with Dark Rabbit. It "destroys" Kaiba's Minotaur. Pegasus, now in the driver's seat, plays the Blue Eyes White Dragon he stole. Toon World turns it into the Blue Eyes Toon Dragon, however. Since Kaiba has figured out Pegasus and his hand reading scheme, he discards his hand and starts playing from the deck. He draws and plays the Blue Eyes

White Dragon. After the Blue Eyes White Dragon attacks, Pegasus reveals that with Toon World in play, toon monsters can't be attacked by non-toon monsters. This is shown by the Blue Eyes Toon Dragon shape shifting out of the White Lightning's way. Pegasus plays Shine Castle, raising the Blue Eyes Toon Dragon to 3500 attack points strong. He attacks, but Kaiba activates Shadow Spell. This stops Blue Eyes Toon Dragon in its tracks and reduces its attack by 700. Kaiba orders his Blue Eyes to annihilate it with White Lightning and does so. Pegasus then counters with Dragon Capture Jar and plays Dragon Piper as well. With his Blue Eyes White Dragon trapped, Kaiba orders his Rude Kaiser to attack the Jar Demon. Pegasus has other plans, though, as he activates Copycat and copies the Crush Card Virus, which annihilates Kaiba's deck. Kaiba's soul is then trapped in a card. ✪

Yu-Gi-Oh!
Season 3 Introduction

— By Mika Matsumoto

There are so many different sides to Yu-Gi-Oh, it's almost hard to say how it can be any better than it already is. Well, hold on to your horses because the ride into the dark side is only beginning! If you're not big on spoilers, you probably shouldn't be reading this...

THE BATTLE CITY SAGA CONTINUES

But since you ARE reading this, here's what you can look forward to! Battle City heats up with the arrival of the next god card: Saint Dragon – The God of Osiris! Malik's pantomime attacks Yugi with the fiendish god card, but somehow Yugi manages to escape from its attacks.

All the while, Joey continues his quest to be a true duelist, fighting against Maco in a friendly duel. The duel gets intense, with Joey playing in a sea field, which isn't his best setting. Maco gives it a good run, but in the end Joey wins the duel. In the process, he gains "The Legendary Fisherman", a card that ends up helping Joey more often than he realizes.

Malik takes his time showing his true face and instead plays against Yugi and Seto through the Ghouls. These creepy creatures with light and dark masks force Yugi and Seto to work together as a team. Seto is reluctant to accept the idea of teamwork, but when a quick move by Yugi saves him from near elimination, Seto changes his tune. Their teamwork and Seto's Obelisk card gives them the win over the Ghouls.

The battle isn't over for Seto and Yugi, who are whisked away to the Domino City docks by Mokuba and the Kaiba Corp. helicopter. Malik, using Yugi's best friend Joey against him, takes over Joey and plays him in a deadly duel between the two! Tea is also possessed by Malik, tying both Joey and Yugi to an anchor that is set to drop when the time limit for the duel ends. Fighting for their friendship, Yugi appeals to everything that Joey remembers about him and their friendship, all the fun and rough times

they had been through. Yugi even gives Joey his Millennium Puzzle, hoping for the best. He has a lot of faith in Joey, so when he starts to falter Malik grips tighter on Joey. It takes the power of the Red Eyes Black Dragon, Joey's prize card, to bring him around. Joey uses it on his friend, intending to finish him but Yugi surprises him by gladly taking the blow. His self-sacrifice breaks Malik's hold on Joey, just enough for him to even the score by finishing himself off, which saves them both.

The dueling stage changes once the semi-finalists make their way onto the Battle Ship. Now the REAL duel begins! Before they get to the Battle Stadium on Alcatraz Island, a dark battle rages between Yugi and Bakura and the two of them face off against each other. Bakura has tons of traps to fool Yugi, but he fights back against his occult deck, defeating Bakura's powerful card, "Dark Necrophia".

Joey faces off against who he believes is Malik, but really is Rashid, one of Malik's long-time companions. He has a hard time getting in damage on Rashid, especially when he counters with magic and trap cards at every turn. Joey gets left wide open with no monsters when Rashid plays "Anubis' Judgment", destroying all of his cards! With next to nothing left, Rashid takes advantage of the opportunity to use his Ra card to finish off Joey, but his card is nothing but a copy of Malik's real one. While Joey fights back with the cards he's won along his dueling journey, Rashid plays his Ra card, but it rebels against him and instead attacks everyone playing! Joey, even though he only has 200 lifepoints, wins by default because Rashid couldn't get back up.

Mai gets her chance to prove herself in the arena, this time against the real Malik. He takes no prisoners, warning her that her game will be one of darkness; the consequences would be devastating. She faces it bravely, dueling hard against him with her Harpies. Malik is unstoppable though, grinding through her monsters and leaving her tied up. He plays his Ra card, but from nowhere, Joey races in to take the damage of the blow for Mai. Unable to hold on any longer, Joey is forced to give up and drops from sheer exhaustion. Under the rules of the dark game, her spirit is held captive by Malik.

Seto is up once again, fighting against the mysterious duelist number 8: Isis Ishtar, Malik's sister. Able to see the future of their match, Isis is not intimidated by Seto in any way. As expected, he plays expertly with Isis countering his moves, but in a sudden change of the future, Seto sacrifices his god card Obelisk for his favored Blue Eyes White Dragon! Isis' assured win is gone and Seto comes out on top with the win.

Isis and Malik's history all comes to light after she loses to Seto, particularly how they got their Millennium items and why Malik has all that raging darkness inside him. A lot of things happened to them when they were younger in Egypt, with Sha-di returning to the picture, but a lot of it practically destroyed their family.

To top it all off, the dark versus dark battle ensues between Malik and Bakura. Their dark sides go out of control, fighting for the win. The match is secured early in Malik's favor and made final when he attacks Bakura with his god card Ra. Against that kind of power, he never has a chance.

And think about this: Battle City isn't over yet!! There's still more to come from Yu-Gi-Oh, so there's only one thing left to say.

It's time to duel! ○

Top 10
Legend of Blue Eyes - Creatures

Legend of Blue eyes White Dragon Top 10 list

— By DeQuan Watson

10. Final Flame

Some people might argue this card being on any top ten lists. The reason I think it should make the list is that it is quick easy free damage. If you are playing a deck with lots of fast early hitters, you can definitely take advantage of this. Once you get your opponents life total low, your opponent might even stop attacking. If he is unsure of what magic cards you have down or what your creature in defense mode is that's face down, you get the advantage. It's a card that if used well can deal some damage AND buy you some time.

9. Blue Eyes White Dragon

I know. I know. Some people are wondering how the most expensive card in the set is only number nine on the list. Not only is this card the most expensive, it's also the most popular. However, the fact that you have to sacrifice two monsters in a tribute is what keeps it so low on the list. I don't see anything wrong with this card. Without some tricks in your deck to get it in play, I wouldn't recommend playing more than one in a deck.

8. Swords of Revealing Light

I'll be fair; this card could possibly be one or two spots higher. However, I've seen this card in action many times. Sometimes its great, sometimes is not. A lot of times, I just see it buying time to delay the inevitable. I've seen several tournament decks win without it. I think in the future with more cards available this card will become a staple card in decks with control and delay tactics.

7. Man Eater Bug

For such a little monster, this guy packs a mean punch. Man Eater Bug is in nearly every good deck. The card is fairly easy to get and it has a strong effect. Most people play it face down and wait for it to be attacked. The thing they are good for is outright killing your opponent's face down monster so you don't get surprised. It's a great low level monster that has earned its place in tournament winning decks.

6. Monster Reborn

This card is simply amazing. It lets you get multiple uses out of key monsters in your deck that have already gone to the graveyard. What makes it even better though, is that you can choose to take a monster from your opponents graveyard. You can take advantage of what your opponent is playing as well as your own. Unfortunately this card is restricted in tournament play, so you can only use on in a deck.

5. Fissure

Raise your hand if you like to kill monsters. I know I do. This card is good for helping that along. It does have two restrictions though. It has to kill a face up monster. Also, it destroys a face up monster with the lowest attack (ATK) value. Even though this seems limited, it is definitely worth having in your deck. As more sets come out, players will start using more small creatures with good effects. This will make this card much more useful.

4. Trap Hole

If Fissure is on the list, then Trap Hole definitely deserves to be on the list. The only limitation Trap Hole has, is that it can only destroy a creature that has 1,000 ATK value or higher. This isn't much of a limitation. It kills most large problem monsters. It also helps take out scary tribute monsters such as Blue Eyes White Dragon.

3. Pot of Greed

This is such a simple and harmless looking card. However, when you only have 40 cards in your deck, getting to race through them faster can be a huge advantage. We all knew from day one that this card was going to end up on the restricted list. Card advantage in a game like this can be so devastating. This card is an absolute must have in every deck. It is two free cards as soon as you draw it. That is hardly ever a bad thing.

2. Dark Hole

Dark Hole is a great comeback card. I have seen so many games won from a bad position because of Dark Hole. It's a good thing this card is on the restricted list as well. It does destroy ALL monsters (this includes yours). That's not a bad thing though. If you need to get caught up, this card will help you do it.

1. Raigeki

Finally, we've reached the top. If Dark Hole is good, then Raigeki is simply better. You get to destroy your opponent's monsters while getting to keep your own. You can keep your opponent from putting anything in the way of your attacking monsters. It's a great card to help you finish out a game. It hardly seems fair. Well, it probably isn't. That's why it too is on the restricted list. ❂

Top 10
Legend of Blue Eyes - Magic & Trap

— By Nick Moore (a.k.a. NickWhiz1)

It's a basic consensus that the first set of a Trading Card Game needs to be a foundation to build the game on. In Yu-Gi-Oh!'s case, the Legend of Blue-Eyes White Dragon set needs to be a strong enough foundation to support the game that has grown into a phenomenon. These cards were originally difficult to find, as there was a limited production run that was supposedly cancelled with the release of Metal Raiders in June, but they have begun to surface again.

To be perfectly honest, in my opinion, Legend of Blue-Eyes White Dragon is, as a whole, the weakest set so far. Except for the few good cards (that are among the best in the game), the set isn't that strong. Those good cards, however, end up being game breakers. The following list is a look at the top 10 Legend of Blue-Eyes White Dragon Magic and Trap cards, in this writer's humble opinion. If not for these strong cards, the set would be a dud, with nothing more than weak and overpriced monsters.

(NOTICE: I also included cards that can only be found in the Starter Decks as well, because, technically, they're part of the Legend of Blue-Eyes White Dragon set.)

10. Card Destruction

The poor man's Pot of Greed. For the cost of discarding your hand, you get a new hand of the same size, and your opponent does the same. This is used in the infamous Monster Reborn combo, and can counter Exodia, but other than that, for the time being, it's dead weight. If they had made it similar to Professor Oak (lower the number from 7 to 5, of course), everyone would have it in their deck. As it stands, however, it's just not up to par. With Pharaoh's Servant and future sets, however,

comes great promise for this card, as discard decks will get very popular. You can try a Bistro Butcher + Giant Trunade + Card Destruction combo deck if you want to, but it's too inconsistent for my tastes. Restricted to 2 per deck.

9. Trap Hole

I am sure to get a lot of disagreement about this card, but I think this card is more of a waste of space than anything now, because of the number of staple cards growing exponentially with each new set. When the game first came out, everyone packed 3 of these things as easy monster removal. That number has slowly declined in the past couple of months as people are trying to streamline their decks and are ending up getting rid of these guys. Trap Hole is all but dead in the Japanese environment, and soon, this card won't be used in English circles anymore. For a while, though, it was one of the most popular cards in the game. May you rest in peace, oh Pit Trap. Not restricted.

8. Polymerization

OK, I know all of you will probably disagree with me on this one too,

because of how hot this card is and it's the only way you can play Fusions. I will give one simple little counter: Fusion decks are really weak right now. There aren't many good Fusions to play, and in my opinion, with Magic Jammer polluting the environment, as well as the upcoming Imperial Decree in Pharaoh's Servant, Polymerization can simply be countered, ruining your entire strategy. The only good way to play Fusions is with the Devil Franken (English: Cyber-Stein), that lets you pay 5000 LP to Special Summon a Fusion monster. It's 1/3 of the one turn KO combo, but that will come in due time. I would take advantage of the popularity of this card and trade it for other good cards, unless you wish to build a Fusion deck. If so, good luck. Not restricted.

7. Waboku

I like this card. I like it even more because of the ruling that it prevents Battle Damage from all of your opponent's monsters. In a way, it's kind of like Negate Attack from the anime. Think of it as a Swords of Revealing Light for one turn, if you wish to. Nowadays, this card isn't used that much anymore, because of newer stalling methods, like Messenger of

Peace. However, it's always a nice surprise to put into your deck, or at least your side deck. Not restricted.

6. Swords of Revealing Light

Probably the best card that is currently restricted to 2 (although Heavy Storm makes a convincing argument). Stopping your opponent dead in their tracks for 3 turns can be the thing that you need to pull off a game-winning combo. Flipping over your opponent's monsters is both a blessing and a curse, as you

Card Game - Top 10 LOB Magic and Trap

can see what you'll be attacking, but you may also activate Flip effects, and if it's Magician of Faith or Man-Eater Bug, you're in trouble. This card is weakened by the fact that Mystical Space Typhoon from Magic Ruler can destroy this card before your turn ends (they won't need to use Magic Jammer on it, as this card has the properties of a Continuous Magic card). It's still a good card to have, and will be restricted to 1 within the next couple of months. Restricted to 2 per deck.

5. Monster Reborn

This and the next two cards were hard to put in order, but this is the best order I could come up with. Monster Reborn has the unique ability of being able to bypass the Tribute Summon rule, as it can Special

Summon any monster from either player's graveyard (unless it has a Special Summon requirement, like a Ritual Summon or a Toon monster, and it hasn't entered play normally yet). A classic combo is to set Monster Reborn on the field, then use a discard card (Card Destruction is a popular choice) to discard a high-level monster, then activate Monster Reborn to bring back said monster from the

Graveyard. The only downside to Monster Reborn is that it can't Special Summon monsters in facedown defense position. That shouldn't stop you from playing this card, however. Restricted to 1 per deck.

4. Dark Hole

While not as good as Raigeki, Dark Hole has its uses. The most obvious of these uses is when your monster field is clear. If you don't have any monsters on the field, this card acts as a Raigeki, which hurts, badly.

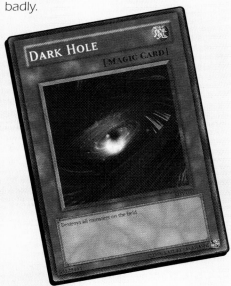

It's also good to use with Witch of the Black Forest and Sangan in your Exodia deck, as it will speed it up and eliminate your opponent's threatening monsters as well. A good candidate to bring back with Magician of Faith's effect, unless you have Raigeki in the Graveyard. Restricted to 1 per deck.

3. Change of Heart

This card has combo possibilities. I'm serious, it does. While you can use it to swipe one of your opponent's monsters and either attack with it or Tribute it, there is a really sinister thing you can do that will make your opponent cringe. Aim for facedown cards. If you Flip Summon a facedown

monster card with a Flip effect while it is under your control, you get the effect. Man-Eater Bug is nice to have, but by far, the best Flip effect monster to get is Magician of Faith. With Magician of Faith, you could bring back Change of Heart and steal another opposing monster, or bring up a Raigeki, Pot of Greed, or other game-breaker. Experiment with it, you'll love it. Restricted to 1 per deck.

2. Pot of Greed

If this could draw one more card, it would be in the #1 spot. However, then we couldn't call it the Bill of the Yu-Gi-Oh! universe. This card is powerful enough as it is. For the simple cost of one

little card, you get 2 free draws. Yep, that simple. This card dramatically increases your deck's speed and also thins it out, giving you a better chance of drawing any single card that you need to win the game. This is probably the best card to bring back with Magician of Faith's effect, because having hand advantage is crucial in this game, due to the low hand size and the nasty discard cards in Magic Ruler and upcoming sets. Restricted to 1 per deck.

1. Raigeki

Oh, come on, who didn't see this coming? Raigeki is quite possibly the biggest gamebreaker in the entire game, including the Japanese version. One spray of this Thunderbolt, and your opponent's Monsters are obliterated. Follow up with a Heavy Storm from Metal Raiders, and your opponent might as well concede the game. It's best to use this card when your opponent's field has a lot of monsters, or if you feel there are threatening facedown monsters that could shift the game in their favor. I would highly recommend clearing your opponent's

Magic/Trap cards first (Heavy Storm is a good candidate), so they don't pull a Magic Jammer on you. Highly recommended as a recovered card with Magician of Faith's effect. Restricted to 1 per deck.

Honorable Mention: Soul Exchange

This card had great promise, and was frequently used in the early days of the game. However, people started noticing that the loss of Battle Phase was more trouble than it was worth, and their newly Tributed monster always managed to get destroyed before they could utilize it. A single Trap Hole will make your opponent's efforts all for naught and they still lose their Battle Phase. It works wonders in defensive decks, but those aren't extremely strong right now. They will be, though... Not restricted.

This concludes my look at the top 10 Magic/Trap cards of the Legend of Blue-Eyes White Dragon. You may feel free to disagree with this list, because, in the end, it all comes down to personal preference anyways. Feel free to use it as a reference list, though. I don't mind that. ✪

Top 10 Metal Raiders - Creatures

— By Augustine Choy

Metal Raiders wasn't really a set for monsters. It was based hugely on traps, such as mirror force and those 4 counter trap cards. But there were some good very good monsters released, albeit rather few. Here is my opinion on the top ten monsters from Metal Raiders.

10. Cannon Soldier

This monster is perfect in a late game situation. When you need a quick 1000-2000 damage, this monster can easily clinch the game for you. However, this is a very specialized monster. It does one job and one job only. It becomes useless when you really need a strong offensive monster. You should only think of putting this monster in your deck if your main goal is direct damage.

9. Barrel Dragon

One of the best parts about this monster is that it is a machine type, which saves it from many debilitating effects such as paralyzing potion or germ infection. This definitely has one of the best effects in the game. You have a 50% chance of destroying any monster on the field. Basically, you have a chance to attack twice with this monster; once with the effect and then again with the regular attack. The reason I didn't rate this monster higher is that it requires 2 tributes to get out. If you're going to pay 2 monsters to get out a monster, you might as well bring out a Blue Eyes White Dragon instead. Also, it's rather unlikely that you'll be able to use the effect more than once, as it will probably be destroyed by magic in the blink of an eye.

8. Kuriboh

This is certainly one of the more interesting effects that were released in Metal Raiders. You can discard Kuriboh from your hand in order to prevent any Life Point damage from 1 monster. The reason I think this card is good is because it is impossible to counter the activation of this effect. The other reason is that soon, this card will become so versatile. Fans of the animé know of the multiply combo that was used. When multiply is released, this card will let you stall for some time. Fans of the animé will also know how devastating the Deck Destruction Virus of Death was. While it isn't quite as powerful as in the animé, it is still quite deadly, and Kuriboh qualifies as the required tribute needed to unleash the virus.

7.7 Colored Fish

A great addition to the small group of level 4 1800 attack monsters. This monster was the first monster with 1800 attack and no detrimental effect since La Jinn. Definitely a must for any beatdown deck as it is one of the most powerful monsters you can summon without tribute. However, this card isn't as good as La Jinn due to the fact that Sea monsters aren't all that popular yet. Future sets will definitely increase the popularity of them.

6. Dark Elf

This was a great addition to the beat down decks. It has the second highest attack for 4 star monsters so far. The only downside is that you have to pay 1000LP every time you attack with it. But that shouldn't really hamper it at all. You can simply leave it in attack mode and create an offensive wall early in the game. When you do choose to attack with it, do not use it to attack defense monsters. Rather, use it to attack the opponent's LP directly, so that you make a net gain of 1000LP. Also, with the release of Megamorph in Magic Ruler, losing LP can be an advantage because then it will allow you to equip Megamorph to Dark Elf, raising its attack to 4000.

5. Shadow Ghoul

With a measly 1600 attack, this card doesn't look like much, but when you get this card out late in the game, it can rival the power of Blue Eyes White Dragon with only requiring 1 tribute. It gains 100 attack points for each monster in your graveyard, so you want to optimize the effect by saving it for later in the game instead of playing it at the start. In some ways, this can be even greater than Summoned Skull, but with the constant fluctuation in attack power, you don't want to take chances. You're much better off going with a constant attack force.

4. Sangan

This is definitely weaker than its counterpart, Witch of the Black Forest. Witch of the Black Forest is for high attack, low defense monsters. It really

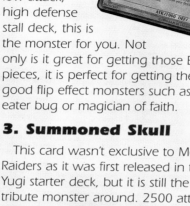

depends on what deck you play for you to decide which of the two best suits your deck. If you have a low attack, high defense stall deck, this is the monster for you. Not only is it great for getting those Exodia pieces, it is perfect for getting the good flip effect monsters such as man eater bug or magician of faith.

3. Summoned Skull

This card wasn't exclusive to Metal Raiders as it was first released in the Yugi starter deck, but it is still the best tribute monster around. 2500 attack for just 1 monster is unrivaled by any other monster. In addition, its defense is just 1200, meaning that it can be easily retrieved via Witch of the Black Forest. But that low defense also makes it very susceptible to shield and sword. Reducing its attack to 1200 will allow even the weakest monsters to eliminate it. However, the pros to this card are just too great for this one downside for it to affect the playability of this card. It belongs in every attack-based deck

2. Witch of the Black Forest

This card should definitely be in every deck. In case you aren't familiar with the effect, when this monster is sent from the field to the graveyard, you can get any monster from your deck that has 1500 defense or less and put it in your hand. Most of the best cards around have less than 1500 defense, for example, Summoned Skull and La Jinn. Also, this is a perfect card

for Exodia decks if you haven't already figured it out already. I really believe this is the best monster from metal raiders as it greatly increases the speed of a deck. There's a reason this card is restricted to 1 in Japan. However, it doesn't match up to...

1. Magician of Faith

If you look down the list of restricted cards, what do you see? 14 of the 24 limited or semi-limited cards are magic cards. That's more than half. And with this card, you can really turn the tide of a game by allowing you to use those great magic cards over and over. A definite must for most decks. Best of all, it isn't restricted at all. Think how devastating it can be if you Raigeki the opponent 4+ times a game. Or stalling for 15+ turns with Swords of Revealing Light. This card can easily bring you back from the brink of defeat and turn the tide of battle. ○

Top 10 Metal Raiders - Trap

— By Chris Schroeder

Greetings duelists! My name is Chris Schroeder. For my first Yu-Gi-Oh article I will be reviewing the top 10 magic/trap cards from Metal Raiders. Metal Raiders introduced some of best trap cards including Magic Jammer and Mirror Force. And power magic cards such as Heavy Storm and Tribute to the Doomed.

1. Magic Jammer (Ultra Rare)

Number 1 on the list is Magic Jammer. A deck staple. This is one powerful trap card. Having 2 or even 3 of these in your deck can prove to be useful in the end. The ability to negate your opponents Pot of Greed, Raigeki, Swords of Revealing Light, etc. is indeed powerful and can tip the game in your favor. Even though you must discard 1 card to use this card it is well worth it in the long run. A must for any deck!

2. Mirror Force (Ultra Rare)

My personal favorite, Mirror Force takes number 2 on the top 10. Even though this card is limit 1 per deck it is a force to be reckoned with. This deck staple is seen in every deck because of its incredible effect. You not only negate your opponents attack but you also destroy all of their monsters that are in attack position. Clearing the field can give you a huge advantage and makes your opponent open for an attack on their life points. A very powerful trap card

3. Change of Heart (Ultra Rare)

Change of Heart takes number 3. Even though this card does come in the starter decks, it also comes in metal raiders packs in an ultra rare version. Anyway, this card is one of the best deck staples in the game. With its effect you

may take control of a face-up or face-down monster and take control of that monster for 1 turn. Doing change of heart on a face down Magician of Faith will stop any plan your opponent may have had. This card is also great for stealing a monster then tributing it for a monster of your own. Or even just stealing their only monster on the field just so you can hit them for direct damage. So many uses for this card. Make sure this is in your deck!

4. Seven Tools of the Bandit (Ultra Rare)

Seven Tools of the Bandit steals number 4 of the top 10. While this card isn't a deck staple it shouldn't be overlooked. For the cost of 1000 of your life points you can negate any trap card. With so many powerful trap cards like Mirror Force, Magic Jammer, Robbin Goblin, etc. you may want to try throwing in 1 or 2 of these in your deck. Even though its costs 1000 life points it can prove useful in times of need.

5. Solemn Judgement (Ultra Rare)

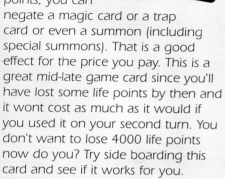

The card that can cost a lot, Solemn Judgement takes number 5. For half of your life points, you can negate a magic card or a trap card or even a summon (including special summons). That is a good effect for the price you pay. This is a great mid-late game card since you'll have lost some life points by then and it wont cost as much as it would if you used it on your second turn. You don't want to lose 4000 life points now do you? Try side boarding this card and see if it works for you.

6. Heavy Storm (Super Rare)

Heavy storm gets number 6 with its awesome power. When you play this card it wipes the field clean of all magic/trap cards including your own.

While some of you may think it sucks to get rid of your cards as well, it's actually not. This is an effective way to get rid of Mirror Force, robbin goblins and trap holes. This card has been restricted to 2 per deck because of its power. Sweeping all trap and magic cards away will give you a fine chance to summon a monster without the fear of Trap Hole. It can even get rid of those Magic Jammers on the field allowing you to use that Raigeki or Pot of Greed (unless your opponent plays 2 Jammers face down and jams the Heavy Storm) with no fear of it getting negated. Thus allowing you to gain an advantage over your opponent. Another great magic staple card.

7. Tribute to the Doomed (Super Rare)

Tribute to the Doomed gets the 7th spot of the top 10. For the cost of 1 card from your hand you may destroy any monster on the field. With this card you can stop those nasty Man-Eater Bugs, Magicians of Faith, Hane-Hanes, etc. from ever flipping over. Its not really a deck staple but it is needed since there are a lot of flip effects out there. Some let you even get magic or trap cards back from your graveyard. It is also great for getting rid of that Summon Skull or other high level monsters that you couldn't trap hole earlier but its works best for set monsters. Its better than fissure so try it out.

8. Robbin Goblin (Rare)

The Robbin Goblin trap card is number 8 and it has one mean effect.

When 1 of your monsters does battle damage to your opponent's life points, you may randomly pick 1 card from his hand and discard it. Robin Goblin teams up nicely with White Magical Hat since his effect does the same thing as robbin goblin but you'll be discarding 2 cards from his hand. Taking out his hand can give you total advantage of the game. Making him discard monsters so they have nothing to defend with. Or taking out their Raigeki or Change of Heart they were saving for later. Although this card is tough to keep on the field with cards like Heavy Storm and Giant Trunade, if you can get it out and get rid of those key cards you can probably win the game. Great trap card and its only a rare!

9. Shield and Sword (Rare)

Shield and Sword takes number 9. This card is feared by Summoned Skull since his defense points are so low while his attack is still high. When using this card all the monsters on the field (Face Up) switch their attack power with their defense power for 1 turn. With Summoned Skull at a low 1200 defense he can be easy picking for La Jinn that is summoned after this magic card is used. This card is also used in wall decks. Wall decks include monsters with defenses 2000 and over that take advantage of switching their defenses into huge attacks. Even the Labyrinth Wall can attack for 3000 points with this card. That is the same thing a Blue Eyes would do but it's a little bit easier to do. A great magic card although it's not a staple card for other decks, it's a key staple card for wall decks.

10. Tremendous Fire (Common)

And the final card of the top 10 is Tremendous Fire. For 500 life points you can inflict 1000 life points of direct damage to your opponent. Great in direct damage decks that do nothing but attack your opponents life points instead of their monsters with cards like Just Desserts , Princess of Tsurugi and other direct damage cards. It doesn't cost that much to use and if your opponent only has 900 life points left you can win the game with this card. But nothing overly great about this card. And its not a staple card but if you like doing direct damage go on and play it. ○

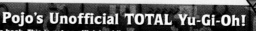

— By Scott Gerhardt

Yeah it's a Tribute monster, but it's got 3000 DEF. That will hold off most anything in the game. Some super defensive decks might try to use this to hold off until they can do things like assemble Exodia or set up a really nasty attack.

#10 – Ceremonial Bell

1850 DEF with the ability that all hands are played face-up. This eliminates some surprise factors. Play some cards face down, then play with this guy and you'll be the only one with any surprise factors. The DEF will be good enough to hold off opponents for a while, especially with some good traps hidden. Not for every deck, but nice to see what's coming.

#9 – Karate Man

This guy can go Kamikaze when you need to lay a whoop down on your opponent for one turn. Not the best permanent attacker, but to be able to boost up 1000 at will

Honorable Mention – Labyrinth Wall.

can make your opponent think twice about serving into him.

#8 – Flash Assailant

Great in Super-Aggro decks. You need to dump your whole hand real fast and just start beating with this guy. Having an empty hand is not easy, but the reward of a 4 start 2000/2000 is worth it. If you find the right deck for him with lots of power-ups, he'll cause your opponent problems.

#7 – Spear Cretin

The trick here is to get a large fattie in your graveyard, then let him die. Once he does, you can get a fattie, regardless of size, into play. There are enough cards

where you can discard cards – use it to set-up the Cretin to die and bring one back.

#6 – Dark Zebra

Keep something – anything on the board, and you have 1800 ATK. Great for beatdown. Just don't get caught with nothing or he goes DEF and that is pretty bad since he's weak there. Keeping things on the board should not be all that hard, though.

#5 – Crab Turtle

Don't forget Ritual Monsters. His cost is hefty, but if you have the set-up, he CAN be first turn. Remember the tribute can come from the hand or the board. Opening hand: 2 Crab Turtles, and a Turtle Oath. Drop one Turtle to summon the other. With 2550 ATK, very little will be able to deal with this threat early.

#4 – Toon Summoned Skull

All the Summoned Skull, going directly for the dome. Unless they have Toons, he's gonna dish at least 2500 to your opponent a turn. Dead in 3-4 turns. Yes you have to have Toon World in play

and keep it safe, but it's a small price to pay for direct death.

#3 – Maha Vailo

There are so many good Magic Enchant cards that this is a natural near the top of the list. Slap it on an Axe of Despair for a complete monster. Horn of the Unicorn and Megamorph can also make this thing nearly unstoppable. He's prone to destruction, but without it, he can end a game in just a couple turns with the right cards.

#2 – Relinquished

What were they thinking? This card can wreck an opponent and REALLY make them not want to attack. Take your creature, affect YOUR life total, and basically have something so large there is nothing you can do about it. They have to catch him naked to kill him and that's really hard to do. He'll blatantly win games.

#1 – Cyber Jar

So good they had to restrict him. The ability to wipe the board and bring down a bunch of Level 4s is just too good. Your opponent gets it too, but you're the one prepared for it. It's like another Dark Hole only the effect can be even more devastating. Basically a must for any deck. ✪

Top 10
Magic Ruler - Magic/Trap

— By Vijay Seixas A.K.A SomeGuy

1. Axe of Despair

Not necessarily THE best Magic / Trap card in the set, but a very good one that gives, what would seem like, mediocre Monsters a chance to shine. A couple examples are Maha Vailo and White Magical Hat. With an Axe of Despair equipped, both of these Monsters, along with others, become a force to deal with. Whether it is super high ATK or excellent effects, Axe of Despair gives the needed boost for weaker Monsters to survive and deal a nice amount of Life Point damage.

This is the card that's making Summoned Skull obsolete. Why Tribute a monster risking a Trap Hole, and wasting your Normal Summon for the turn, when you can just throw an Axe onto it and make it as strong, or stronger than a Summoned Skull?

2. Delinquent Duo

Delinquent Duo is restricted to one for a good reason. Even with the drawback, it has too much power for one card. Being able to strip away two cards from your opponent's hand is definitely worth the mere 1000 Life Point loss. Out of the three hand disruption cards we received from Magic Ruler

(Confiscation, The Forceful Sentry, & Delinquent Duo), this is undoubtedly the best one.

Delinquent Duo is best played during the first turn (Stripping your opponent's opening hand from five to three), or sometime in the mid-game (The average mid-game hand is three). The end of the game isn't a very intelligent time to play Delinquent Duo, because Life Points are usually rather low. And losing 1000 Life Points can severely change the outcome.

3. Snatch Steal

Snatch Steal is basically a permanent Change of Heart. There is one advantage that Change of Heart has over Snatch Steal though. The fact that Change of Heart can take control of face-down Monsters is what makes it more versatile than Snatch Steal. Being able to Change of Heart a face-down Magician of Faith, then using the effect to pull back Change of Heart, is what makes it priceless (This is just one of many uses Change of Heart has). The drawback that Snatch Steal has isn't such a big deal, because most of the Monsters you take control of; will have at least 1000 ATK. And thus, counting each other out.

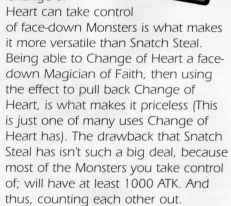

Even though Snatch Steal can be both Heavy Storm-ed and Mystical Space Typhoon-ed, the most annoying counter to it, is Spellbinding Circle.

Picture this, your opponent plays

Snatch Steal on one of your Monsters, you respond by flipping Spellbinding Circle over, targeting the Monster that your opponent took control of. Every turn you will be gaining 1000 Life Points while your opponent won't be able to attack with the Snatch Steal-ed Monster.

4. Megamorph

Megamorph works great with Monsters such as Dark Elf and even the less popular, Jirai Gumo. Megamorph is all about a quick win. Usually one hit with a Megamorph-ed Monster takes off about half of your opponent's Life Points. Other non-Monster cards such as Solemn Judgment, Delinquent Duo, and Confiscation backup decks based on Megamorph greatly. Along with the cards mentioned above, Monster removal (Raigeki, Dark Hole, Fissure, Tribute to the Doomed, ECT.) is also needed. Being able to clear the field for one swift, large attack is what Megamorph is intended for.

5. The Forceful Sentry

Why is this card better than Confiscation? The fact that it has no Life Point payment is the main reason (even though it's better. Though, with all the Magician of Faith going around, shuffling into the deck can be a good thing. I'd much rather have my opponent try and top deck the card, then him being able to revive it

from his Graveyard. And as we all know, the majority of the cards targeted from Confiscation and The Forceful Sentry are Magic cards. If you don't know why, take a look at the Upperdeck restriction list.

6. Confiscation

The 1000 Life Point loss somewhat hurts Confiscation. Being able to discard an important card from your opponent's hand makes up for it though. As stated above, Magician of Faith is probably it's biggest counter. But, since Magician of Faith isn't indestructible, it can be surpassed. Confiscation works best as a first turn play.

7. Mystical Space Typhoon

Not as powerful as Heavy Storm, but still a strong card nevertheless. In Japan, Mystical Space Typhoon (Known as Cyclone) is staple card. As more sets are released, I'm sure it will be the same way here in the USA.

Quickplay Magic is a new mechanic that was released with Magic Ruler. Quickplay Magic cards can be activated during your Battle Phase. Also, when Quickplay Magic cards are set on the field, they can be activated during your opponent's turn. So, if your opponent flipped a Robbin' Goblin during his Battle Phase, you could flip Mystical Space Typhoon in order to destroy the Robbin' Goblin and save your hand. Mystical Space

Typhoon also works well when you have important Magic / Trap cards set on the field that you may not want to Heavy Storm away. Overall, Mystical Space Typhoon is a versatile card that will have more and more uses as the sets go by.

8. Messenger of Peace

This card can be very tough to deal with in the right deck. Both my Exodia deck and my Relinquished deck (Which you will see) abuse this card to the maximum. In Exodia, being able to stall for countless turns, against most decks, will give you plenty of time to search out for all five pieces or just to setup with plenty of Counter Traps. 100 Life Points per turn is nothing, this is what makes the card so combo efficient. Keep in mind; you will need Counter Traps in order to keep it active.

9. Chain Energy

This is probably the most combo based Magic card in the entire Magic Ruler set. It's not one of those cards you just throw into your deck. A lot of skill is needed in order to play Chain Energy correctly. If used inaccurately, it will backfire on you and possibly cost you the game. But, if used at the right time, can easily lock up the game in your favor. Playing a couple of these when your opponent has only a few thousand Life Points remaining, can be extremely aggravating for him/her.

Obviously Chain Energy is best suited for Direct Damage based decks, along with Lock variants. Cards that can work in conjunction with Chain

Energy are Toll, Wall of Illusion, Hane-Hane, and various Direct Damage cards such as Tremendous Fire, Princess of Tsurugi, and possibly Just Desserts.

Why Hane-Hane and Wall of Illusion? Simple, they pay 500-1500 to play the Monster (Because of Chain Energy[s]). Then they go ahead and attack with it (Possibly paying 500-1500 if Toll[s] is in play), then you flip over Hane-Hane / Wall of Illusion and it goes straight back to their hand. All those Life Points wasted for no good reason. Try Chain Energy out, and see what combos you can come up with.

10. Malevolent Nuzzler

This is definitely an underrated card. For only a common, it packs a decent punch. If you're on a tight budget (Or just can't find Axe of Despair in general), don't be afraid to give this card a try. Malevolent Nuzzler even works pretty well with Maha Vailo. A tribute-less 2750 ATK Monster isn't too awful. Though, this is slightly worse than an Axe-ed La Jinn the Mystical Genie of the Lamp or 7 Colored Fish. Another reason I think Malevolent Nuzzler is pretty cool, is the fact that is has a cheap cost to place it back on top of your deck when discarded, unlike Axe of Despair. And it also doesn't force you to put it back on top of your deck when discarded, unlike Horn of the Unicorn.

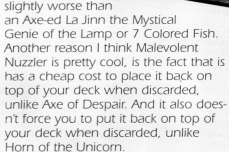

If you can't afford Axe of Despair / Megamorph, or are just playing an Equipment Magic heavy deck, give Malevolent Nuzzler a try. It's much better than Sword of Deep-Seated, Stim-Pack, and even Horn of the Unicorn.

As you can see, Magic Ruler is literally the Magic set. Spellbinding Circle almost made the cut at #10, but lost due to the fact it isn't much stronger than the average Monster removal. I'd much rather destroy a Monster straight up, then just leave it sitting there possibly doing some defending or being used up as Tribute. ○

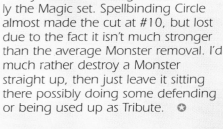

Top 10 Tournament Pack

— By Vijay Seixas AKA Some Guy

1. TP1-001 Mechanical Chaser

Ultra Rare

Here is the card that basically defines the whole TP1 (Tournament Pack Season One) set. The main reason anyone even opens up their TP1 pack is to get a chance to pull one of these babies. Since this is the only Ultra Rare in the set, the ratio in order to pull one is 1:108 TP1 packs. This is unlike the standard 1:12 in all the other sets. Sell wise, Mechanical Chaser goes from anywhere from $100-$200. So yes, getting a playset of these is a tough accomplishment.

What makes Mechanical Chaser a strong card is the fact that he has 50 more ATK then the highly played 7 Colored Fish and La Jinn the Mystical Genie of the Lamp. Of course, now with the release of Magic Ruler, we have good equipment cards such as Megamorph, Axe of Despair, and even Malevolent Nuzzler. These cards make the extra 50 ATK that Mechanical Chaser has, not as good as it once was. But in the end, an Axe-d Mechanical Chaser will always beat an Axe-d La Jinn the Mystical Genie of the Lamp.

2. TP1-013 Goddess with the Third Eye

Rare

Goddess with the Third Eye is better than Versago the Destroyer and Beastking of the Swamps strictly because of ATK power. This little rare (along with the other two like it), are what make Fusions playable right now. The problem is the only decent Fusion right now, in my opinion, is B. Skull Dragon. Now you don't have to worry about playing that crappy Red-Eyes Black Dragon in your deck. Sure it looks cool, but it's very weak for a level seven.

3. TP1-015 Versago the Destroyer

Rare

Unlike Goddess with the Third Eye, Versago the Destroyer is pretty much the same card besides the slightly less ATK and different attributes. The different attributes along with the slightly less ATK doesn't mean much because Versago the Destroyer will, most of the time, be played from the hand in order to complete a Fusion. If you're playing a Dark-based Fusion deck with Mystic Plasma Zone, then Versago the Destroyer can attack for 1600 in a pinch. And if you're really desperate, you can equip some Magic onto him for a bigger punch.

4. TP1-014 Beastking of the Swamps

Rare

Here is the last of the three Fusion-supporters. Like the others, Beastking of the Swamps has different ATK along with different attributes. Of the three Fusion-supporters, this one has the highest DEF. A DEF of 1100 isn't going to be doing a lot of good defending though. Not much else to say about this card that hasn't already been previously stated.

One thing that's for sure, you definitely don't want to max out all three of these guys in your deck.

5. TP1-004 Patrol Rob

Super Rare

Interesting card. The stats are pretty bad, but it's nothing that can't be fixed by Axe of Despair or some other form of Equipment Magic. If used correctly, this card can give you the heads up on if you should, attack, play a certain card, ECT. Being able to know that

your opponent has a Mirror Force on the field can help you better prepare for it. The same goes for Magic Jammer and other forms of Counter-Traps. Although most decks won't have the room for it, Patrol Robo is not that bad of a card. There are just better options.

6. TP1-002 Axe Raider

Type: Normal Monster
EARTH/Warrior
Level 4
1700/1150
Super Rare

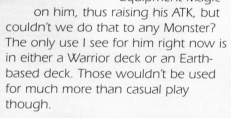

Axe Raider is barely better than Neo the Magic Swordsman and Battle Ox, and are those played? Nope. Not anymore at least. If Axe Raider was released when all we had was SDK/SDY and LOB then, yeah, he would have been "good". But it's a little too late for that. We could always throw Equipment Magic on him, thus raising his ATK, but couldn't we do that to any Monster? The only use I see for him right now is in either a Warrior deck or an Earth-based deck. Those wouldn't be used for much more than casual play though.

7. TP1-005 White Hole

Type: Normal Trap
When your opponent plays "Dark Hole", the monsters on your side of the field are not destroyed.
Super Rare

It can be a smack in your opponent's face if used at the right time. Watching your opponent destroy all his/her Monsters (If any) is priceless. Too bad Dark Hole is a restricted card, or else White Hole would have been three times as good. The fact that Dark Hole is restricted is what makes this card not very playable. Wasting spots in your deck just because of one

card that's limited to one isn't a very good idea. I would much rather be using Magic Jammer or Solemn Judgment in its place. If you must play it, don't use anymore than one.

8. TP1-025 Hercules Beetle

Type: Normal Monster
EARTH/Insect
Level 5
1500/2000
Common

Having to pay Tribute for a 2000 DEF Monster is bad, but not as bad as some of the other cards in this set. There is absolutely nothing that abuses this card, unless you consider Kwagar Hercules a good reason. Besides that (which you really shouldn't play anyway), this card has no use other than to defend. And since there are so many better defensive Monsters without any Tribute, those make this card obsolete.

9. TP1-003 Kwagar Hercules

Type: Fusion Monster
(Kuwagata \ + Hercules Beetle)
EARTH/Insect
Level 6
1900/1700

Here's the Fusion that Hercules Beetle eventually turns into. The only reason that makes it even remotely good is the fact that it can't become Trap

Hole-d (just like every other Fusion out there). Without any Equipment Magic it isn't anything special besides the fact that it can destroy Mechanical Chaser, La Jinn the Mystical Genie of the Lamp, and 7 Colored Fish. That is, if they don't have any Equipment Magic attached.

10. TP1-011 Gust Fan

Type: Normal Magic
A WIND monster equipped with this card increases its ATK by 400 points and decreases its DEF by 200 points.

The only reason why this Equipment Magic made it over the other three is because Harpie Lady Sisters is such a fun casual type deck. Yep, I know that there are better Equipment Magic cards, but the whole point to a casual Harpie Lady Sisters deck is to have fun. This just adds to the theme of the deck. Which in turn, makes the deck more enjoyable. Tournament wise, this card is T-E-R-R-I-B-L-E. Even, the outdated, Stim Pack is better than this. But what can you expect from a thirty-card set?

The set just gets worse and worse as the numbers go by. Cards one through seven were really the only cards worth paying much attention to. Overall, I believe this is a better set for collectors than tournament players. The casual player may find a few fun cards to mess around with though.

Now we wait for TP2… ✪

– By Israel Quiroz

We know some of you guys are on a budget. You don't have a money tree, and can't buy all the rares some Killer Decks contain. But you don't need rare cards to win games. So here are some of the best common cards. These are easily available for a few pennies. These are found in either the YuGi or Kaiba starters, or commons in booster packs.

1. Man-Eater Bug (SDY-046)

This Monster might have an attack of 450 and a defense of 600 but it's the Flip effect that makes him great. Whenever you Flip this monster; whether is a Flip Summon or because your opponent attacked you get to choose a Monster on the Field and destroy it regardless of position. This Monster can get rid of your opponent's Blue Eyes White Dragon or any other thread he might have in play by just Flipping over. With this Monster in play you'll always have something in defense mode to protect you and Monster removal when you need it.

2. Dark Hole (SDY-022)

Talk about clearing the board. Dark Hole is one of the strongest Magic cards in the game because of its ability to destroy all Monsters in play. This card can save you from being over-whelmed by your opponent's army and can help you regain control of the game. With this card you can clear the board then drop one of your Monsters and attack your opponent's life points directly because he won't have any Monsters in play. Dark Hole is a really great and strong card but it also has a great draw back. When this card clears the board it destroys all Monsters on the field including yours. If you ask me that's a fair price to be able to re-set the game because this card will allow you to make a come-back when you're in those tight spots.

3. La Jinn the Jeanie of the Lamp (SDK-026)

If you're looking for the biggest level four monsters in the game this guy is one of the first cards you'll think about. He might not have an effect but he comes with an attack power of 1800 and a defense of 1000, talk about an enforcer. La Jinn is one of the biggest level four Monsters out there, he might not be the biggest Monster out there but he also doesn't come with a draw back. Once you get him in play there isn't much that can stop him, throw a Magic Equip Card on him that'll increase his attack strength and your opponent will have more than enough to worry about.

4. Monster Reborn (SDY-030)

If you thought Change of Heart was good just wait until you see it's older brother. Monster Reborn is what gamers would call a Change of Heart with the Kicker, with this card you get to keep whatever Monster you get until your opponent destroys it instead of just keeping it for one turn. Monster Reborn allows you to choose a Monster on anyone's

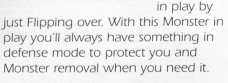

discard pile and special summon it on your side of the field. This card is not only great because you'll always get the biggest Monster you can find but because it will also make your opponent pay for using all those level seven and higher Monsters against you.

5. Change of Heart (SDY-032)

Talk about switching the momentum of the game. This card's ability to let you take control of any one of your opponent's Monsters until the end of the turn is amazing.

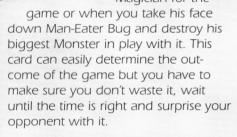

You can take your opponent's stronger Monster on the field and attack his own Monsters with it or finish him off.

Imagine the look on your opponent's face when you attack him with his own Dark Magician for the game or when you take his face down Man-Eater Bug and destroy his biggest Monster in play with it. This card can easily determine the outcome of the game but you have to make sure you don't waste it, wait until the time is right and surprise your opponent with it.

6. Trap Hole (SDY-027)

How many times have you lost because you didn't have any Monsters in play and your opponent played some fatty to finish you off? With this card in play that'll never happen to you again. Trap Hole sits in play waiting for your opponent to play a Monster with an attack power of 1000 or greater and destroys it. This card will not only leave your opponent open for one turn because just about any Monster has a power of 1000 or greater but it will

also take care of your opponent's Level five and higher Monsters.

7. Fissure (SDY-026)

There's nothing greater than seeing your opponent sacrifice all of his Monsters in play to get a level seven Monster on the field only to have it Fissured next turn. This card's ability to destroy your opponent's Monster with the smallest attack power in play is a lot stronger than many players think. Just because this card destroys your opponent's Monster with the lowest attack points, it doesn't mean it can't get rid of your opponent's Barrel Dragon with an attack power of 2600. If all your opponent has in play is his big, fat enforcer this card will make him pay because if he only has one Monster in play this card will get rid of it regardless of the Monster's attack strength.

8. Wall of Illusion (SDY-034)

This Wall is one of the most annoying Monsters on the game and it will frustrate your opponent more than you can imagine. What makes this card playable is not only the fact that it has a defense of 1850 but it also comes with a great effect. The effect on this card returns any Monsters that attack it back to their opponent's hand whether the wall is destroyed or not and irregardless of whether is on attack or in defense mode. This means that this wall is not only defensive but also aggressive. You can attack your

opponent for 1000 life points every turn until he can attack it with a bigger Monster only to have that Monster returned to his hand. Talk about a complete package.

9. Summoned Skull (SDY-004)

We've seen what this Monster has done for Yugi in the past, he's won him more duels than I can remember and he can do it for you too. Summoned Skull is the biggest level six Monster you can find, with an attack power of 2500 only some level sevens can overpower him. You can get this guy in play turn two by sacrificing one of your smaller Flip Effect Monster played on the previous turn and start hitting your opponent for a whopping 2500 life points each turn. The game will be over before you know it because there's nothing your opponent can do to deal with such a huge threat in the early game.

10. Malevolent Nuzzeler (MRL-005)

This card has to be the best equip card in the game because is easy strong and easy to get. This Magic equip card gives one of your Monsters a bonus of +700 life points and if it ever gets discarded you can pay 500 life points to place it on top of your deck. If you don't think this card is that great let me tell you what makes it be on the top 10 list. In this game, the biggest Monster always wins and will keep crushing everything in its path until a bigger Monster is summoned. Malevolent nuzzeler changes that because with this card's bonus to your Monster's attack points you'll be able to get rid of that pesky Monster that keeps picking on your smaller guys. ★

Killer Decks Don't Relinquish Control

— By Scott Gerhardt

This deck in its nature is combo-control. It plays nothing towards beatdown, but rather does everything it can to hold on to board control until you can drop a Relinquished, absorb something, and start swinging. Being able to use your opponent's creature as a shield is rather nice. With any luck, the goal would to be simply hold them off in the early game until you're ready to bring down a Relinquished. Then, hand destroy them as much as you can to keep them from having anything in hand that deals with your friend, drop him, absorb their largest monster (hopefully only monster) and start swinging. Let's run a quick analysis of the deck on the whole.

With Monsters, you obviously have 3 of the required Relinquished. You have to play 3 copies each of Sonic Birds and Senju of the Thousand Hands so you can go find your Relinquished and Black Illusion Rituals. Cyber Jar and Man-Eater Bug are there just to clear out your opponent's creatures in a spot. Magician of Faith is exceptional to be able to recover broken Magic cards like Raigeki and the Hand Destruction spells.

In the realm of Magic cards, Black Illusion Ritual is obviously needed to get out our little fattie. From here it's kind of the run of restricted cards.

Pot of Greed, Change of Heart, Raigeki, Dark Hole, Monster Reborn, Delinquent Duo, Confiscation, The Forceful Sentry, and Snatch Steal are all so broken that they should be in most every deck, and are in this one. Messenger of Peace is insane against beatdown decks to hold them off. I'd rather take 100 than 1800 thank you very much. Fissure stops more creatures from hitting the board, and Swords of Revealing Light is a wonderful 3 turn stopwatch on your opponent to keep him from beating down on you. Heavy Storm is there to deal with nasty traps and magic your opponent may be hiding for you.

Finally, our few traps include the incomparable Mirror Force which is obviously devastating, and Trap Hole to clear out some beatdown creatures your opponent may play.

This deck will not fit everyone's style. If you're a beatdown player, you're not going to like the idea of sitting back and having to react to your opponent for the majority of the game. This will be too slow a deck for you. If you like being the one who controls the pace of the game, though, I think you'll find that this deck is exceptional in doing that.

The only major drawback I can find about this deck is that it is a bit pricey on the wallet. That is, unfortunately, a game flaw. It seems all the really good cards cost a fair deal of money. You can always work to trade for the cards or play on-line.

I hope you have found this article informative and useful. I think if you try this deck you'll agree that it's a blast to play and a pretty strong alternative to the beatdown decks that seem to dominate the environment.

Thanks for reading and I hope you enjoyed! ✪

DARK HOLE

[MAGIC CARD]

Monsters:
3x Relinquished
3x Sonic Bird
3x Sunju of the Thousand Hands
1x Cyber Jar
3x Magician of Faith
3x Man-Eater Bug

Magic:
3x Black Illusion Ritual
1x Pot of Greed
1x Change of Heart
1x Raigeki
1x Dark Hole
1x Monster Reborn
1x Delinquent Duo
1x Confiscation
1x Forceful Sentry
1x Snatch Steal
3x Messenger of Peace
2x Fissure
2x Swords of Revealing Light
2x Heavy Storm

Trap:
1x Mirror Force
2x Trap Hole

Card Game
Killer Decks
RELINQUISHED's Weenie Swarm

— By Vijay Seixas A.K.A. SomeGuy

Strategy

The initial strategy of the deck is to get a Relinquished into play while having a Messenger of Peace on the field as well as a mess of Monsters. Messenger of Peace allows every single one of my Monsters to attack (They're all 1400 ATK and below) while negating most of my opponent's Monsters (Beatdown is the most widely played deck, and as we all know, contains few 1400- Monsters).

This is when Relinquished does his job. Since my opponent can only play one Normal Summon Monster per turn, I just simply use Relinquished's effect to absorb every Monster they put into play (They can Normal Summon one monster per turn and I can absorb one Monster per turn). Thus leaving a clear field for my Weenies to go to work. And if I have a Robbin' Goblin on the field, things just get worse and worse for my opponent.

The deck works like a machine. Every Monster in the deck gives me card advantage. Whether it is Sonic Bird or White Magical Hat, my opponent is either going to be losing cards or I'm going to be gaining cards. This is what makes the deck so unique.

Now I'm going to go into a card-by-card analysis to advise you exactly why I chose the cards for this deck. I will also explain why I didn't choose some particular cards.

Relinquished

The core of the deck. Gives me an infinite supply of removal (At least until it's destroyed). Rarely ever attacks, it's best to keep it in DEF mode to remain safe from Mirror Force.

Senju of the Thousand Hands

It speeds up the deck by directly searching for Relinquished. It also has 1400 ATK; just enough to attack with while Messenger of Peace is in play. Not to mention it is a 2-for-1 card. You're getting a Monster to attack with, as well as a Relinquished for just one card.

Sonic Bird

This searches for the other half of the transaction. Allowing me to directly search for Ritual of Dark Illusions speeds up the deck immensely. Just like Senju of the Thousand Hands, Sonic Bird also has 1400 ATK and is a 2-for-1 card.

Masked Sorcerer

When the whole combo is on the field, this is a great card to be attacking with. A couple of attacking Masked Sorcerer's can fill up my hand quickly. Thus, giving me plenty of options.

White Magical Hat

Another card that works excellently when the whole combo is up and going. Stripping away my opponent's hand will help lock up the game in my favor.

Witch of the Black Forest

Since none of the Monsters in this deck has a DEF higher than 1500, Witch of the Black Forest can potentially search out for any Monster.

Magician of Faith

The main reason Magician of Faith is included in the deck, is in case they Counter / Discard Dark Illusion Ritual or Messenger of Peace. Both of these Magic cards are essential to the strategy of the deck and therefore are worth pulling back from the Graveyard. Only two Magician of Faith are necessary, though.

Cyber Jar

At times, this can be an alternate way of getting Relinquished into play. Most of the time Cyber Jar will be used for when you're in a tight situation.

Black Illusion Ritual

Crucial for bringing Relinquished into play.

Messenger of Peace

This is another card that is very important to the strategy. With this in play, most of the Monsters you see on a normal basis cannot attack (Every Monster with 1500 or more ATK to be exact). These include La Jinn the Mystical Genie of the Lamp, 7 Colored Fish, Dark Elf, Summoned Skull, Maha Vailo, ECT.

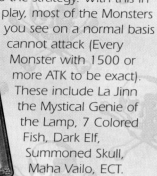

Mystical Space Typhoon

This was added due to the fact that most decks play Swords of Revealing Light, Snatch Steal, and Mirror Force. And since Heavy Storm would hurt me too much, these made the cut.

Dark Hole

Not really needed, but helps out in dismal situations.

Raigeki

Arguably the best Magic card in the game.

Monster Reborn

This allows me to revive one of my destroyed Relinquished if I manually summoned it. In which the deck always does.

Pot of Greed

More card advantage. Simple as that.

Magic Jammer

With so much card advantage in the deck, the "draw-back" is nothing. Magic Jammer protects my Relinquished and Messenger of Peace from cards such as Raigeki and Heavy Storm.

Solemn Judgment

Some more protection… Great late game counter when life totals aren't too high.

Robbin' Goblin

If the combo goes as planned, there will be plenty of direct attacking done to my opponent. Might as well add some insult to injury.

Mirror Force

It's a Mirror Force, do I need to explain?

Now for a few cards that were NOT added to the deck…

Change of Heart and Snatch Steal

With Relinquished's effect, these aren't necessary at all.

Deck Name: Weenie Swarm

Monster -20-
- 3 – Relinquished
- 3 – Senju of the Thousand hands
- 3 – Sonic Bird
- 3 – Masked Sorcerer
- 3 – White Magical Hat
- 2 – Witch of the Black Forest
- 2 – Magician of Faith
- 1 – Cyber Jar

Magic -12-
- 3 – Black Illusion Ritual
- 3 – Messenger of Peace
- 2 – Mystical Space Typhoon
- 1 – Dark Hole
- 1 – Raigeki
- 1 – Monster Reborn
- 1 – Pot of Greed

Trap -8-
- 3 – Magic Jammer
- 2 – Solemn Judgment
- 2 – Robbin' Goblin
- 1 – Mirror Force

Delinquent Duo, Confiscation, and The Forceful Sentry

There wasn't enough space, and I intended to keep the deck at 40 cards. These three cards aren't required anyway.

There it is, Relinquished's Weenie Swarm. If you have the cards, I prompt you to try out the deck. You will be surprised at how well it actually fares. ◐

Killer Decks
The Standard Beatdown

— By Nick Moore (a.k.a. NickWhiz1)

I'll come out and say this before I get started: I'm a bog standard beatdown user. Feel free to criticize me for it, but the fact stands, beatdown is still the strongest deck now (although weenie rush decks with Messenger of Peace are quickly picking up steam). Today we're going to look at an example of a basic beatdown deck.

The general premise of a beatdown deck is just that, to beat your opponent to a fine pulp. We do this by using the strongest Level 4 monsters we can find, combined with a couple of mid-level hard hitters and nasty effect monsters, and some speedy and downright unpleasant Magic and Trap cards. I have also included a little controlling aspect in the discarding cards, so we can limit our opponent's options to counter us. This deck is by no means perfect, it is simply a basis for a beatdown deck in the post-Magic Ruler era.

Monsters:

For the most part, we have assembled the hardest hitters for the lowest price possible to make this a hard-hitting deck. 7 Colored Fish, La Jinn the Mystical Genie of the Lamp, and Dark Elf make for a strong attacking force. I have omitted Jirai Gumo because that is up to personal preference due to the great risk invloved, and Mechanicalchaser just because it's so darn rare. You could even throw in Dark Zebra, Boar Soldier and Flash Assailant if you want to be creative. Summoned Skull makes for our mid-level hard-hitter. We have no need for high-level monsters (Level 7 and above), as they would just slow the deck down. Witch of the Black Forest fetches out any other monster

Note:
Pendulum Machine isn't used in this deck, He's just cool lookin'.

in our deck (that's why all of our monsters have low defense). Don't be surprised if in the future, Witch of the Black Forest is restricted to 1, because of its insane speed factor and Exodia will get tons more powerful starting in Pharaoh's Servant. Magician of Faith is to recycle any of our Magic cards, each gamebreakers in their own right. Cyber Jar is considered by many to be one of the top 5 Monster cards in the game, even in Japan, where they are at least two years ahead of us. Not only does it clear the field of Monsters, it replenishes it as well. Follow up with Raigeki, and your opponent basically loses.

Magic:

Fairly standard as well. We've basically put in all the strongest Magic cards to support our heavy hitters. Pot of Greed speeds us up. Raigeki, Dark Hole, and Tribute to the Doomed clear the field of Monsters. Monster Reborn lets us recycle monsters from the graveyard. Change of Heart and Snatch Steal give us control of opposing monsters. Heavy Storm and Mystical Space Typhoon clear the field of Magic/Trap cards. Swords of Revealing Light stops the opponent dead in their tracks. Delinquent Duo and The Forceful Sentry empty out your opponent's hand. Axe of Despair follows up with the beatdown theme, giving our monsters 1000 more points

of pure beatdown power, and it can regenerate itself as well (albeit a little steep cost, though). 18 Magic Cards may seem like a lot to most people, but I'm fine with using a lot of Magics, as long as I can get victory. As I said before, any deck you make should be suitable to your playing style. Using someone else's deck with a different playing style can be bad for your chances of victory.

Traps:

Nothing special here, really. I've limited my Traps to just five (most people use around 7 or 8, depends on preference). You will notice a lack of Trap Hole. Trap Hole just isn't as important a card anymore, as any monster in attack mode is likely to be destroyed quickly anyways. And for those high level monsters, we have plenty of ways to get rid of them. Mirror Force is one of those ways. The last thing your opponent will want is for their entire attack force to be destroyed by one single card. It makes for probably the nastiest surprise in the game. Magic Jammer is our only way to counter Magic cards right now, but it does its job well. There is a card in English Pharaoh's Servant called Imperial Decree (tentative name) that will negate all Magic cards, and it's a Continuous Trap, so people will start using that. The downside is the 700 LP upkeep cost during each of your Standby Phases and your Magic cards are negated too. Think of it as a free Magic Jammer for one turn, should you wish to. Robbin' Goblin supplements Delinquent Duo and The Forceful Sentry in wiping out your opponent's hand. Limiting your opponent's options is one major key to victory for any kind of deck, even a beatdown deck.

This is a general look at a basic beatdown deck. You will also notice that this is an expensive deck to make, because of all the Super and Ultra Rare Magic and Trap cards. Editing your

deck for card availability is good if you use cards that serve a similar purpose to the cards you are getting rid of. And, of course, the most important thing is to playtest any deck you make and edit it until it runs the way you want it to. I haven't included a side deck here, I'll leave that to your imagination, as that comes down to your local metagame. ✪

Deck Name: "Bog Standard Beatdown"

Monsters: (18)
3x Summoned Skull
3x Dark Elf
3x 7 Colored Fish
3x La Jinn the Mystical Genie of the Lamp
2x Witch of the Black Forest
3x Magician of Faith
1x Cyber Jar

Magic: (18)
1x Pot of Greed
1x Raigeki
1x Dark Hole
1x Monster Reborn
1x Change of Heart
1x Snatch Steal
2x Heavy Storm
2x Swords of Revealing Light
2x Tribute to the Doomed
1x Delinquent Duo
1x The Forceful Sentry
2x Axe of Despair
2x Mystical Space Typhoon

Traps: (5)
1x Mirror Force
2x Magic Jammer
2x Robbin' Goblin

Total Cards: 41

Killer Decks
Toon/Stall Deck

— By Wartortle32

I'm supposed to create a killer deck that would be able to stand up to many tests in the current environment of Yu-gi-oh. And what is that deck? Beatdown. Everywhere you go, every deck has its La Jinn, 7 Colored Fish, Dark Elf, etc... Where is the originality? So I am not going to create a beatdown deck here. Rather, I'm going to try and create a successful toon deck.

This deck I'm about to create is not some magic bullet that will destroy anything in it's path. It is up to the duelist to make this deck work. Without further ado, I give you my toon-based deck. Keep in mind that toons and toon related cards are quite expensive, so if you choose to mimic this deck, it may take some lavish resources.

Wartortle32's "Can't Touch This" Toon/Stall Deck

Yeah, I know the title is corny. So sue me.

At first glance, this deck seems a bit odd. What is messenger of peace and Blue Eyes Toon Dragon doing in the same deck? Well hear me out first.

This is basically a stall/toon deck. The plan is to get out one of the Messenger of Peace while you get a combo of Toon World / Giant Trunade / Megamorph / and maybe a Magic Jammer in your hand. You'll want to have a Magic Jammer set down for at least a turn before you play your Toon World for protection. Then, play the Toon World, and play your toon monsters. On the next turn, use Giant

Trunade to cancel the effects of Messenger of Peace, play the Megamorph, and then attack. The great upside of this is that you also returned your Toon World back to your hand so that it can't be destroyed, keeping your toons safe. If you played the cards right, you should effectively kill the opponent in 1 – 2 turns. Do not attempt to pull off the combo until you are sure it will work, because if there is a small slip, such as running into a Mirror Force, it can ruin the entire match.

Also, Toon Mermaid works great with Messenger of Peace. You can chip away at the opponent's LP while being safe from any attack. Just try to get a weaker monster face up first before playing the Mermaid, as it is vulnerable to Fissure.

An interesting card to also note is Soul Exchange. Soul Exchange works perfect in a toon deck. Since you can't attack with toons the turn you summon them, there's no drawback with using Soul Exchange.

Also a few rulings to note about toon monsters:

1. They are special summon although they require tribute.

2. You cannot use the opponent's

Toon World to summon your toons.

And also, I'd like to raise an interesting point about Messenger of Peace. The Life Point loss every turn actually works to your advantage as it allows you to use the Megamorph effectively.

So how does this measure up against other decks that are being played right now? I'll give an analysis how this deck stands against the current popular decks.

Beatdown

This deck should effectively shut down the beatdown as long as you are able to get those Messenger of Peaces out and protect them with the Magic Jammers. In the meantime, you can stall until you get the cards required for the combo described above. If you can't get the Messengers out, you should have enough defenses and monster removal cards to hold them off long enough.

Burners

This is definitely the deck that will give you the most trouble. You're already draining your LP with your Messengers and using toons. If you are to be successful in defeating a burner, you must get your toons out quickly before the opponent can take away too much of your LP. The Magic Jammers should provide you with some cover, but don't expect it to save you for long. One helpful tip: don't set too many traps or magics as you will be vulnerable to Princess of Tsurugi.

Exodia

Exodia decks were certainly hampered by Magic Ruler, but they can still be quite deadly, depending on the opponent. If you're facing an Exodia deck, you can be sure they'll be running Messengers of Peace, which is great for you because this way, they'll be losing the LP instead of you. When you have the combo ready, use Giant Trunade to get rid of the Messenger of Peace and attack their LP directly. Keep in mind that your attack must work in 1 turn or else they'll just put the Messenger back down. If that happens, get another Giant Trunade and repeat the process. Don't stall for too long or else it gives the opponent ample time to get Exodia.

Weenie Rush

This type of deck relies also on Messenger of Peace and Gravity Bind when Pharoah's Servant comes out. Basically, they chip away at your LP with Jinzo #7 while they hide behind the Messenger of Peace or the Gravity bind. You should have enough Monster Removal cards to take out those LP damaging monsters before they cause too much damage, but you must get the combo out quickly because they will still be coming at you at every turn. You might want to throw some Eatgaboons in the side deck to counter this if you run into such a deck.

Deck Name: "Cant Touch This" Toon/Stalle

Monsters (20)
2x Blue Eyes Toon Dragon
3x Toon Summoned Skull
2x Witch of the Black Forest
3x Magician of Faith
3x Man Eater Bug
2x Aqua Madoor
2x Sangan
3x Toon Mermaid

2x Swords of Revealing Light
2x Megamorph
3x Soul Exchange
1x Monster Reborn
1x Change of Heart
1x Snatch Steal
1x Pot of Greed
3x Messenger of Peace

Magic (22)
3x Toon World
3x Giant Trunade
1x Raigeki
1x Dark Hole

Traps (8)
1x Mirror Force
2x Trap Hole
3x Magic Jammer
2x Waboku

Toon Decks

Basically, you will be fighting a replica of this deck, except that the opponent in all likelihood will play an offensive toon deck instead. Just treat this just the way you would do with beatdown. In the meantime, you must get out some Magic Jammers fast to prevent early toons from attacking you. It basically comes down to who can get out the toons first, and who can protect them the longest.

Well there you go. I know it will be rather hard to construct this deck as there are so many rare cards. But when you get your hands on this deck, the right duelist can be quite unstoppable. Of course you can feel free to change this to your liking. Happy dueling! ☺

YOUR CARD'S DEF IS NOW D.O.A.!

— By Israel "IQ" Quiroz

You've all heard the expression "Burn baby burn" but I bet you never expected to see anything like this. This deck will burn your opponent to ashes with pure direct damage; he'll be fried before he knows what hit him.

Top Cards

Messenger of Peace will make sure your opponent doesn't overrun you with all his big, fat, evil Monsters. This card is your main defense when you're facing aggressive beat down decks. While this Magic card is in play, Monsters with a power greater than 1500 attack cannot attack. This card will not only keep you safe but it will also frustrate your opponent because all his Monsters won't be able to do anything to you.

Cyber Jar will set up your main combo by forcing your opponent to get Monsters into play weather he wants to or not. The effect of Cyber Jar forces your opponent to reveal the top five cards of his deck and to bring all Monsters of level four of lower into play. This effect would normally be a bad thing, but when you have traps cards like Just Desserts in play the more Monsters your opponent has in play, the More Damage you can deal him.

Let's not forget about Raigeki and Dark Hole, these two magic cards will wipe out all of your opponent's monsters in the blink of a second. Raigeki is one of the strongest cards in the game because it nukes all of your opponent's Monsters in play and leaves him open so you can attack him with anything and everything. Dark Hole in the other hand is not as great, it will get rid of your opponent's monsters but it will also take out yours. Make sure you have a Monster in your hand when you play this card so you won't leave yourself open.

How it Beats You

Simple, just make your opponent pays for anything he tries to do and deal as much direct damage as you can. Trust me when I say this is a lot harder than it sounds, because there is no room for mistakes. Your main weapon in this deck is

I'LL SEE YOU IN THE GRAVEYARD!

Note:
Black Luster Soldier isn't used in this deck, He's just cool lookin'.

YBER JAR

[ROCK / EFFECT]
FLIP: Destroys all monsters in the field (including this monster). Both players then pick up five cards from the top of their respective Decks and show the cards to each other. Immediately Special Summon any Monster Cards of Level 4 or lower among them on the field in face-up Attack Position or face-down Defense Position. The rest of the cards picked up are placed in the players' hands.

ATK/ 900 DEF/ 900

©1996 KAZUKI TAKAHASHI
34124316

MYSTICAL ELF

[SPELLCASTER]
A delicate elf that lacks offense, but has a terrific defense backed by mystical power.

ATK/ 800 DEF/2000

Chain Energy, it will make your opponent lose 500 life points every time he plays a card but it will also hurt you in the same way. Now that you can see why there's no room for mistakes lets talk about the strategy behind the deck.

With this deck, you will be racing your opponent. The only way you can win is to stay ahead of him while your cards are dealing damage to both of you. This deck doesn't try to gain life points to stay ahead; instead you'll be trying to make sure your opponent takes more direct damage than you do. What would be the fun of playing it safe?

Cards like Just Desserts, Princess of Tsurugi and Ookazi will allow you to hit your opponent's life points directly to stay ahead in the race. You also have Magician of Faith, which allows you to recover Ookazi to deal even more damage to your opponent so you can finish him off.

Most of your cards will deal more damage in the late game once your opponent has a lot of Monsters or Magic and Trap cards on the field, which makes the early game a little hard on you. For the early game you have Giant Stone Soldier, Mystical Elf, Aqua Maddor and Giant Germ. These cards will allow you to set up your defense until you can get a Messenger of Peace in play and will make your opponent think twice before attacking you. Giant Germ inflicts

500 life points of direct damage to your opponent when it's destroyed as a result of battle, and you get to search your deck for up to two other Giant Germs and Special Summon them into play. Talk about direct damage in a can. Giant Stone Soldier and your other Monsters with 2000 defense will stop just about anything that's attacking you and will most likely deal damage to your opponent at the same time. These Monsters are hard to breakthrough because not even a Dark Elf can take them out, they will keep you safe while punishing your opponent for attacking you.

That's pretty much what the deck is all about. It's easy to play but you have to make sure you don't ever leave yourself open. If your opponent manages to get ahead of you in life points, you'll find yourself in a tight spot. But don't panic! Because with this deck, you can easily make a come back! Remember to think things trough and like Yugi says, "Believe in the Heart of the cards". =) ✪

CHANGE OF HEART

[MAGIC CARD]

Select and control 1 opposing monster (regardless of position) on the field until the end of your turn.

Deck Name: Kamikaze

Monsters: (17)
1x Cyber Jar
1x Mystical Elf
3x Giant Stone Soldier
3x Aqua Maddor
3x Magician of Faith
3x Giant Germ
3x Princess of Tsurugi

Trap Cards: (7)
1x Mirror Force
3x Trap Hole
3x Just Desserts

Magic Cards: (16)
1x Raigeki
1x Pot of Greed
1x Dark Hole
1x Monster Reborn
1x Change of Heart
2x Swords of Revealing Light
3x Messenger of Peace
3x Chain Energy
3x Ookazi

Killer Decks
High Dollar Drama

— By DeQuan Watson

irst of all, let's explain the name. This eck can be expensive to make. It has lot of rare, super rare, and ultra rare. his is a serious deck that is going o cost you a little bit of money. ut that's ok, for the price of some ood tournament action.

his deck uses a lot of cards from the estricted and limited lists. If they are ood enough to be restricted or limited, ney should be in almost every deck. hey are that good. Most of the cards nat fit into that category are magic nd trap cards. However, several of the seful ones that are fairly easy to get ren't on either of those lists. Cards like rap Hole, Fissure, and Sword of the Deep Seated are perfect examples. ruthfully, I think a player can expect early every opponent in a tournament o have a full set of three Trap Hole and issure in their deck.

hose cards aside lets look at the rest of the deck. The deck seems to be a little creature light at first. That's not a real big deal when you look at the creature selection. Monsters like La Jinn the Mystical Genie of the Lamp, Neo the Magic Swordsman, and 7 Colored Fish can all hold their own pretty well in combat. A real surprise factor can be the Dark Elf. Muka Muka and Man-Eater Bug seem to be the only real effect monsters in the deck. All of the other monsters you are swinging with are straightforward power monsters. You don't need a ton of monsters in this deck though. You have several magic and trap cards to help remove your opponent's monsters, so you shouldn't need a whole lot of them on the board at one time.

Two of the most unappreciated cards in this deck are probably Waboku and Sword of the Deep Seated. Waboku, is a great surprise card. It can reduce your opponents creatures to a zero attack value until the end of the turn. All the while, it lets your monsters keep swinging for the fences. Using good equipment cards like Sword of the Deep Seated can be a real trick. You have to understand how it works. Having it go to the graveyard can be a bad thing or a good thing depending on the situation. Remember, when it goes to the graveyard, it goes back on top of your deck instead, so be aware of that. Don't let it come back to burn you. On the other hand, playing with the sword allows this deck to get away with not having any larger

tribute monsters. With the help of the sword, many of the creatures in this deck are as big as the average tribute monster. Between that and the magic and trap cards helping to remove your opponent's monsters, you should be good to go.

The main advantage that this deck has is that it can hit hard and fast early. Take advantage of that. This deck doesn't have a whole lot of extras. There aren't a lot of tricks. This deck does not pack a lot of extra frills. This deck is made to go to your opponents dome and do what you can as fast as you can. However, be aware that this deck has fewer monsters than many other tournament decks that I have seen. This means you should be

careful not to play too many monsters out at a time. If you ever get three monsters out, I would just hold tight there.

Don't forget to take advantage of your effects from Man-Eater bug and Robbin' Goblin.

This is a really good tournament deck for beginner level tournament players. If you can get the cards together and are fairly new to the game, I would highly recommend this deck. Good luck, and may your opponent's monsters be weaker than yours! ✪

The List:

- 1 Pot o' Greed
- 1 Change of Heart
- 1 Dark Hole
- 1 Raigeki
- 1 Monster Reborn
- 1 Mirror Force
- 2 Witch of the Black Forest
- 2 Swords of Revealing Light
- 2 Card Destruction
- 3 Trap Hole
- 3 Fissure
- 3 La jinn the Mystical genie of the Lamp
- 2 Robin Goblin
- 3 Dark Elf
- 2 Muka Muka
- 2 Waboku
- 3 Neo the Magic Swordsman
- 3 7 Colored Fish
- 3 Sword of the Deep Seated
- 3 Man-Eater Bug

Note:
Magician of Black Chaos isn't used in this deck, He's just cool lookin'.

Cheap @$$ Decks
Combining the Two Starter Decks

— By Scott Gerhardt

Okay, so you're new to Yu-Gi-Oh, and you're ready to duel! One problem – your deck's not all that good and you don't have much money to spend. Well, let me be your answer! I'm sure you all know Yu-Gi-Oh is a pretty expensive game and a lot of people can't even afford to get anything more than the Yugi and Kaiba starter deck.

Well, no need to fear. What we've done here is taken these two decks and made one of the most killer decks you can. Now while this might not be the best deck you'll ever see, it will at least give your friends a run for their money until you can improve it some.

Of course, I need to explain how I came up with this 40 card monster. That's easy. Let's start at the beginning. First of all, you have the Yugi and Kaiba starter decks.

from here, take all the cards and separate them into Monster, Trap, and Magic. Now to build these decks, you have to understand one initial fundamental truth about the game – too many tributes are bad. I understand it is fun to beat people down with big creatures, but if you can't get them into play, then they are worthless. Yugi may be able to bring out his Dark Magician for free, but if you want yours, you have to tribute (sacrifice) 2 monsters – that's a lot. So, I started by separating all the 4 star and less monsters in one pile, and all the 5 star and more monsters into another pile. From there, look at the smaller pile. This will make up most of your deck.

Unfortunately, the starters do not provide for much in the way of defensive measures, so the majority of your deck will be offensively-oriented. So, go through your 4 stars and find all your big monsters. Anything with 1500 or more ATK. This will be mostly what you will be using. Now your deck can't be completely offense – you need a couple good defensive creatures to hold off your opponent. This said,

find all your creatures with a DEF of more than 1800. From here, find other creatures that are useful, but maybe not just for attacking and defending. I found two that I felt were worth playing anyway. Man-Eater Bug's ability to flip and destroy anything on the field makes it worth playing for sure. Hane-Hane's ability to return something to its owner's hand is great as well. It's not as good as Man-Eater Bug, but since we only get one Bug, we need something else. Mysterious Puppeteer is nice because creature summons will give you some life back. Plus, with a 1500 DEF, it can hold off a couple things too. It's worth running with. Now, I know you need a little big fat beef to punch through your opponent's army with.

This said, let's go grab those tribute monsters and have a look. Immediately, Summoned Skull pops out. This guy is 2500 ATK for only a single tribute. That is awful nice. Judge Man is not quite as good, but he still has a 2200 ATK, though, and can still break through a stalemate. Outside of that, let's leave the rest of the single tributes out. Just for kicks and for a real game breaker, let's run a single double tribute card. That monster known as the Blue Eyes White Dragon basically beats anything in the game. If it doesn't get killed, it will mow your opponent down in no time flat. Let's run him just in case he's got the chance to rule the board.

Now we're sitting with 26 cards. That's a great start. Now, onto Magic. One thing I should point out here. I wanted this deck to be tournament legal. That meant if something was on the restricted list, I only put one of it in the deck, even if two were available. This way people understand why some broken cards are only in here in multiples of one. Starting with that restricted list, put in 1 copy each of Dark Hole, Monster Reborn, and

they think they're going to win a match-up. Play both you have. Last we have Ultimate Offering. There are 2 copies available, but I don't think it's that useful, so we only need to run 1 copy of it. Having multiples in play just doesn't do you any good here.

We are now at 41 cards and really should shave one down. Looking at our monsters we find a weak link in Uraby. It's barely at our 1500 ATK requirement, but has an ultra-low DEF of only 800. We now have a deck of exactly 40 cards. Perfect.

Hopefully this low-cost solution to beatdown will help you beat your opponent during your next duel. As you get more cards, feel free to alter this deck and work to make it even stronger. ●

as well use your opponent's creatures, especially for something big like Blue Eyes, so let's play the Soul Exchange. Last Will is nice to keep from getting too far behind on the creature count when your opponent is winning. Last we have 3 creature boosters. Since our deck is mostly Earth creatures with a lot of Fiends, Invigoration, Dark Energy, and Yami are all wonderful additions to help push ATKs over the edge.

Our count is now 36 cards and it's time for traps. Here I found 5 total cards I felt would be good. Trap Hole is just awesome and you need to play both copies you have. The same goes for Castle Walls. You can really surprise an opponent with this card when

Change of Heart. They are all vicious cards that can turn a game in your favor very quickly. Next, you get 2 Fissures, and you sure should use them. Direct creature removal is great. Since we're playing 3 Tribute Monsters, you might

Deck Name: Two Decks Combined

Traps:
1x Ultimate Offering
2x Trap Hole
2x Castle Walls

Magic:
1x Yami
1x Dark Energy
1x Invigoration
1x Last Will
1x Soul Exchange
2x Fissure
1x Change of Heart
1x Monster Reborn
1x Dark Hole

Non-Tribute Creatures:
1x Mystical Elf
1x Giant Soldier of Stone
1x Wall of Illusion
1x Skull Red Bird
1x Great White
1x Battle Ox
1x Rogue Doll
1x Neo the Magic Swordsman
1x Baron of the Fiend Sword
1x Man-Eating Treasure Chest
1x Ryu-Kishin Powered
1x La Jinn the Mystical Genie of the Lamp
2x Mystical Clown
1x Koumori Dragon
1x Destroyer Golem
1x Kojikocy
1x Pale Beast
1x The Stern Mystic
1x Man-Eater Bug
1x Hane-Hane
1x Mysterious Puppeteer

Tribute Creatures:
1x Summoned Skull
1x Judge Man
1x Blue Eyes White Dragon

Cheap @$$ Decks
No-Rares Deck: A Modified Beatdown

— By Nick Moore (a.k.a. NickWhiz1)

Low on money? Not able to get all the cards that you want? Still want a deck that has a shot at winning a tournament? It's difficult to do, but it's still very possible. This is an example of a "cheap deck", assembled using 1 of each of the Starter Decks and commons from Legend of Blue-Eyes White Dragon, Metal Raiders, and Magic Ruler. It's basically a watered-down beatdown deck. Since beatdown decks can be very expensive, we're going to look at one that you can build really cheap and still win with.

We took some of the basic elements of a beat-down deck (strong, hard-hitting monsters and supporting Magic/Trap cards), swapped out some of the rarer cards for cards that serve a similar purpose, and we have ourselves a deck.

Deck Name: "I Can't Afford a Stapler"

Monsters: (19)
1x Blue-Eyes White Dragon
1x Dark Magician
1x Judge Man
1x Summoned Skull
2x Jirai Gumo
1x La Jinn the Mystical Genie of the Lamp
2x Dark Zebra
3x 7 Colored Fish
2x Big Eye
1x Wall of Illusion
1x Spear Cretin
1x Hane-Hane
1x Man-Eater Bug
1x Trap Master

Magic: (14)
1x Change of Heart
1x Dark Hole
1x Monster Reborn
1x Upstart Goblin
1x Card Destruction
1x Soul Exchange
2x Gravekeeper's Servant
2x Fissure
2x Block Attack
2x Malevolent Nuzzler

Traps: (7)
2x Trap Hole
1x Ultimate Offering
2x Reverse Trap
1x Just Desserts
1x Waboku

Total Cards: 40

Monsters:

Thanks to the starter decks, we are able to get some pretty hard-hitting Tribute monsters. Normally, you wouldn't consider using a Level 7 or higher monster in a beatdown deck, but since we're dealing with a limited card base, our best bet is to hit the opponent as hard as we possibly can. To do this, I've included one Blue-Eyes White Dragon and one Dark Magician. For our mid-level monsters, Summoned Skull and Judge Man make good attackers. As for our low-level monsters, we need monsters with an attack power of 1800 or higher to stand up against the rich person's beatdown deck. We were able to get 1 La Jinn the Mystical Genie from the Kaiba starter deck, 3 7 Colored Fish and 2 Jirai Gumo from Metal Raiders, and 2 Dark Zebra from Magic Ruler. We also need strong effect monsters. 2 Big

Eyes will give us the necessary manipulation over what cards we draw. The Man-Eater Bug, Hane-Hane, and Wall of Illusion can help clear the field. Spear Cretin acts as a second Monster Reborn. Sure, it lets your opponent revive a card as well, but that's a risk we have to take. And finally, Trap Master gives you a shot to get rid of your opponent's Mirror Force or Magic Jammer, currently the two most important traps in the game. This deck may lack some of the more powerful cards, like Dark Elf, Magician of Faith, and Witch of the Black Forest, but we can compensate for that.

Magic:

Since we are not able to access powerful staple cards like Raigeki, Swords of Revealing Light, and Pot of Greed, we must compensate somehow. Upstart Goblin is probably the closest you're going to get to a Pot of Greed, although the 1000 LP cost and only drawing 1 card can slow you down. We managed to get Dark Hole, Change of Heart, and Monster Reborn, however, which are among the 5 strongest Magic cards in the game right now. Card Destruction and Soul Exchange are powerful additions from the Yugi structure deck, as they essentially give us a Pot of Greed and a Snatch Steal, respectively, but not without a cost, whether it be your current hand or your Battle Phase. Fissure and Block Attack make it easier to get rid of threatening monsters. With Block Attack, almost any decent attacking monster can destroy Summoned Skull. Fissure just plain gets rid of them. Gravekeeper's Servant will make your opponent reluctant to attack, because they may lose a key card from the top of their deck. Malevolent Nuzzler is the best common equip card in my opinion, giving you a 700 point boost and having an optional regeneration ability (500 LP to put on top of your deck). As with the monsters, we can compensate for the Magics we are missing by putting similar, but slightly weaker, cards in our deck.

Traps:

This is where the cheap deck gets hurt most. The three most useful traps in the game right now are Mirror Force, Magic Jammer, and Robbin' Goblin, and we don't have access to any of them. Instead, we're going to customize this deck for the possible current metagame (which I predict may be beatdown decks with heavy equipment). Trap Hole gets rid of the attacking threats before they even settle themselves on the field, and Reverse Trap will just devastate any Maha Vailos that come into play (0 attack power, anyone?). Ultimate Offering will give you a monster advantage, which we need to finish the opponent off quickly before they can really beat us up. Just Desserts gives us a little direct damage to bring our opponent that much closer to defeat, and Waboku acts as a one turn Swords of Revealing Light.

This deck probably stands a 40-50% chance against the standard beatdown deck. As with most card games, games with decks of similar composition come down to luck and skill. A really good player playing this deck with a lot of luck can beat a not so good player using a rich man's beatdown deck that's having a bad day, and, of course, vice versa. Nothing is for certain in this game.

If you can get your hands on some of the Normal Rares below, you can make this deck stronger. These cost a little more than most of the cards that we used above, but if you can get at least some of them, you'll be in excellent shape:

Pot of Greed (probably the toughest of these to get)

Dark Elf (one of the strongest beatdown monsters)

Magician of Faith (Magic recovery)

Witch of the Black Forest (speed demon)

Robbin' Goblin (hand depletion)

Cyber Jar (just plain fun) ○

Cheap @$$ Decks

— By Israel Quiroz

The element of surprise can be what determines the outcome of the battle. This deck is not only built with the element of surprise in mind but it's also designed to throw off your opponent. This deck is built with all the tools you need to outsmart your opponent, to counter his strategy and the best cards in the game.... that you can get for under 99 cents.

Top/Cheap Cards

Believe it or not, one of the most underrated cards in the game is what will give you the upper hand in this duel to the death… or until your mommy calls you. "Reinforcements" gives you the element of surprise when your opponent decides to attack you. This cards' bonus of 500 extra attack points is what will allow your Monster to defeat your opponent's when he was sure he had the battle won. A trap card that gives you a bonus of +500 attack points might not seem like much but when that Dark Elf is coming after you, getting ready to run over all of your Monsters you'll be glad you have this card.

Fairy's Hand Mirror is another one of those cards that not many players think highly of but when your card pool is limited this card is pretty amazing. With the

release of Magic Ruler the amount of Magic Equip cards has increased a lot which makes this card that much stronger. Fairy's Hand Mirror is not only good when facing decks with a lot of equip cards but it also works against those power cards every deck uses. This card is what you can use to force your opponent to waste his Monster Reborn on a Magician of Faith or make his Change of Heart useless by making him take control of your face up Man-Eater Bug.

Malevolent Nuzzler is another card you will rely on to be able to take down your opponent. This item is one of the best in the game; it's a nice bonus of +700 attack that you can recover when it gets discarded by paying 500 life points. Granted Horn of the Unicorn comes back to the top of your deck without you having to pay any life points but that's not always a good thing. There are times when you need to draw new cards in order to stay alive or to be able to finish your opponent. When you reach that point in the game you'll realize that paying an extra 500 life points to be able to decide whether or not you draw a new card or not is not that bad.

How it Beats You

This deck will not only beat your opponent but it'll also destroy his ego once you tell him you're not using a single rare card. This deck is living proof that you don't need one of those fancy Raigeki or Mirror Force cards to be able to win. Just rely on your skill and on the element of surprise to defeat your opponent.

This deck is really easy to play and really basic, you could even teach a new player how to play with it. But just because it is simple doesn't mean it is weak or inferior to those super complicated Exodia decks. It simply

back with it was a deck made out of commons after all. The best part is when you defeat him; he'll never hear the end of it from you or anybody that was watching the game. Losing to a deck made out of just commons will crush just about anyone's ego on the spot. Never forget that the game is not about winning, it is about having fun while destroying your opponent. >;~) ☆

means that you don't need all those high dollar cards to be able to foil your opponent's plans, and that you need to get a job and stop depending on your allowance to be able to buy new cards.

This deck may be made of nothing but commons but you still have your bases covered, you have your beefy monsters like Summoned Skull, La Jinn and the Seven Colored Fish to attack your opponent head on. You have your removal with cards like Trap Hole, Fissure, Man-Eater Bug and even Reinforcements if you use them at the right time. Every deck needs to have that little something that makes it fun, what would the game be with out the cool effects like Hane-hane's and the effects from Waboku? Hane-hane is there to take care of your opponent's level 5 and higher monsters and Waboku will help you stay alive when you're in those tight spots.

The really cool thing about using this deck is that your opponent will never get bragging rights. If he ever tries to say anything about how bad he crushed you, you can always come

Deck Name: Surprise!!!

Monsters: (20)
- 2x Neo the Magic Swordsman
- 3x Man-Eater Bug
- 3x Hane-Hane
- 3x Wall of Illusion
- 3x La Jinn the Mystical Genie of the Lamp
- 3x Seven Colored Fish
- 3x Summoned Skull

Trap Cards: (10)
- 3x Trap Hole
- 2x Waboku
- 3x Reinforcements
- 2x Fairy's Hand Mirror

Magic Cards: (10)
- 1x Pot of Greed
- 1x Dark Hole
- 1x Monster Reborn
- 1x Change of Heart
- 3x Malevolent Nuzzler
- 3x Fissure

What's Up Your Sleeve?

— by DeQuan Watson

As much as we like playing our games, we have to remember that our cards are still collectibles. Sure, we shuffle them. However, we don't have to destroy them while we do it. The easiest, and most likely the best, way to take care of your cards is by sleeving them.

For those of you that are unaware, there are card sleeves specially made to protect your cards individually. For years, the leader in the protective product business has been Ultra-Pro. Ultra-Pro makes almost anything you can think of to protect any type of popular collectible. Originally, they had just clear sleeves. The brand name is called Deck Protector. Those were all fine and good for a while, but then a problem came up in tournaments. If a card is worn, then it still shows through the back of a clear sleeve, making it a "marked" card. Ultra-Pro remedied that problem by coming out with Black Deck Protectors. Later they came out with red sleeves. They also followed later with a blue and a deep forest green style o sleeve. For the longest time, they were the only ones being carried and distributed heavily in the United States.

Well, during this time, a couple of Japanese companies starting producing sleeves. Almost all Japanese brands follow the trend of being slightly taller than Ultra-Pro brand Deck Protectors and are a little bit softer. The fact that they are taller provides the player with extra protection on their cards while shuffling. Also, being slightly softer allows them to bend a little easier and allows for better shuffling. Being softer also makes the sleeves mark up a little slower. However, for some reason or another, Ultra-Pro sleeves tend to last forever. Ultra-Pro sleeves do mark up fairly easily, so replace them often. They are good for keeping around for an old test deck though.

There is also another company called Arcane-Tinmen that produces a popular line of card sleeves called Dragon Shields. Dragon Shields tend to give you the best of both worlds. You get tall sleeves with a midsize thickness. I'm personally a big fan of Dragon Shield brand sleeves. Dragon Shields are probably the second most popular line of protective card sleeves in the United States.

Sleeves are a bit different when it comes to Yu-Gi-Oh! however. Since Yu-Gi-Oh! cards are smaller than the average trading card on the market. Therefore, they don't fit properly into the average card sleeve. They leave too much room. This can lead to damage on your cards during shuffling. To answer this problem, all of the card sleeve manufacturers have created a line of protect sleeves especially for Yu-

Gi-Oh sized cards.

Most of these sleeves are in colors similar to what is available in the larger sizes, but they are scaled down to fit Yu-Gi-Oh cards. This provides Yu-Gi-Oh players with better shuffling protection. Also, for players that want EXTRA card protection, the card sleeves fit just fine into a nine-pocket page for storing card cards in any binder.

I personally like Dragon Shields. They are available nearly everywhere, they give you a good decent cut, and they shuffle well. I think that the Japanese are the second best. Part of that is due to the lack of availability. The main reason I put Ultra-Pro in third is that they often give you an uneven cut and

they break more often when shuffling. However, to be fair, I have to say that Ultra-Pro sleeves last nearly forever (when they don't break) and they have a huge variety of colors to choose from. Ultra-Pro even has more colors coming out before Christmas.

Regardless of what company and/or sleeves you choose to use, just be sure to use something. There's no reason to devalue your cards while having fun. With protective sleeves, you can preserve their value AND have your fun. ✪

FAQ's

— By Augustine Haw-Ken Choy

A lot of people have questions about playing the Yu-Gi-Oh CCG. Upper Deck (http://www.yugioh-card.com) does have a small FAQ up on their site, but duelists still have many questions unanswered. Add that to the vagueness of the Upperdeck FAQ as well as the lack of frequent updates, and many players are lost. So, we figured we'd try to help everyone understand the rules better. This is not an Official Q&A. But it will help answer many questions players have. We try to keep this up to date at www.pojo.com.

General Gameplay

Q: I saw a such and such combo on the show! Am I really allowed to do this?

A: For the most part, no. Don't follow anything you see on the show. The rules are much different.

Q: Is there a Card Limit on the number of cards I can hold in my hand?

A: Yes, you cannot have more than six cards in your hand during your End Phase. You must discard cards during your End Phase until you have six. During your turn, you can hold as many as you want.

Q: How many cards can I draw per turn?

A: You can only draw 1 card per turn unless otherwise instructed by another card (i.e. Pot of Greed)

Q: Can I discard cards whenever I want?

A: No, you cannot just discard a card. If you do discard a card,

that must be because a card told you to or you have more than 6 at the end of your turn.

Q: Can I attack with more than 1 monster per turn?

A: Yes, all of your monsters can attack once per turn.

Monsters

Q: Can I flip a face up monster back face down?

A: No. Once it is face up, you are not allowed to flip it back face down unless otherwise specified by another card.

Q: Can I set a level 5+ monster without tributing?

A: No you cannot. You must tribute monsters before you set down a level 5+ monster.

Q: Do monsters have to be on the field in order to fuse them?

A: No. You can fuse monsters from your hand.

Q: When I have control of one of my opponent's monsters where does it go if it must be returned to my hand? to the discard?

A: It goes to whoever OWNS the card; thus it will go to your opponent's hand/discard/deck.

Q: Can parts of Exodia be on the field for me to gain the auto-win?

A: No, they must all be in your hand.

Q: Can I Set a monster, then flip it face-up on the same turn?

A: No, by playing a monster you are choosing its position when you play it.

Q: Can I play a monster in face down attack mode?

A: The only way to get a monster into face down attack mode is to summon it in face up attack mode, and then use darkness approaches to put it in face down attack mode.

Q: Can I summon a monster straight into face up defense mode?

A: No, you cannot. You can either set the monster or play it in attack mode.

Q: What happens when a fusion monster is returned to my hand?

A: If a fusion monster is returned to your hand, it goes back into the fusion deck. You should never be holding a fusion monster in your hand.

Q: Can a monster have negative stats?

A: No, the lowest stats that a monster can have is 0.

Q: Are toon monsters considered special summons?

A: Yes. When you summon a toon monster, it is a special summon. Therefore, you cannot set toon monsters or trap hole them. You still have to tribute however.

Q: Can I reborn a fusion monster?

A: You can only reborn a fusion monster if it was first summoned by using polymerization on the fusion material monsters.

Q: Are ritual monsters considered special summons?

A: Yes. When you summon a ritual monster, it is a special summon. Therefore, you cannot set them.

Magic Cards

Q: Can I play Magic Cards from my hand?

A: As long as you have a free space in your Magic/Trap zone, yes.

Q: Can I play more than one Magic Card per turn?

A: As long as you have a free space in your Magic/Trap zone, yes.

Q: Can I play/activate Magic Cards during my opponent's turn?

A: Only if the Magic card has a Quick-Play icon on it; if not, no.

Q: Does Remove Trap / De-spell stop Traps / Magics?

A: No, first of all, it simply destroys the card, not negate its effects. Second, the Chain system does not allow Traps or magic cards to be countered by Magic cards, except Quick-Play ones. Remove trap, currently will only be useful for removing face up permanent traps that are still there on YOUR turn. You can't use it on the opponent's turn. De-spell, however, can be used on face down cards.

Q: Can I use quick play magic cards on the opponent's turn?

A: Yes, but the magic card must be set if you want to use it on the opponent's turn.

Trap Cards

Q: Can I lay more than one Trap card on a turn?

A: The maximum amount of traps you can set are 5 since there are only 5 m/t slots in your m/t zone.

Q: Can I play/activate Trap Cards on my own turn?

A: As long as the Trap you wish to activate has been set on the field for at least one turn, yes.

Q: Can I activate traps after I have declared an attack?

A: Yes, as long as the trap has been set for 1 turn.

Q: If the opponent summons a monster through Ultimate Offering, can Trap Hole it?

A: Yes, Ultimate Offering is NOT a Special Summon, it simply allows you extra normal summons at the cost of 500 LPs per summon.

Miscellaneous FAQ

Q: If they play Change of Heart on one of my monsters and it attacks my Wall of Illusion, whose hand does it go? Where does it go if it is discarded?

A: It will go to the OWNER's hand, not the CONTROLLER's. Since you own that monster, it'll go to your hand, not his. If it got discarded, it will be placed into your graveyard for the same reason.

Q: Does De-Spell destroy Swords of Revealing Light and negate its effects?

A: Yes, but not in a chain. You may play De-Spell to remove its monster-stopping effects on your turn, however. That is because Swords of Revealing light stays on the field during the duration of it's effect.

Q: How does Lord of D.'s effect work?

A: This has caused great controversy. Lord of D. will only protect dragons from targeted effects. Upperdeck made 2 Lord of Ds. The correct one is the one that says it protects dragons from targeted effects. Basically, a targeted effect is where the player manually chooses a target for an effect. (For example, the player chooses which monster he wants to use change of heart on. He chooses which

This book is not sponsored, endorsed, or otherwise affiliated with any of the companies or products featured in this book. This is not an official publication.

monster he wants to kill with Man Eater Bug's effect.) A non-targeting effect is where the player has no say in which monster the effect targets. (For example, the player does not choose which monster will be targeted by Dark Hole. It simply destroys everything on the field.)

Q: Am I allowed to use Japanese cards?

A: For unofficial tournaments, you have to check with the tournament officials. As for the official Upperdeck tournaments, they are banned. As for casual play, you and your opponent must agree to using Japanese cards before play.

Q: How do I get tournament packs?

A: You have to get tournament packs from stores that have bought them from Upperdeck. Those stores will hold tournaments and if you are the winner of that tournament, you will win some tournament packs. You cannot buy them off the shelves.

Individual Card Rulings

These are extensive rulings on many cards in the English game, listed alphabetically for your convenience. Of course some cards require no explanation (i.e. Skull Servant). These cards are not listed.

Acid Trap Hole

This card only destroys monsters face down with 2000 defense strength or less.

If the monster face down has defense strength of 2000 or less and has a flip effect, the flip effect activates before it is destroyed.

If the monster has a defense greater than 2000, it is flipped back face down. If it has a flip effect, it is NOT activated.

This card is NOT legal in Official Upperdeck tournaments.

This is a targeted effect.

Ameba

You cannot simply give this monster to the opponent. He has to take it either by change of heart or snatch steal or some other effect.

It has to be taken face up for the effect to work.

Ancient Telescope

You look at the top 5 cards of the opponent's deck and return it in the SAME order.

Armed Ninja

You MUST activate the effect when it flips, even if it means destroying your own cards.

It CAN target face down cards in the m/t zone.

This is a targeted effect.

Axe of Despair

If you choose to bring it back to the top of your deck, you must tribute one of your own monsters. You cannot tribute the opponent's monsters.

Banisher of the Light

If you use some magic or trap card to destroy this monster, that magic or trap card is not removed from the game (i.e. Tribute to the Doomed).

Barrel Dragon

If you flip 3 heads, the effect still works.

You are allowed to use the effect and still attack with Barrel Dragon.

This is a targeted effect.

Beast - King of the Swamps

If you use this as a substitute for a fusion material monster, you cannot use another monster that takes the place of a fusion material monster and combine them together.

Can be fused from your hand.

Beast Fangs

You can only equip this on a beast sub-type monster. If you attach it on a monster other than a beast, the Beast Fangs are returned to your hand, not destroyed.

This is a targeted effect.

Big Eye

The effect must activate when it is flipped.

Black Illusion Ritual

This is the only way you can summon Relinquished.

You cannot reborn a Relinquished unless you first summoned it by using this card.

You can sacrifice monsters from your hand to satisfy the requirements.

Black Pendant

The effect happens if it goes from the field to the grave for any reason.

This can be equipped to any monster.

This is a targeted effect.

Bladefly

It does gain a power boost from it's own effect so it CAN be trap holed.

This is a non targeted effect.

Blast Juggler

The monsters you destroy can be either yours or your opponent's.

This is a targeted effect.

84   **Pojo's Unofficial TOTAL Yu-Gi-Oh!**

This book is not sponsored, endorsed, or otherwise affiliated with any of the companies or products featured in this book. This is not an official publication.

Block Attack

You CANNOT use this on your own monster.

The effect lasts for 1 turn only.

This is a targeted effect.

Blue Eyes Toon Dragon

You cannot summon this in any way if Toon World is not on the field.

This monster cannot attack on the turn that it is summoned. That includes if you Monster Reborn it.

This monster can attack the opponent's LP directly if they have no Toon Monsters.

You cannot play this card if your opponent has Toon World out and you don't. You need your own Toon World to summon Toon Monsters.

This monster can be attacked by a regular monster, contrary to what the anime says.

When you summon this from your hand, it is a special summon, but you still have to tribute.

This monster can only be reborn if it was summoned normally. (same rules for Gate Guardian)

Boar Soldier

If you normal summon this monster, it is destroyed right away.

Burning Spear

You can only equip this on a fire sub-type monster. If you attach it on a monster other than a fire type, the Burning Spear is returned to your hand, not destroyed.

This is a targeted effect.

Cannon Soldier

You can use the effect as many times during your turn as you want.

You CANNOT use this with Last Will to bring an infinite amount of monsters into play. Only 1 monster per last will.

You are allowed to make the Cannon Soldier kill itself to use the effect.

Card Destruction

The Card Destruction does not count in the number of the cards you draw after you discard your hand.

Castle of Dark Illusions

Since the effect is a flip effect, no zombie monsters will get any power up from this card if it is summoned face up.

If the castle is destroyed, all power ups that zombie monsters have received from the castle remain.

Any zombie monsters that were summoned AFTER the castle flipped DO NOT gain anything from the castle.

The power bonuses received are cumulative.

Castle Walls

You can use this card before or after the opponent has declared an attack on your monster.

This is a targeted effect.

Catapult Turtle

You can use the effect as many times as you want.

You CANNOT use this with Last Will to bring an infinite amount of monsters into play. Only 1 monster per last will.

You are allowed to make the Catapult Turtle launch itself.

Ceremonial Bell

The effect works while it is in face up attack or defense mode.

Chain Energy

The effect works for both players

If you activate something already face down on the field, you don't have to pay for that.

If there is more than 1 chain energy on the field, you will lose 500 for each Chain Energy on the field when you play a card from your hand.

The card must go from the hand to the field in order for the player to lose LP (i.e. discarding cards don't count)

Change of Heart

If you take a face down monster with a flip effect, you can flip it to use the flip effect in your favor.

You cannot use the Change of Heart to give your opponent your monster.

This is a targeted effect.

Chorus of Sanctuary

You can play this if your m/t zone is full because it goes in it's own field magic card zone.

The effect works for both players

This card affects both face up and face down monsters.

This is a non-targeted effect.

Cockroach Knight

If it goes to the graveyard for any reason (either from the field, deck, or hand) it is returned to the top of your deck.

Cocoon of Evolution

You are allowed to play this as a regular monster without attaching it to Petit Moth.

Playing this monster counts as your 1 summon/set per turn.

If equipped on petit moth, it goes in your m/t zone. If played regularly, it goes in the monster zone.

It CAN be destroyed by cards that destroy magic cards (i.e. De-spell, Heavy Storm, etc.)

Card Game - F A Q's

Commencement Dance

This is the only way to summon Performance of Swords. You cannot reborn Performance of Swords if you didn't first summon it with this card.

You can sacrifice monsters from your hand when sacrificing monsters to fufill the requirement.

Confiscation

If this card is countered and negated, you must still pay 1000LP.

Crab Turtle

This monster can only be summoned with the Turtle Oath.

When summoned with the ritual card, it is a special summon.

Crass Clown

The effect works if the monster goes from defense to attack for any reason .

If you return a monster that has changed possesion, (i.e. through Change of Heart) the monster goes back to the OWNER's hand. So if they use Monster Reborn on your monster, you can use the effect to bring it back to your hand.

You can use this effect as many times as you want, but only once per defense mode to attack mode switch.

This is a targeted effect.

Curse of Fiend

This card can only be activated in the standby phase.

If a monster is set when this card is used, it goes to face down attack mode.

This is a non-targeted effect.

Cyber Jar

You must show the 5 cards that you draw to your opponent.

Any monsters that you draw that are level 4 are lower can be placed in attack mode or face down defense.

If the effect happened as a result of being attacked, the battle phase is not yet over and the opponent can still attack with the monsters that he summoned with the effect.

This is a non-targeted effect.

Dark Elf

You must pay the 1000LP EVERY time you attack, not just the first time.

Dark Energy

You can only equip this on a fiend sub-type monster. If you attach it on a monster other than a fiend type, the Dark Energy is returned to your hand, not destroyed.

This is a targeted effect.

Dark Hole

It destroys all monsters on the field, including face down monsters.

If a face down monster has a flip effect, the flip effect does not activate.

This is a non targeted effect.

Darkness Approaches

If this card is countered and negated, you must still discard 2 cards.

This is a targeted effect.

If used on a face up monster in attack position, it goes to face up attack mode.

Delinquent Duo

If this card is countered and negated, you must still pay 1000LP.

The first card you discard is chosen at random by the player who used this card. The second card discarded is chosen by the oppo-

nent. He can discard whichever one he wants.

De-spell

It can be used on face down cards. If it is a trap, the trap is not activated and placed back face down.

It can destroy Swords of Revealing Light.

It can destroy field magic cards.

This is a targeted effect.

Dragon Capture Jar

It is a non-targeting effect, so Lord of D. cannot protect dragons from it.

If you play stop defense on a dragon while Dragon Capture Jar is active, the dragon will go to attack mode, and then revert right back to defense mode.

Dragon Piper

You CANNOT target a face down trap, hoping that it is a Dragon Capture Jar. You can only use the effect on a face up DCJ.

This is a targeted effect.

Dragon Treasure

You can only equip this on a dragon sub-type monster. If you attach it on a monster other than a dragon type, the Dragon Treasure is returned to your hand, not destroyed.

This is a targeted effect.

Dream Clown

You can use this effect as many times as you want, but only once per attack mode to defense mode switch.

The effect works if it switches from attack to defense for any reason.

This is a targeted effect.

Eatgaboon

If you use this on a monster that has been flip summoned, it does not negate the effect of that monster.

This is a non-targeted effect.

Electric Lizard

The effect is mandatory if the opponent discards it.

The effect does not work if you discard it.

Electro Whip

You can only equip this on a thunder sub-type monster. If you attach it on a monster other than a thunder type, the Electro Whip is returned to your hand, not destroyed.

This is a targeted effect.

Elegant Egotist

This is the ONLY way to summon the Harpie Lady Listers.

The Harpie Lady required for the use of this card is NOT destroyed in the process.

This is a special summon and you can bring the Harpie Lady Sisters from out of your deck or from your hand.

Elf's Light

You can only equip this on a light main type monster. If you attach it on a monster other than a light type, the Elf's Light is returned to your hand, not destroyed.

This is a targeted effect.

Eternal Rest

This will destroy monster equipped with any card, not just magic cards.

This is a non-targeted effect.

Exodia the Forbidden One

All 5 pieces must be in your HAND in order for the automatic victory to be declared.

Fairy's Hand Mirror

You can only switch targets if the card that was played has a targeting effect. (Hence, you cannot switch the target of Fissure to another monster).

This only applies to monsters on the field. (So you can't redirect a Monster Reborn or a Delinquent Duo).

You can only switch the target to another legal target. (So you can't make the opponent change of heart his own monster).

Fake Trap

You CANNOT use this to save your traps from 7 Tools of the Bandit or Solemn Judgement because it is too slow.

Does not save your set magic cards from being destroyed.

Final Destiny

If this card is countered and negated, the user must still discard 5 cards because that is the cost of using the card.

The effect destroys everything on the field, monsters and m/t.

This is a non-targeted effect.

Fissure

When the opponent has 2 monsters equal with the lowest attack power, the player who played Fissure is allowed to choose which of the 2 monster will die.

This is a non targeted effect.

Flash Assassin

You reduce the attack of this monster by 400 for each card in the controller's hand, not the owner's hand.

Flying Kamakiri #1

You can only use the effect to bring a wind monster to the field, not your hand.

Follow Wind

You can only equip this on a winged beast sub-type monster. If you attach it on a monster other than a winged beast type, the follow wind is returned to your hand, not destroyed.

This is a targeted effect.

Forest

You can play this if your m/t zone is full because it goes in it's own field magic card zone.

This is a non targeted effect.

Gaia Power

The effect works for both players

You can play this if your m/t zone is full because it goes in it's own field magic card zone.

This is a non-targeted effect.

Gate Guardian

This monster can ONLY be summoned by sacrificing the 3 pieces (Suijin, Sanga, and Kazejin).

When you sacrifice the 3 pieces, they must be from the field, not in your hand.

It must be summoned from your hand. You can't search your deck for it.

You cannot discard it and use Monster Reborn to get it back. You can only use Monster Reborn on it if it was already summoned in the normal fashion.

Germ Infection

All decreases in attack due to this card are all cancelled if Germ Infection is destroyed. (It goes back to the original attack power).

This is a targeted effect.

Giant Germ

When you use the effect, you can only bring out other Giant Germs. You cannot bring out any other monster with the effect.

Card Game - F A Q's

Giant Rat

The monster that you choose gets summoned to the field, not brought to your hand.

Giant Trunade

This will not activate the effects of any face down traps or magics. This is a non-targeted effect.

Goddess with the Third Eye

If you use this as a substitute for a fusion material monster, you cannot use another monster that takes the place of a fusion material monster and combine them together. Can be fused from your hand.

Gravekeeper's Servant

The effect works every single time the opponent attacks.

Great Moth

This monster can ONLY be summoned by tributing a Petit Moth that has been equipped with the cocoon of evolution for 4 of your turns.

If the cocoon is destroyed a few turns before your 4th turn, you have to start those turns all over if you equip another cocoon.

You cannot discard it and use Monster Reborn to get it back. You can only use Monster Reborn on it if it was already summoned in the normal fashion.

Griggle

You cannot simply give it to the opponent.

The effect only happens if it is face up when the opponent gains control of it.

Gust Fan

You can only equip this on a wind-type monster. If you attach it on a monster other than a wind type, the gust fan is returned to your hand, not destroyed.

This is a targeted effect.

Hamburger Recipe

This is the only way to summon Hungry Burger. You cannot reborn Hungry Burger if you did not first summon him with this card.

You can sacrifice monsters from your hand when fulfilling the tribute requirements.

Hane-Hane

When this monster is flipped, you MUST use the effect. Even if that means you are returning the Hane-Hane itself.

If you return a monster that has changed possesion, (i.e. through change of heart) the monster goes back to the OWNER's hand. So if they use Change of Heart on your monster, you can use Hane-Hane to bring it back to your hand.

This is a targeted effect.

Harpie Lady Sisters

This monster can only be summoned by using Elegant Egotist on a Harpie Lady.

You cannot discard it and use Monster Reborn to get it back. You can only use Monster Reborn on it if it was already summoned in the normal fashion.

Heavy Storm

Destroys all magic and trap cards on the field, including your cards, as well as the field magic card currently in play.

The opponent is allowed to play traps in response to this card such as Reinforcements or Waboku. When they do, the trap card is used, discarded, and then any magic or trap cards remaining will be destroyed.

This is a non targeted effect.

Hiro's Shadow Scout

The cards that are not magic cards stay in the opponent's hand.

Horn of Heaven

Since this negates a summon, if the opponent were to summon a Sangan or Witch of the Black Forest from their hand, using Horn of Heaven would prevent the effects of both monsters from happening because they were never considered summoned and therefore were never on the field. However, if the opponent were to FLIP SUMMON the Sangan/Witch of the Black Forest, the effect will work.

If this card is countered, (i.e. 7 Tools of the Bandit) you still have to pay the cost of tributing 1 monster.

If you use this against a monster that is being flip summoned, this card will negate the flip effect of that monster, if any.

This is a non targeted effect.

Horn of Light

You are not required to return it to the top of your deck when it is destroyed.

You can equip this on any monster.

This is a targeted effect.

Horn of the Unicorn

It only goes to the top of your deck if it was sent from the FIELD to the grave. If it goes form the hand or deck, it does not go back to the deck.

This is a targeted effect.

Hoshiningen

This monster will gain a power boost from it's own effect, so it can be trap holed.

This is a non targeted effect.

House of Adhesive Tape

If you use this on a monster that has been flip summoned, it will not negate the effect of that monster.

This is a non-targeted effect.

Hungry Burger

This monster can only be summoned by the Hamburger Recipe.

When summoned with the ritual card, it is a special summon.

Insect Soldiers of the Sky

The effect does not activate if a wind type were to attack it. It only works when it attacks a wind type.

This is a non targeted effect.

Invader of the Throne

The effect is mandatory and cannot be activated in the battle phase.

Invigoration

You can only equip this on an earth main-type monster. If you attach it on a monster other than an earth type, the invigoration is returned to your hand, not destroyed.

This is a targeted effect.

Jigen Bakudan

You can only use the effect during the standby phase.

This is a non-targeted effect.

Monsters that have flip effect that are face down do not get their flip effects activated when sacrificed for this effect.

Jinzo #7

This monster can either attack the opponent's LP directly, or attack a monster. It is NOT allowed to do both.

You are allowed to use this in conjunction with Robbin' Goblin to activate the effect of Robbin' Goblin.

Jirai Gumo

You must flip for the effect every time you attack, not just the first time.

If you are attacked, you don't have to flip for the effect.

If his attack is negated, you still must flip for the effect (i.e. Waboku).

Just Desserts

The damage calculation is only for the opponent's monsters. You don't take your own monsters into account for the damage calculation.

Karate Man

You can only double the original attack power. You can't double the modified attack power of the monster.

Kazejin

The effect reduces the ATTACK of a monster to 0. It doesn't reduce the damage to 0. That means that if a Blue Eyes White Dragon were to attack Kazejin, and you activate the effect, BEWD's attack is reduced to 0. That means that a monster with 0 attack power has attacked your monster. That means the BEWD will die and the opponent loses 2400 LP.

If you use the effect, and then Kazejin leaves the field somehow, you can use the effect again if Kazejin re-enters play.

If someone uses the effect on you, you cannot use Reverse Trap to reverse the effect and make your monster twice as powerful.

If you use Monster Reborn on your opponent's Kazejin, you are not allowed to activate the effect because you are not the owner of Kazejin. Only the owner of Kazejin is allowed to use the effect.

Kotodama

When the effect says same name, it means exactly the same name (i.e. Winged Guardian of the fortress #1 and Winged Guardian of the Fortress #2 can both exist at the same time.

This is a non-targeted effect.

Kuriboh

The effect can only be activated from your hand, not from the field

Currently, there is no way you can counter Kuriboh's effect.

The effect will only protect your LP from 1 of your opponent's monsters. It will not save your monsters from dying. It only protects your LP.

Larvae Moth

You cannot discard this monster and use Monster Reborn to get it back. You can only use Monster Reborn on it if it was already summoned in the normal fashion.

You can only summon it by sacrificing a Petit Moth that has been equipped with Cocoon of Evolution for 2 turns.

You cannot revert back to the Petit Moth and Cocoon of Evolution stage after you summon this monster.

Laser Cannon Armor

You can only equip this on an insect sub-type monster. If you attach it on a monster other than an insect type, the Laser Cannon Armor is returned to your hand, not destroyed.

This is a targeted effect.

Last Will

The effect only lasts for the duration of your turn.

You can only summon 1 monster per last will.

Lava Battleguard

You can gain multiple attack boosts from multiple Swamp Battleguards on the field.

Left Arm of the Forbidden One

All 5 pieces must be in your HAND in order for the automatic victory to be called.

Left Leg of the Forbidden One

All 5 pieces must be in your HAND in order for the automatic victory to be called.

Legendary Sword

You can only equip this on a warrior sub-type monster. If you attach it on a monster other than a warrior type, the Legendary Sword is returned to your hand, not destroyed.

This is a targeted effect.

Leghul

This monster can either attack the opponent's LP directly, or attack a monster. It is NOT allowed to do both.

You are allowed to use this in conjunction with Robbin' Goblin to activate the effect of Robbin' Goblin.

Lord of D.

Only protects dragons from targeted effects (Change of Heart, Equip Magic, Tribute to the Doomed, Man Eater Bug's effect, etc...)

Does not protect dragons from non-targeted effects (Dark Hole, Raigeki, Field Magic cards, Wall of Illusion's effect, Fissure, etc...)

The correct wording is the second one that Upperdeck released, the one that says it protects dragons from targeted effects.

Luminous Spark

The effect works for both players

You can play this if your m/t zone is full because it goes in it's own field magic card zone.

This is a non-targeted effect.

Machine Conversion Factory

You can only equip this on a machine sub-type monster. If you attach it on a monster other than a machine type, the machine conversion factory is returned to your hand, not destroyed.

This is a targeted effect.

Magic Jammer

You MUST pay the cost of discarding 1 card from your hand in order to use the effect.

If the Magic Jammer is negated by another counter trap, you still have to pay the cost of discarding 1 card from your hand.

You cannot activate this card if you have no cards in your hand

This is a non targeted effect.

Magical Labyrinth

Equipping this to Labyrinth Wall is the only way to summon Wall Shadow. You cannot reborn Wall Shadow until you have summoned him first using this.

Magician of Faith

You MUST use the effect if it is flipped.

If there are no magic cards in your graveyard, you don't retrieve any card from the grave.

Maha Vailo

In addition to gaining 500 ATK for magic cards equipped to this monster, it also gains the boost from the actualy card itself. (so if you attach Malevolent Nuzzler, you gain 1200 ATK points).

Malevolent Nuzzler

You are not required to return it to the top of your deck if it is destroyed.

You can equip this on any monster.

This is a targeted effect.

Man Eater Bug

If this monster is flipped, you MUST use the effect, even if that means you must kill the MEB himself.

This is a targeted effect.

Manga Ryu-Ran

You cannot summon this in any way if Toon World is not on the field.

This monster cannot attack on the turn that it is summoned. That includes if you Monster Reborn it.

This monster can attack the opponent's LP directly if they have no toon monsters.

You cannot play this card if your opponent has Toon World out and you don't. You need your own Toon World to summon toon mosnters.

This monster can be attacked by a regular monster, contrary to what the anime says.

When you summon this from your hand, it is a special summon, but you still have to tribute.

This monster can only be reborned if it was summoned normally. (same rules for Gate Guardian)

Mask of Darkness

You MUST use the effect if it is flipped.

If there are no trap cards in your graveyard, nothing happens.

Masked Sorcerer

The effect only works when this monster does damage to the opponent's LP.

If you do damage to the opponent's LP with this monster, you MUST use the effect.

Megamorph

This doubles the attack power of the original stats. (i.e. if you use Karate Man's effect and then use Megamorph, Karate Man only goes up to 2000).

Do not take into account any additional power boosts when doubling the attack power.

This is a targeted effect.

Messenger of Peace

Monsters with attacks modified over 1500 still cannot attack.

You can choose to not pay the LP, but the card will be destroyed.

Milus Radiant

This monster does get a power boost from its own effect.

Minar

The effect is mandatory if discarded by the opponent.

The effect does not happen if you discard it.

Mirror Force

This only kills the opponent's monsters that are in attack mode, not defense mode.

You can only use this when a monster attacks.

This is a non targeted effect.

Molten Destruction

The effect works for both players
You can play this if your m/t zone is full because it goes in it's own field magic card zone.

This is a non-targeted effect.

Monster Reborn

You cannot reborn monsters that have special summon requirements that have not been fulfilled.

If you reborn a level 5+ monster,

you don't have to tribute to bring back.

Mother Grizzly

The effect will bring a water type to the field, not your hand.

Mountain

You can play this if your m/t zone is full because it goes in it's own field magic card zone.

This is a non targeted effect.

Muka Muka

If you have 2 cards in your hand when you summon this monster, it can be trap holed.

Mushroom Man #2

You MUST pay 300LP if this monster is under your control during your standby phase.

Mysterious Puppeteer

You gain 500LP for every monster summoned by you and your opponent while MP is face up on the field.

You DO NOT gain LP for monsters already on the field or for the MP himself.

You can gain 1000LP for every monster summoned by having 2 MP in play.

You gain 500LP if you attack a face down monster and it is flipped face up.

Mystic Lamp

This monster can either attack the opponent's LP directly, or attack a monster. It is NOT allowed to do both.

You are allowed to use this in conjunction with Robbin' Goblin to activate the effect of Robbin' Goblin.

Mystic Plasma Zone

The effect works for both players
You can play this if your m/t zone is full because it goes in it's

own field magic card zone.

This is a non-targeted effect.

Mystic Tomato

You can only use the effect to bring a dark monster to the field, not to your hand.

Mystical Moon

You can only equip this on a beast sub-type monster. If you attach it on a monster other than a beast type, the Mystical Moon is returned to your hand, not destroyed.

This is a targeted effect.

Mystical Space Typhoon

If you use this on the opponent's turn, it must be set.

It will not negate any effect if used in a chain. (i.e. playing this in response to trap hole does not save your monster).

If you target a trap that is face down, the opponent is allowed to activate that trap in response if the timing for the trap is correct.

Nimble Momonga

You can only bring out other Nimble Momongas with this effect. You cannot use the effect to bring out any other monster.

Ooguchi

This monster can either attack the opponent's LP directly, or attack a monster. It is NOT allowed to do both.

You are allowed to use this in conjunction with Robbin' Goblin to activate the effect of Robbin' Goblin.

Paralyzing Potion

This does not affect machine sub-type monsters.

Monsters equipped with this card can still use their effect, if they have any.

This is a targeted effect.

Card Game - F A Q's

Patrol Robo

You can only use the effect during your standby phase.

Penguin Knight

At the moment, the only way I think the effect can work is if it is discarded through Gravekeeper's Servant.

Performance of Sword

This can only be summoned by commencement dance.

When summoned with the ritual card, it is a special summon.

Polymerization

You can use this to fuse the fusion material monsters from either the field or your hand.

This is a targeted effect.

Pot of Greed

You can use this even if you have more than 6 cards in your hand. The only thing that matters is that you cannot have more than 6 cards at the end of your turn.

Power of Kaishin

You can only equip this on an aqua sub-type monster. If you attach it on a monster other than an aqua type, the power of Kaishin is returned to your hand, not destroyed.

This is a targeted effect.

Princess of Tsurugi

If your opponent has a field magic card in play, that also counts in the damage calculation.

Pumpking the King of Ghosts

If you use castle of Dark Illusions' effect, the Pumpking gains 300 attack and defense every turn.

Queen's Double

This monster can either attack the opponent's LP directly, or attack a monster. It is NOT allowed to do both.

You are allowed to use this in conjunction with Robbin' Goblin to activate the effect of Robbin' Goblin.

Raigeki

It destroys all opponent monsters in play, even if they are face down.

If the opponent's monster is face down and has a flip effect, the flip effect does not activate.

This is a non targeted effect.

Rainbow Flower

This monster can either attack the opponent's LP directly, or attack a monster. It is NOT allowed to do both.

You are allowed to use this in conjunction with Robbin' Goblin to activate the effect of Robbin' Goblin.

Raise Body Heat

You can only equip this on dinosaur sub-type monster. If you attach it on a monster other than a dinosaur type, the raise body heat is returned to your hand, not destroyed.

This is a targeted effect.

Reaper of the Cards

If this monster is flipped, it MUST use the effect, even if that means you target your own cards.

If the face down card that you target is a magic card, the magic card is flipped back face down.

This is a targeted effect.

Reinforcements

You can use this before or after you declare an attack, as long as it has been face down for 1 turn.

This is a targeted effect.

Relinquished

You cannot absorb more than 1 monster at a time.

If this monster absorbs another relinquished that has absorbed another monster, this monster will have stats of 0/0.

You cannot use the effect on the opponent's turn.

You can only summon this by using the ritual card.

You cannot reborn this monster unless you summoned it first by using the ritual card.

The monster you absorb stays on your m/t zone.

The effect can be used only once per turn.

Once you have absorbed a monster, you cannot simply discard that monster.

Remove Trap

You cannot target face down cards with this card.

You can only play it on your turn, so it is only good for removing permanent traps.

This is a targeted effect.

Reverse Trap

It makes all increases in ATK and DEF decreases and all decreases in ATK and DEF increases. For example, I equip a Sword of Dark Destruction to La Jinn. Normally it gives La Jinn a 400 attack boost and a 200 defense penalty. By activating reverse trap, you can subtract 400 from La Jinn instead and add 200 to it's defense, making its stats 1400/1200.

You cannot use a reverse trap against another reverse trap. Using 2 against each other does not return things to normal.

This card cannot counter the effect of the Gate Guardian pieces.

Right Arm of the Forbidden One

All 5 pieces must be in your HAND in order for the automatic victory to be called.

Right Leg of the Forbidden One

All 5 pieces must be in your HAND in order for the automatic victory to be called.

Ring of Magnetism

It is now official as it is on the Upperdeck FAQ. You CANNOT equip Ring of Magnetism on the opponent's monster.

When equipped on your monster, it does not force the opponent to attack. They can choose to skip their battle phase entirely if they so choose to do so.

This is a targeted effect.

Rising Air Current

This effect works for both players

You can play this if your m/t zone is full because it goes in it's own field magic card zone.

This is a non-targeted effect.

Robbin' Goblin

You cannot combine this with the effects of Catapult Turtle or Cannon Soldier to force the opponent to discard a card.

You cannot combine this with cards like Ookazi to force the opponent to discard a card.

The effect only happens when a monster does damage to the opponent's LP.

If multiple monsters do damage to the opponent's LP, then the opponent discards equal to the amount of monsters that did damage to their LP. (so if 2 monsters do damage to their LP, they discard 2 cards.)

If you have multiple Robbin'

Goblins active, then if 1 monster does damage to the opponent's LP, you can force them to discard cards equal to how many Robbin' Goblins you have in play. (so if you have 3 Robbin' Goblins active, and 2 monsters do damage, the opponent discards 6 cards.)

Rush Recklessly

If you want to use this on the opponent's turn, you must have it set.

The increase in attack is gained for 1 turn only.

You can use this during the battle phase.

Salamandra

This card is NOT legal in official Upperdeck tournaments.

You can only equip this on pyro sub-type monster. If you attach it on a monster other than a pyro type, the Salamandra is returned to your hand, not destroyed.

This is a targeted effect.

Sanga of the Thunder

The effect reduces the ATTACK of a monster to 0. It doesn't reduce the damage to 0. That means that if a Blue Eyes White Dragon were to attack Sanga, and you activate the effect, BEWD's attack is reduced to 0. That means that a monster with 0 attack power has attacked your monster. That means the BEWD will die and the opponent loses 2400 LP.

If you use the effect, and then Sanga leaves the field somehow, you can use the effect again if Sanga re-enters play.

If someone uses the effect on you, you cannot use reverse trap to reverse the effect and make your monster twice as powerful.

If you use monster reborn on your opponent's Sanga, you are

not allowed to activate the effect because you are not the owner of Sanga. Only the owner of Sanga is allowed to use the effect.

Sangan

The effect only works if it goes from the field to the graveyard. If it goes from your hand to the graveyard, the effect doesn't work.

When you use the effect, you must show the monster you searched for to your opponent or an impartial judge.

Seiyaryu

This monster is not legal in official Upperdeck tournaments.

Senju of the Thousand Hands

The effect is not mandatory.

Seven Tools of the Bandit

If this card is countered, you must still pay 1000 LP for the activation cost.

You cannot activate this card if you have less than 1000 LP.

This is a non targeted effect.

Shadow Ghoul

The effect only adds power to this monster for monsters in YOUR graveyard. It doesn't count monsters in the opponent's graveyard.

Share the Pain

The monster you tributed cannot be allowed as a tribute to bring out a level 5+ monster.

The monster you tributed cannot be used as a tribute for Cannon Soldier/Catapult Turtle's effect.

The monsters you tributed are simply destroyed. You cannot use them as tributes for anything.

If this card is negated, you must still destroy one of your monsters as the activation cost

Card Game - F A Q's

Shield and Sword

The effect lasts for 1 turn only.

If you summon a monster after you play Shield and Sword, Shield and Sword does not affect its stats.

This is a non targeted effect.

Shining Angel

The effect will bring a light monster to the field, not your hand.

Silver Bow and Arrow

You can only equip this on fairy sub-type monster. If you attach it on a monster other than a fairy type, the Silver Bow and Arrow is returned to your hand, not destroyed.

This is a targeted effect.

Snake Fang

The effect lasts for 1 turn only.

Snatch Steal

You can only use this on face up monsters.

The opponent gains 1000LP during EACH of his standby phases, as long as this card remains in play.

If the Snatch Steal is returned to the owner's hand or destroyed, the monster is returned to the owner of that monster.

This is a targeted effect.

Sogen

The effect works for both players.

You can play this if your m/t zone is full because it goes in it's own field magic card zone.

This is a non targeted effect.

Solemn Judgement

If this card is negated, you still have to pay half your LP as an activation cost.

If you ever have a decimal in your LP, round off to the nearest whole number.

This card can negate the flip

summon of a monster and will negate the flip effect of that monster if there is any.

This is a non targeted effect.

Sonic Bird

The effect is not mandatory.

Soul Exchange

The tribute monster you bring out with this card counts as a NORMAL summon.

You cannot play this card in main phase 2 at all.

You are allowed to use this in combination with Catapult Turtle / Cannon Soldier to use their effect to launch the opponent's monster back at the opponent.

Despite what the picture looks like, you DO NOT switch monsters with the opponent.

If this card gets countered and negated, you can still have a battle phase.

Soul Release

You cannot use this card to remove cards from both graveyards. You must choose 1 graveyard and remove up to 5 cards from that graveyard.

Spear Cretin

The effect happens after the monster is destroyed after it has been flipped. The effect does not happen right as it is flipped.

You cannot use Spear Cretin's effect to bring itself back into play. However, if you have 1 Spear Cretin on the field and 1 in the graveyard, you can use one to bring the other back in a continuous loop.

Spellbinding Circle

If the monster this is equipped to is tributed, the circle is not destroyed. Rather, it stays in your m/t zone, taking up space.

This can target face down monsters.

This is a targeted effect.

Star Boy

This monster does gain a power boost from its own effect so it can be trap holed.

This is a non targeted effect.

Steel Scorpion

Upperdeck also made 2 versions of this card. One version says to destroy the monster that attacked this card after 2 turns. The other one says 3 turns. The correct text is the one that says 3 turns. That is the ruling you must play by regardless of which copy of the monster you have.

This is a non targeted effect.

Steel Shell

You can only equip this on water main-type monster. If you attach it on a monster other than a water type, the Steel Shell is returned to your hand, not destroyed.

This is a targeted effect.

Stim-Pack

This card will continue to reduce a monster's attack points until it reaches 0.

If it is destroyed, the monster reverts back to its original attack.

This is a targeted effect.

Stop Defense

You cannot use this on your own monster.

If the monster is face down, it's flip effect activates immediately.

The effect lasts for 1 turn only.

This is a targeted effect.

Suijin

The effect reduces the ATTACK of a monster to 0. It doesn't reduce the damage to 0. That means that if a Blue Eyes White Dragon were to attack Suijin, and you activate the effect, BEWD's attack is reduced to 0. That means that a monster with 0 attack power has attacked your monster. That means the BEWD will die and the opponent loses 2400 LP.

If you use the effect, and then Suijin leaves the field somehow, you can use the effect again if Suijin re-enters play.

If someone uses the effect on you, you cannot use reverse trap to reverse the effect and make your monster twice as powerful.

If you use Monster Reborn on your opponent's Suijin, you are not allowed to activate the effect because you are not the owner of Suijin. Only the owner of Suijin is allowed to use the effect.

Swamp Battleguard

You can gain multiple attack boosts from multiple Lava Battleguards on the field.

Sword of Dark Destruction

You can only equip this on dark main-type monster. If you attach it on a monster other than a dark type, the Sword of Dark Destruction is returned to your hand, not destroyed.

This is a targeted effect.

Sword of Deep Seated

It goes back to the top of your deck if it goes to the graveyard for any reason.

It can be equipped on any monster.

This is a targeted effect.

Swords of Revealing Light

The effect ends after the end phase of your opponent's third turn.

The SORL stays on the field when you play it.

None of the opponent's monsters may attack during the time that SORL is in play, even if they summon it after you played SORL.

All of your opponent's face down monsters are flipped face up. All flip effects are activated.

If your opponent sets a monster after you play SORL, that monster stays face down.

SORL can be despelled and destroyed by anything that destroys magic cards.

If the opponent destroys your Sword of Revealing Light, they can't attack until the turn after they destroyed the swords.

This is a non targeted effect.

Tailor of the Fickle

If you want to use this on the opponent's turn, it must be set.

You cannot switch the equip magic to an illegal target (i.e. putting a Dark Energy on a Rogue Doll.)

You can use this during the battle phase.

This is a targeted effect.

Tainted Wisdom

When the monster goes from attack mode to defense mode, you must activate the effect.

The Bistro Butcher

The effect only activates when this monster does damage to the opponent's LP. It doesn't activate every time it attacks.

If your opponent is not able to draw the 2 cards due to the effect, he loses the game.

The Flute of Summoning Dragon

You are allowed to use this card if your opponent has a Lord of D. on the field and you don't.

The Immortal of Thunder

The owner of the Immortal loses the 5000LP when it is sent to their graveyard.

If this card is destroyed while face down without being flipped, no one will lose or gain and LP from the effect because it was never flipped.

The Inexperienced Spy

The card you look at must be randomly selected.

The Little Swordsman of Aile

You can use this effect as many times as your want, but the power boost only lasts until the end of the turn.

The Reliable Guardian

If you want to use this on the opponent's turn, it must be set

The defense bonus is gained for 1 turn only.

You can activate this during the battle phase.

The Stern Mystic

The effect will flip over all face down cards on the field, including your cards.

No cards or flip effect are activated when they are flipped.

After you have looked at everything, the cards that were flipped face up are flipped back face down.

This is a non targeted effect.

The Unhappy Maiden

The effect only activates if the maiden is destroyed by battle.

The Wicked Worm Beast

The effect only works if the monster is face up and alive at the end of your turn. If it is destroyed, it does not return to your hand.

The effect does not work if you set the beast.

Thunder Dragon

The effect only works by discarding it from your hand.

Card Game - F A Q's

When you get the other 2 thunder dragons from your deck, you must show them to your opponent or an impartial judge.

Time Wizard

The effect can be used every turn, but only once per turn.

If this effect causes someone's LP to have a decimal in there, round to the nearest whole number.

Toll

The effect works for both players.

You must pay the 500LP to attack before any damage by the attack is calculated.

This is a non-targeted effect.

Toon Mermaid

You cannot summon this in any way if Toon World is not on the field.

This monster cannot attack on the turn that it is summoned. That includes if you Monster Reborn it.

This monster can attack the opponent's LP directly if they have no toon monsters.

You cannot play this card if your opponent has Toon World out and you don't. You need your own Toon World to summon toon monsters.

This monster can be attacked by a regular monster, contrary to what the anime says.

When you summon this from your hand, it is a special summon, but you still have to tribute.

This monster can only be reborned if it was summoned normally. (same rules for gate guardian)

Toon Summoned Skull

You cannot summon this in any way if Toon World is not on the field.

This monster cannot attack on the turn that it is summoned. That

includes if you Monster Reborn it.

This monster can attack the opponent's LP directly if they have no toon monsters.

You cannot play this card if your opponent has Toon World out and you don't. You need your own Toon World to summon toon monsters.

This monster can be attacked by a regular monster, contrary to what the anime says.

When you summon this from your hand, it is a special summon, but you still have to tribute.

This monster can only be reborned if it was summoned normally. (same rules for Gate Guardian)

Toon World

If this card is negated as it is played, you do not get the 1000LP back.

If this card is returned to your hand when you already have toons in play, the toons are not destroyed. You cannot summon anymore toons though, until you put the toon world back into play.

Trap Hole

You can only trap hole a monster that has just been summoned.

You can trap hole monsters that were normal, tribute, or flip summoned.

You cannot trap hole a monster that was summoned a few turns ago.

You cannot trap hole set monsters.

You cannot trap hole special summon monsters or monsters with attack less than 1000.

This is a non targeted effect.

Trap Master

If the monster is flipped face up, you MUST activate the effect, even if that means you have to target

your own cards.

This is a targeted effect.

Tremendous Fire

If you have 500 or less LP and the opponent has 1000 or less LP, you can create a draw by playing this card.

Tribute to the Doomed

You can destroy face down monsters with this card.

You can target your own monsters with this card.

If this card is negated, then you must still discard a card from your hand because that is the activation cost.

This is a targeted effect.

Turtle Oath

This is the only way to summon Crab Turtle. You cannot reborn a Crab Turtle unless it was summoned by using this card.

You can tribute monsters from your hand when fulfilling the tribute requirements.

Two-Pronged Attack

The 2 monsters you destroy must be on the field. They can't be in your hand.

If this card is negated, you DO NOT have to sacrifice 2 monsters because that is not the cost of activation.

This is a targeted effect.

UFO Turtle

The monster you choose gets summoned to the field. It does not go to your hand.

Ultimate Offering

Only the owner of the Ultimate Offering can use the effect. This is official now. Upperdeck has released the ruling on this.

This card can be activated and used during your 2 main phases or the opponent's battle phase. Using it during the battle phase causes a replay.

If you want to bring out a tribute monster with the effect, you still have to tribute the required monsters.

You can use the effect as much as you want, provided that you have enough LP to pay the cost.

Umi

The effect works for both players. You can play this if your m/t zone is full because it goes in it's own field magic card zone.

This is a non targeted effect.

Umiiruka

The effect works for both players. You can play this if your m/t zone is full because it goes in it's own field magic card zone.

The is a non-targeted effect.

Versago the Destroyer

If you use this as a substitute for a fusion material monster, you cannot use another monster that takes the place of a fusion material monster and combine them together.

Can be fused from your hand.

Vile Germs

You can only equip this on plant sub-type monster. If you attach it on a monster other than a plant type, the Vile Germs is returned to your hand, not destroyed.

This is a targeted effect.

Violet Crystal

You can only equip this on zombie sub-type monster. If you attach it on a monster other than a zombie type, the Violet Crystal is returned to your hand, not destroyed.

This is a targeted effect.

Waboku

This card will protect your LP and your monsters from all of your opponent's monsters.

It reduces the battle damage taken from the opponent's monsters to 0.

This card will not protect you from cards like Ookazi or from the effects of Catapult Turtle / Cannon Soldier.

This is a non targeted effect.

Wall of Illusion

If the monster attacking this card destroys it, it is still returned to the owner's hand.

If the opponent attack your wall of illusions with your own monster, the monster is returned to your hand because you are the owner.

This is a non targeted effect.

Wall Shadow

This monster can only be summoned by sacrificing a Labyrinth Wall equipped with Magical Labyrinth.

Wall Shadow can only be special summoned, so it cannot be set.

This can be summoned from your hand or deck.

Wasteland

The effect works for both players. You can play this if your m/t zone is full because it goes in it's own field magic card zone.

This is a non targeted effect.

Weather Report

If you use the effect, you get your second battle phase right after the first one.

White Hole

Activating this when the opponent plays Dark Hole will save your monsters and destroy all oppo-

nent's monsters. Any flip effects will not work.

This is a non targeted effect.

White Magical Hat

If this monster does damage to the opponent's LP while you have Robbin' Goblin active, you can make the opponent discard 2 cards.

Witch of the Black Forest

The effect only works if it goes from the field to the graveyard. If it goes from your hand to the graveyard, the effect doesn't work.

When you use the effect, you must show the monster you searched for to your opponent or an impartial judge.

Witch's Apprentice

This monster does gain a power boost from it's own effect so it can be trap holed.

This is a non targeted effect.

Wodan the Resident of the Forest

You also increase that attack of this monster for plant types that your opponent has.

Yado Karu

When using the effect, you can put 0 cards at the bottom of the deck if you wish.

Yami

The effect works for both players. You can play this if your m/t zone is full because it goes in it's own field magic card zone.

This is a non targeted effect. ✪

Read More At
www.pojo.com

by Adam Forristal

In this index, we have all the English (Upper Deck) cards in alphabetical order, with their stats, effects, level, type, etc. Adam maintains an up to date list at www.pojo.com

Deck Key: MR=Metal Raiders; DDSp=Dark Duel Stories Promotional Card; KSD=Kaiba Starter Deck; YS=Yugi Starter Deck; LoBEWD=Legend of the Blue Eyes White Dragon; TpS=Tournament Promotional Series; MgRl=Magic Ruler; SD(ky)=Starter Decks (Kaiba and Yugi);

NAME	LEVEL	TYPE	ATTRIBUTE	ATK	DEF	DECK	DESCRIPTION
7 Colored Fish	4	Fish	Water	1800	800	MR	
Acid Trap Hole	T	Trap	Norm. Trap			DDSp	DDS-005 Flip 1 face-down monster face-up. If the monster's DEF is 2000 points or less, it is destroyed. If the DEF is more than 2000 points, flip the monster face-down
Ameba	1	Aqua	Water	300	350	MgRl	When this card is face-up on the field and control shifts to your opponent, inflict 2000 points of Direct Damage to your opponent's Life Points. This effect can only be used once as long as this card remains face-up on the field
Ancient Brain	3	Fiend	Dark	1000	700	MR	
Ancient Elf	4	Castr	Light	1450	1200	MR	
Ancient Lizard Warrior	4	Rep	Earth	1400	1100	MR	
Ancient one of the deep forest	6	Beast	Earth	1800	1900	MgRl	
Ancient Telescope	M	Magic	Norm. Magic			KSD	See the top 5 cards of opp. deck. Return in same order
Ansatsu	5	War	Earth	1700	1200	YS	
Aqua Madoor	4	Castr	Water	1200	2000	LoBEWD	
Armaill	3	War	Earth	700	1300	LoBEWD	
Armed Ninja	1	War	Earth	300	300	LoBEWD	Flip – Destroys 1 magic card on the field (same rules as De-spell)
Armored Lizard	4	Rep	Earth	1400	1200	MR	
Armored Starfish	4	Aqua	Water	850	1400	LoBEWD	
Armored Zombie	3	Zomb	Dark	1500	0	MR	
Axe of Despair	M	Magic	Equip Magic			MgRl	A monster equipped with this card increases its ATK by 1000 points. When this card is sent from the Field to the Graveyard, you can offer 1 monster from the field as a Tribute to place it on top of your Deck
Axe Raider	4	War	Earth	1700	1150	TpS	TP1-002
Baby Dragon	3	Drag	Wind	1200	700	MR	
Banisher of the Light	3	Fairy	Light	100	2000	MgRl	As long as this card remains face-up on the field, any card sent to the Graveyard is removed from play
Baron of the Fiend Sword	4	Fiend	Dark	1550	800	YS	
Barrel Dragon	7	Mach	Dark	2600	2200	MR	Flip a coin 3 times – 2 heads, destroy 1 opp. Monster. Can be used once/turn
Basic Insect	2	Ins	Earth	500	700	LoBEWD	
Battle Ox	4	B-War	Earth	1700	1000	KSD	

NAME	LEVEL	TYPE	ATTRIBUTE	ATK	DEF	DECK	DESCRIPTION
Battle Steer	5	B-war	Earth	1800	1300	MR	
Bean Soldier	4	Plant	Earth	1400	1300	TpS	TP1-018
Beast Fangs	M	Magic	Equip Magic			LoBEWD	Beast type with this card gains 300/300
Beast-King of the Swamps	4	Aqua	Water	100	1100	TpS	TP1 –014 You can substitute this card for any 1 Fusion-Material Monster. You cannot substitute for any other Fusion-Material Monster in the current Fusion.
Beaver Warrior	4	B-War	Earth	1200	1500	LoBEWD	
Bickuribox	F	Fiend	Dark	2300	2000	MR	Crass Clown + Dream Clown
Big Eye	4	Fiend	Dark	1200	1000	MR	See top 5 of your deck, arrange them how you want, and put them back on top of your deck
Black Illusion Ritual	M	Magic	Ritual Magic			MgRl	this card is used to Ritual Summon "Relinquished". You must also offer monsters whose total Level Stars equal 1 or more from the field or your hand as a Tribute
Black Pendant	M	Magic	Equip Magic			MgRl	A monster equipped with this card increases its ATK by 500 points. When this card is sent from the Field to the graveyard, inflict 500 points of direct damage to your opponent's Life Points
Black Skull Dragon	F	Drag	Dark	3200	2500	MR	Summoned Skull + Red Eyes Black Dragon
Blackland Fire Dragon	4	Drag	Dark	1500	800	MR	
Bladefly	2	Ins	Wind	600	700	MR	As long as it is face up, ATK of wind + 500, ATK of earth – 400
Blast Juggler	3	Mach	Fire	800	900	MR	Offer as a tribute in standby phase to destroy 2 monsters with ATK 1000 or less
Block Attack	M	Magic	Norm. Magic			MR	Shift 1 opp. Monster into defense position
Blue Eyes Toon Dragon	8	Dragon Toon	Light	3000	2500	MgRl	This card cannot be summoned unless "Toon World" is on the field. This card cannot attack in the same turn that it is summoned. Pay 500 life points each time this monster attacks. When "Toon World" is destroyed, this card is destroyed. If your opponent doesn't control a Toon monster on the field, this card may inflict direct damage to your opponents life points. If a Toon monster is on your opponents side of the field, your attacks must target the toon monster
Blue Eyes White Dragon	8	Drag	Light	3000	2500	LoBEWD	LOB-001 & DDS-003
Blue Medicine	M					TpS	TP1-008 Increase both yours and your opp. LP by 400
Blue-Winged Crown	4	Wng-B	Wind	1600	1200	MR	
Boar Soldier	4	B-War	Earth	2000	500	MgRl	This card can only be summoned by a Flip Summon. If summoned by a normal summon, the card is destroyed. If your opponent has 1 or monsters under his/her control, the ATK of this monster is decreased by 1000 points
Book of Secret Arts	M	Magic	Equip Magic			LoBEWD	A Spellcaster equipped with this card is + 300/300
Bottom Dweller	5	Fish	Water	1650	1700	MR	
Burning Spear	M	Magic	Equip Magic			TpS	TP1-010 A Fire monster with this card is +400/0 and –0/200
Cannon Soldier	4	Mach	Dark	1400	1300	MR	Tribute 1 monster on your side of the field to inflict 500 points direct damage on your opponent LP. Cannot be used for tribute summon also.
Card Destruction	M	Magic	Norm Magic			YS	Both players discard their entire hands and draw the same number of cards from their deck
Castle of Dark Illusions	4	Fiend	Dark	920	1930	MR	FLIP: Increases the ATK and DEF of all Zombies by 200 points. As long as this card remains face up on the field, the ATK and DEF of Zombie-type monsters continues to increase during each of your standby phases. This effect continues until your 4th turn after the card is activated.
Castle Walls	T	Trap	Norm. Trap			SD(k,y)	The selected monster is +0/500 for turn activated
Catapult Turtle	5	Aqua	Water	1000	2000	MR	Tribute 1 monster on your side of the field to do direct damage to your opp. Equal to half the tribute's ATK points. Cannot be used as tribute summon.
Celtic Guardian	4	War	Earth	1400	1200	LoBEWD	

NAME	LEVEL	TYPE	ATTRIBUTE	ATK	DEF	DECK	DESCRIPTION
Ceremonial Bell	3	Castr	Light	0	1850	MgRI	As long as this card remains face-up on the field, you and your opponent must show your respective hands to each other
Chain Energy	M	Magic	Cont. Magic			MgRI	As long as this card remains face up on the field, both you and your opponent must pay 500 Life Points per card to play or set cards from your respective hands
Change of Heart	M					MR	Control one of your opponents monsters until the end of your turn
Changing Disguises	M	Magic	Quick Magic			MgRI	Move 1 Equipment Magic card to another legal target
Charubin the Fire Knight	3	Pyro	Fire	1100	800	LoBEWD	MonsterEgg + Hinotama Soul
Chorus of Sanctuary	M	Magic	Field Magic			MgRI	increases the DEF of all Defense position monsters by 500 points
Claw Reacher	3	Fiend	Dark	1000	800	YS	
Cockroach Knight	3	Insct	Earth	800	900	TpS	TP1-029 When this card has been sent to the Graveyard, it is returned to the top of your Deck.
Cocoon of Evolution	3	Insct	Earth	0	2000	MR	Can be used as equip on Face up Petit Moth. Petit Moth's ATK and DEF becomes equal to that of Cocoon of Evolution
Commencement Dance	M	Magic	Ritual Magic			MgRI	This card is used to Ritual Summon "Performance of Sword". You must also offer monsters whose total Level Stars equal 6 or more as a tribute from the field or your hand
Confiscation	M	Magic	Norm. Magic			MgRI	pay 1000 Life Points to look at your opponent's hand. Select 1 card and discard it to the graveyard
Corroding Shark	3	Zomb	Dark	1100	700	TpS	TP1-020
Crab Turtle	8	Aqua Ritual	Water	2550	2500	MgRI	This monster can only be Ritual Summoned with the Ritual Magic Card, "Turtle Oath"
Crass Clown	4	Fiend	Dark	1350	1400	MR	When this monster is changed from DEF to ATK position, return one monster on your opp. Side of the field to its owners' hand.
Crawling Dragon	5	Drag	Earth	1600	1400	MR	
Curse of Dragon	5	Drag	Dark	2000	1500	LoBEWD	
Curse of Fiend	M	Magic	Norm. Magic			MgRI	Changes the battle positions of all attack position monsters to defense position and vice-versa. These positions cannot be changed during the turn this card is activated except by the effect of a Magic, Trap, or Effect Monster Card. You can activate this card only during your standby phase
Cyber Jar	3	Rock	Dark	900	900	MgRI	FLIP: Destroys all monsters on the field (including this monster). Both players then pick up (not draw) 5 cards from the top of their respective decks and show the cards to each other. Immediately Special Summon any Monster Cards of Level 4 or lower among them on the field in face-up Attack Position or in face-down Defense Position. The rest of the cards picked up are place in the player's hands
Cyber Saurus	5	Mach	Earth	1800	1400	MR	Blast Juggler + Two Headed King Rex
Cyber Soldier of Darkworld	4	Mach	Dark	1400	1200	TpS	TP1-028
D. Human	4	War	Earth	1300	1100	KSD	
Dark Assailant	4	Zomb	Dark	1200	1200	KSD	
Dark Elf	4	Castr	Dark	2000	800	MR	Attacking with Dark Elf requires a sacrifice of 1000 of your own LP
Dark Energy	M	Magic	Equip Magic			LoBEWD	Fiend Equipped with this becomes + 300/300
Dark Grey	3	Beast	Earth	800	900	LoBEWD	
Dark Hole	M	Magic	Norm. Magic			LoBEWD	Destroys all monsters on the field
Dark King of the Abyss	3	Fiend	Dark	1200	800	LoBEWD	
Dark Magician	7	Castr	Dark	2500	2100	LoBEWD	LOB-005 & DDS-002
Dark Titan of Terror	4	Fiend	Dark	1300	1100	KSD	

NAME	LEVEL	TYPE	ATTRIBUTE	ATK	DEF	DECK	DESCRIPTION
Dark Witch	5	Fairy	Dark	1800	1700	MgRl	
Dark Zebra	4	Beast	Dark	1800	400	MgRl	If this is the only card in your control during your standby phase, it is automatically placed in Defence Position. You cannot change the position of this card during the same turn
Darkfire Dragon	4	Drag	Dark	1500	1250	LoBEWD	Firegrass + Petit Dragon
Darkness Approaches	M	Magic	Norm. Magic			MgRl	Discard 2 cards from your hand. Select 1 face up monster and flip it face down, but do not change its
battle position							
Darkworld Thorns	3	Plant	Earth	1200	900	LoBEWD	
Deepsea Shark	5	Fish	Water	1900	1600	MR	Bottom Dweller + Tongyo
Delinquent Duo	M	Magic	Norm. Magic			MgRl	Pay 1000 Life Points. Randomly select and discard 1 card from your opponent's hand. Your opponent then selects and discards another card from his/her hand
De-Spell	M	Magic	Norm. Magic			SD(k,y)	Destroys 1 magic card on the field. If this card's target is face down, flip it face up. If it is not a magic card, flip it face down.
Destroyer Golem	4	Rock	Earth	1500	1000	MR	
Dian Keto The Cure Master	M	Magic	Norm. Magic			YS	Increases your LP by 1000
Disk Magician	4	Mach	Dark	1350	1000	MR	
Dissolverock	3	Rock	Earth	900	1000	LoBEWD	
Doma The Angel of Silence	5	Fairy	Dark	1600	1400	MR	
Dragon Capture Jar	T	Trap	Perm. Trap			LoBEWD	All Dragon-type monsters on the field are switched to DEF position and remain like that as long as this card is active
Dragon Piper	3	Pyro	Fire	200	1800	MR	Destroys Dragon Capture Jar and switches all dragons to ATK position
Dragon Treasure	M	Magic	Equip Magic			LoBEWD	Dragon with this card is +300/300
Dragon Zombie	3	Zomb	Dark	1600	0	YS	
Dragoness the Wicked Knight	3	War	Wind	1200	900	LoBEWD	Armaill + One Eyes Sheild Dragon
Dream Clown	3	War	Earth	1200	900	MR	When changed from ATK to DEF position, select and destroy 1 monster on your opponents field
Drooling Lizard	3	Rep	Earth	900	800	LoBEWD	
Eatgaboon	T	Trap	Norm. Trap			MgRl	If the ATK of a monster summoned by your opponent (excluding Special Summon) is 500 points or less, the monster is destroyed
Electric Lizard	3	Thndr	Earth	850	800	MR	A non-Zombie type monster attacking Electric Lizard cannot attack again on its next turn
Electric Snake	3	Thndr	Light	800	900	MgRl	When this card is sent directly from your hand to the Graveyard by your opponent's card effect, you can draw 2 cards from your Deck
Electro Whip	M	Magic	Equip			LoBEWD	A Thunder-type monster equipped with this card is + 300/300
Elegant Egotist	M	Magic	Norm Magic			MR	If you have 1 or more Harpie Lady cards on the field, you can special summon another Harpie Lady or Harpie Lady Sisters from your deck
Elf's Light	M	Magic	Equip Magic			TpS	TP1-006 A light monster with this card is +400/0 and −0/200
Empress Judge	6	War	Earth	2100	1700	MR	Queens Double + Hibikime
Enchanting Mermaid	3	Fish	Dark	1200	900	LoBEWD	
Eternal Rest	M	Magic	Norm. Magic			MgRl	Destroy all monsters equipped with Equip Cards
Exodia the Forbidden One	3	Castr	Dark	1000	1000	LoBEWD	If you have Exodia the Forbidden One, Right Arm of Exodia, Right Leg of Exodia, Left Arm of Exodia and Left Leg of Exodia in your hand – you automatically take victory. LOB-124 & DDS-001

NAME	LEVEL	TYPE	ATTRIBUTE	ATK	DEF	DECK	DESCRIPTION
Fairy's Hand Mirror	T	Trap	Norm. Trap			MgRl	Switch the opponent's Magic Card effect that specifically designates 1 monster as a target to another correctly targeted monster
Fake Trap	T	Trap	Norm. Trap			MR	When your opponent has the ability to destroy a trap card, this card may take the place of a trap card
Feral Imp	4	Fiend	Dark	1300	1400	MR	
Fiend Reflection #2	4	Wng-B	Light	1100	1400	LoBEWD	
Final Destiny	M	Magic	Norm. Magic			MgRl	Discard 5 cards from your hand to destroy all cards on the field
Final Flame	M	Magic	Norm. Magic			LoBEWD	Inflicts 600 points direct damage to opp. LP
Fire Kraken	4	Aqua	Fire	1600	1550	MgRl	
Firegrass	2	Plant	Earth	700	600	LoBEWD	
Fireyarou	4	Pyro	Fire	1300	1000	LoBEWD	
Fissure	M	Magic	Norm. Magic			LoBEWD	Destroys one opp. face-up monster with the lowest attack
Flame Cerebrus	6	Pyro	Fire	2100	1800	MR	
Flame Ghost	3	Zomb	Dark	1000	800	LoBEWD	Skull Servant + Dissolverock
Flame Manipulator	3	Castr	Fire	900	1000	LoBEWD	
Flame Swordsman	5	War	Fire	1800	1600	LoBEWD	Flame Manipulator +Masaki the Legendary Swordsman
Flash Assailant	4	Fiend	Dark	2000	2000	MgRl	Decrease the ATK and DEF of this card by 400 points for every card in your hand
Flower Wolf	5	Beast	Earth	1800	1400	LoBEWD	Silver Fang + Darkworld Thorns
Flying Kamakiri #1	4	Insct	Wind	1400	900	MgRl	When this card is sent to the graveyard as a result of battle, you may select 1 FIRE monster with an attack of 1500 or less from your deck and Special Summon it to the field in face-up Attack Position (no Tribute is required for monsters of Level 5 or more). The deck is then shuffled
Follow Wind	M	Magic	Equip Magic			LoBEWD	A Winged Beast type equipped with this card is + 300/300
Forest	M	Magic	Field Magic			LoBEWD	Insect, Beast, Plant, Beast-Warrior + 200/200
Frenzied Panda	4	Beast	Earth	1200	1000	LoBEWD	
Fusionist	3	Beast	Earth	900	700	LoBEWD	Petit Angel + Mystical Sheep 2
Gaia Power	M	Magic	Field Magic			MgRl	Increases the ATK of all EARTH monsters by 500 points and decreases their DEF by 400 points
Gaia The Dragon Champion	7	Drag	Wind	2600	2100	LoBEWD	Gaia the Fierce Knight + Curse of Dragon
Gaia The Fierce Knight	7	War	Earth	2300	2100	LoBEWD	
Garnecia Elefantis	7	B-War	Earth	2400	2000	MR	
Gate Guardian	11	War	Dark	3750	3400	MR	This card can only be special summoned by offering "Sanga of the Thunder", "Kazejin" and "Suijin" on your side of the field as a tribute
Gazelle the King of Mythical Beasts	4	Beast	Earth	1500	1200	MR	
Germ Infection	M	Magic	Equip Magic			MR	The ATK of a non-machine monster is decreased by 300 in each of its standby phases
Giant Flea	4	Ins	Earth	1500	1200	TpS	TP1-017
Giant Germ	2	Fiend	Dark	1000	100	MgRl	When this card is sent to the Graveyard as a result of battle, inflict 500 points of Direct Damage to your opponents Life Points. You can also take cards with the same name from your Deck and Special summon them to the field in face-up Attack Position Then Deck is then shuffled

NAME	LEVEL	TYPE	ATTRIBUTE	ATK	DEF	DECK	DESCRIPTION
Giant Rat	4	Beast	Earth	1400	1450	MgRl	When this card is sent to the graveyard as a result of battle, you may select 1 EARTH monster with an attack of 1500 or less from your deck and Special Summon it to the field in face-up Attack Position (no Tribute is required for monsters of Level 5 or more). The deck is then shuffled
Giant Soldier of Stone	3	Rock	Earth	1300	2000	LoBEWD	
Giant Trunade	M	Magic	Norm. Magic			MgRl	Return all Magic and Trap cards on the Field to their respective owner's hands
Giant turtle who feeds on flame	5	Aqua	Water	1400	1800	MgRl	
Giga-Tech Wolf	4	Mach	Fire	1200	1400	MR	
Giltia the D. Knight	5	War	Light	1850	1500	MR	Guardian of the Labyrinth + Protector of the Throne
Goblin's Secret Remedy	M	Magic	Norm. Magic			LoBEWD	Increases a players LP by 600
Goddess with the Third Eye	4	Fairy	Light	1200	1000	TpS	TP1-013 This monster can be substituted for any other fusion material monster. You cannot substitute any other fusion monster in the current fusion.
GraveDigger Ghoul	M	Magic	Norm. Magic			LoBEWD	Select 2 monsters from your opp. Graveyard. These monsters are removed from play
Gravekeeper's Secret	M	Magic	Cont. Magic			MgRl	Each time your opponent attacks with a monster, the opponent must send 1 card from the top of his/her Deck to the Graveyard
Great Moth	8	Ins	Earth	2600	2500	MR	This monster can only be special summoned by offering Petit Moth as a tribute on your 4th turn after Petit Moth is equipped with Cocoon of Evolution
Great White	4	Fish	Water	1600	800	YS	
Green Phantom King	3	Plant	Earth	500	1600	LoBEWD	
Griggle	1	Plant	Earth	350	300	MgRl	when this card is face up on the field and control shifts to your opponent, you gain 3000 Life Points. This effect can only be used once as long as this card remains face up on the field
Ground Attacker Bugroth	4	Mach	Earth	1500	1000	MR	
Guardian of the Labyrinth	4	War	Earth	1000	1200	MR	
Guardian of the throne room	4	Mach	Light	1650	1600	MgRl	
Gust Fan	M	Magic	Equip Magic			TpS	TP1-011 A Wind monster with this card is +400/0 and −0/200
Gyakutenno Megami	6	Fairy	Light	1800	2000	KSD	
Hamburger Recipe	M	Magic	Ritual Magic			MgRl	This card is used to Ritual Summon "Hungry Burger". You must also offer monsters whose total Level Stars equal 6 or more as a tribute from the field or your hand
Hane-Hane	2	Beast	Earth	450	500	LoBEWD	Flip – Select one monster card on the field and return it to its owner's hand
Hard Armor	3	War	Earth	300	1200	LoBEWD	
Harpie Lady	4	Wng-B	Wind	1300	1400	MR	
Harpie Lady Sisters	6	Wng-B	Wind	1950	2100	MR	This card can only be special summoned by using the card "Elegant Egotist"
Heavy Storm	M	Magic	Norm. Magic			MR	Destroys all magic and trap cards on the field
Hercules Beetle	5	Ins	Earth	1500	2000	TpS	TP1-025
Hibikime	4	War	Earth	1450	1000	MR	
Hige Tide Gyojin	4	Aqua	Water	1650	1300	MgRl	
Hinotama	M	Magic	Norm. Magic			LoBEWD	Inflicts 500 direct damage on your opponents LP
Hinotama Soul	2	Pyro	Fire	600	500	LoBEWD	
Hiro's Shadow Scout	2	Fiend	Dark	650	500	MgRl	FLIP: Your opponent draws 3 cards. Both players check the cards and any Magic Cards among them must be immediately discarded to the graveyard
Hitotsu-Me Giant	4	B-War	Earth	1200	1500	LoBEWD	

Card Game - List of Cards

NAME	LEVEL	TYPE	ATTRIBUTE	ATK	DEF	DECK	DESCRIPTION
Horn of Heaven	T	Trap	Count. Trap			MR	Offer 1 of your own monsters to negate the summon of an opp. Monster and destroy it
Horn of Light	M	Magic	Equip Magic			MgRI	a monster equipped with this card increases its DEF by 800 points. when this card is sent from the field to the graveyard, you can pay 500 Life Points to place it on top of your deck
Horn of the Unicorn	M	Magic	Equip Magic			MgRI	a monster equipped with this card raises its attack and def by 700 points. when this card is sent from the field to the Graveyard, it returns to the top of your Deck
Hoshiningen	2	Fairy	Light	500	700	MR	As long as this card is face up ATK of Light monsters + 500, ATK of Dark monsters – 400
House of Adhesive Tape	T	Trap	Norm. Trap			MgRI	If the DEF of a monster summoned by your opponent (excluding Special Summon) is 500 points or less, the monster is destroyed
Hungry Burger	6	Ritual War	Dark	2000	1850	MR	This monster can only be Ritual Summoned with the Ritual Magic Card, "Hamburger Recipe"
Hunter Spider	5	Ins	Earth	1600	1400	MR	
Hyosube	4	Aqua	Water	1500	900	MR	
Hyozanryu	7	Dragon	Light	2100	2800	MgRI	
Illusionist Faceless Mage	5	Castr	Dark	1200	2200	MR	
Insect Soldiers of the Sky	3	Ins	Wind	1000	800	MR	The ATK of this Card increases by 1000 points when it ATKs a wind-type monster
Invader of the Throne	4	War	Earth	1350	1700	MgRI	FLIP: Select 1 opponent's monster and switch control of it with this card. This effect cannot be activated during the Battle Phase
Invigoration	M	Magic	Equip Magic			KSD	Earth monster equipped with this card becomes + 400/0, - 0/200
Jellyfish	4	Aqua	Water	1200	1500	MR	
Jigen Bakudan	2	Pyro	Fire	200	1000	MgRI	FLIP: After this card is flipped, offer it as a Tribute during your standby phase to destroy all monsters on your side of the field and inflict direct damage equal to half of the total ATK of the destroyed cards (excluding this monster) to your opponent's LP
Jinzo #7	2	Mach	Dark	500	400	MR	This monster may ATK your opponents LP directly
Jirai Gumo	4	Ins	Earth	2200	100	MR	When you attack with this card, toss a coin and call it. If it is heads, attack normally. If it is tails, take away half your LP before attacking
Judge Man	6	War	Earth	2200	1500	KSD	
Just Desserts	T	Trap	Norm. Trap			KSD	Inflict 500 damage to your opponents LP for every monster your opponent has on the field
Kagemusha of the Blue Flame	2	War	Earth	800	400	LoBEWD	
Kaminari Attack	5	Thndr	Wind	1900	1400	MR	Ocubeam + Mega Thunderball
Karate Man	3	War	Earth	1000	1000	MgRI	Once per turn, the original ATK of this card can be doubled. When this effect is applied, the card is immediately destroyed at the end of the turn
Karbonala Warrior	4	War	Earth	1500	1200	LoBEWD	M-Warrior #1 +M-Warrior #2
Kazejin	7	Castr	Wind	2400	2200	MR	Reduce the ATK of an opp. Monster to 0. This effect can only be used once. The card's owner chooses when to activate this effect.
Killer Needle	4	Ins	Wind	1200	1000	MR	
King Fog	3	Fiend	Dark	1000	900	LoBEWD	
King of Yamimakai	5	Fiend	Dark	2000	1530	MR	
Kojikocy	4	War	Earth	1500	1200	MR	

NAME	LEVEL	TYPE	ATTRIBUTE	ATK	DEF	DECK	DESCRIPTION
Kotodama	3	Fairy	Light	0	1600	MgRl	As long as this card remains face up on the field, monsters of the same name cannot exist on the field at the same time (face-down cards not included). If a card of the same name is summoned in a later turn, that card is destroyed. If 2 cards of the same name are played at the same time, both cards are destroyed
Koumori Dragon	4	Drag	Dark	1500	1200	KSD	
Kumootoko	3	Ins	Earth	700	1400	LoBEWD	
Kurama	3	Wng-B	Wind	800	800	LoBEWD	
Kuriboh	1	Fiend	Dark	300	200	MR	Discard one card from your hand to the graveyard to make the damage inflicted to your LP by one of your opp. Monsters 0. This effect must be activated during your opp. Battle Phase
Kuwagata Ü	4	Ins	Earth	1250	1000	TpS	TP1-030
Kwagar Hercules	6	Ins	Earth	1900	1700	TpS	TP1-003 Kuwagata U + Hercules Beetle
La Jinn The Mystical Genie	4	Fiend	Dark	1800	1000	KSD	
Labyrinth Tank	7	Mach	Dark	2400	2400	MR	Giga-Tech Wolf + Cannon Soldier
Labyrinth Wall	5	Rock	Earth	000	3000	MgRl	
Lady of Faith	3	Castr	Light	1100	800	MR	
Larvae Moth	2	Ins	Earth	500	400	MR	This monster can only be special summoned by offering Petit Moth as a tribute on the 2nd turn after Petit Moth has been equipped with Cocoon of Evolution
Larvas	3	Beast	Earth	800	1000	LoBEWD	
Laser Cannon Armor	M	Magic	Equip Magic			LoBEWD	An insect type monster equipped with this card is + 300/300
Last Will	M	Magic	Norm. Magic			YS	If a monster of yours is sent to the graveyard on the turn this card is played, you may select a monster with an ATK power of 1500 or less from your deck and play it as a special summon. Shuffle your deck afterwards. This card is active for 1 turn only.
Launcher Spider	7	Mach	Fire	2200	2500	MR	
Lava Battleguard	5	War	Earth	1550	1800	MR	Raise the ATK of this card by 500 for every face-up Swamp Battleguard on your side of the field
Left Arm of Exodia	1	Castr	Dark	200	300	LoBEWD	One of Exodia's arms
Left Leg of Exodia	1	Castr	Dark	200	200	LoBEWD	One of Exodia's legs
Legendary Sword	M	Magic	Equip Magic			LoBEWD	A Warrior type monster with this card is + 300/300
Leghul	1	Insct	Earth	300	350	MR	This monster may attack your opp. LP directly
Leogun	5	Beast	Earth	1750	1550	MR	
Lesser Dragon	4	Drag	Wind	1200	1000	LoBEWD	
Liquid Beast	3	Aqua	Water	950	800	MgRl	
Little Chimera	2	Beast	Fire	600	550	MR	As long as this card is face up on the field, all Fire monsters become +500/500 and all Water monsters become -400/400
Lord of D.	4	Castr	Dark	1200	1100	KSD	All Dragon-type monsters are not affected by magic, traps or other effects while this card is face up on the field
Luminous Spark	M	Magic	Field Magic			MgRl	Increases the ATK of all LIGHT monsters by 500 points and decreases their DEF by 400 points
Machine Conversion Factory	M	Magic	Equip Magic			LoBEWD	Machine monster with this card is +300/300
Magic Jammer	T	Trap	Count. Trap			MR	Discard 1 card from your hand to negate the activation of a magic card and destroy it
Magical Ghost	4	Zomb	Dark	1300	1400	YS	
Magical Labyrinth	M	Magic	Equip Magic			MgRl	Equip "Labyrinth Wall" with this card. If you offer "Labyrinth Wall" equipped with this card as a tribute, you can Special Summon "Wall Shadow" from your hand
Magician of Faith	1	Castr	Light	300	400	MR	FLIP: Select 1 magic card from your graveyard and return it to your hand

NAME	LEVEL	TYPE	ATTRIBUTE	ATK	DEF	DECK	DESCRIPTION
Mahar Vairo	4	Castr	Light	1550	1400	MgRI	In addition to the effects of equip cards, the ATK of this monster is increased by 500 points for each card equipped to this monster
Malevolent Nuzzler	M	Magic	Equip Magic			MgRI	A monster equipped with this card increases its attack by 700 points. When this card is sent from the field to the Graveyard, you may pay 500 Life Points to place it on top of your Deck
Mammoth Graveyard	3	Dino	Earth	1200	800	LoBEWD	
Man Eater	2	Plant	Earth	800	600	LoBEWD	
Man Eating Treasure Chest	4	Fiend	Dark	1600	1000	YS	
Man-Eater Bug	2	Insct	Earth	450	600	LoBEWD	FLIP: Destroy one monster on the field
Manga Ryu-Ran	7	Dragon Toon	Fire	2200	2600	MgRI	This card cannot be summoned unless "Toon World" is on the field. This card cannot attack in the same turn that it is summoned. Pay 500 life points each time this monster attacks. When "Toon World" is destroyed, this card is destroyed. If your opponent doesn't control a Toon monster on the field, this card may inflict direct damage to your opponents life points. If a Toon monster is on your opponents side of the field your attacks must target the toon monster
Masaki the Legendary Swordsman	4	War	Earth	1100	1100	LoBEWD	
Mask of Darkness	2	Fiend	Dark	900	400	MR	FLIP: Select one trap card from your graveyard and return it to your hand
Masked Sorcerer	4	Castr	Dark	900	1400	MR	When you inflict damage on your opp. LP with this card, draw 1 card from your deck
Master & Expert	4	Beast	Earth	1200	1000	KSD	
Mechanical Chaser	4	Mach	Dark	1850	800	TpS	TP1-001
Mechanical Snail	3	Mach	Dark	800	1000	MgRI	
Meda Bat	2	Fiend	Dark	800	400	LoBEWD	
Mega Thunderball	2	Thndr	Wind	750	600	MR	
Megamorph	M	Magic	Equip. Magic			MgRI	If your Life Points less than your opponent's, the original ATK of a monster equipped with this card is doubled. If your Life Points are greater, the original ATK is halved
Messenger of Peace	M	Magic	Norm. Magic			MgRI	You must pay 100 Life Points at each of your standby phases. If you cannot pay, this card is destroyed. All monsters with an ATK of 1500 points or higher cannot attack
Metal Dragon	6	Mach	Wind	1850	1700	LoBEWD	Steel Ogre Grotto #1 + Lesser Dragon
Metal Fish	5	Mach	Water	1600	1900	MgRI	
Milus Radiant	1	Beast	Earth	250	300	MR	If this card is face up on the field, Earth is +500/0 and Wind is −400/0
Minar		Insct	Earth	850	750	MgRI	When this card is sent directly from your hand to the Graveyard by your opponent's card effect, inflict 1000 points of direct damage to your opponent's LP
Mirror Force	T	Trap	Norm. Trap			MR	When an opp. Monster atks, negate the attack and destroy all opp. Monsters in ATK position
Misairuzame	5	Fish	Water	1400	1600	LoBEWD	
Molten Destruction	M	Magic	Field Magic			MgRI	Increases the ATK of all FIRE monsters by 500 points and decreases their DEF by 400 points
Monster Egg	3	War	Earth	600	900	LoBEWD	
Monster Reborn	M	Magic	Norm.Magic			LoBEWD	Select 1 Monster from either graveyard and place it on the field face up (attack or defense). This is a special summon
Morinphen	5	Fiend	Dark	1550	1300	MR	
Mother Grizzly	4	B-War	Water	1400	1000	MgRI	When this card is sent to the graveyard as a result of battle, you may select 1 WATER monster with an attack of 1500 or less from your deck and Special Summon it to the field in face-up Attack Position (no Tribute is required for monsters of Level 5 or more). The deck is then shuffled

NAME	LEVEL	TYPE	ATTRIBUTE	ATK	DEF	DECK	DESCRIPTION
Mountain	M	Magic	Field Magic			LoBEWD	Increases all Dinosaurs, Winged Beast, and Thunder type monsters by 200/200
Muka Muka	2	Rock	Earth	600	300	MR	Increase this monster by 300/300 for every card in their hand
Mushroom Man #2	3	War	Earth	1250	800	MR	A player controlling this monster loses 300 LP during each of his/her Standby phases when this card is on the field face up. Control of this monster can be shifted to your opponent during your end phase for a cost of 500 LP
Musician King	5	Castr	Light	1750	1500	MR	Witch of the Black Forest + Lady of Faith
M-Warrior #1	3	War	Earth	1000	500	LoBEWD	
M-Warrior #2	3	War	Earth	500	1000	LoBEWD	
Mysterious Puppeteer	4	War	Earth	1000	1500	KSD	When a monster is summoned (or flipped face up) and this card is face up on the field, the LP of this cards owner increase by 500 (excluding special summon, but including your opp. monsters)
Mystic Clown	4	Fiend	Dark	1500	1000	SD(k,y)	
Mystic Horseman	4	Beast	Earth	1300	1550	MR	
Mystic Lamp	1	Castr	Dark	400	300	MR	This monster may ATK your opp. LP directly
Mystic Plasma Zone	M	Magic	Field Magic			MgRl	Increases the ATK of all DARK monsters by 500 points and decreases their DEF by 400 points
Mystic Tomato	4	Plant	Dark	1400	1100	MgRl	When this card is sent to the graveyard as a result of battle, you may select 1 DARK monster with an attack of 1500 or less from your deck and Special Summon it to the field in face-up Attack Position (no Tribute is required for monsters of Level 5 or more). The deck is then shuffled
Mystical Elf	4	Castr	Light	800	2000	LoBEWD	
Mystical Moon	M	Magic	Equip Magic			LoBEWD	A Beast-type with this card is 300/300
Mystical Sheep #2	3	Beast	Earth	800	1000	LoBEWD	
Mystical Space Typhoon	M	Magic	Quick Magic			MgRl	Destroy 1 Magic or Trap card on the Field
Nemuriko	3	Castr	Dark	800	700	LoBEWD	
Neo the Magic Swordsman	4	Castr	Light	1700	1000	YS	
Nimble Momonga	2	Beast	Light	1000	100	MgRl	When this card is sent to the graveyard as a result of battle, increase your Life Points by 1000 points. You can also take cards of the same name from your Deck and Special Summon them to the field in face-down Defense Position. The Deck is then shuffled
Niwatori	3	Wng-B	Earth	900	800	MR	
Octoberser	5	Aqua	Water	1600	1400	MgRl	
Ocubeam	5	Fairy	Light	1550	1650	MR	
Ogre of the Black Shadow	4	B-War	Earth	1200	1400	KSD	
One-Eyed Shield Dragon	3	Drag	Wind	700	1300	LoBEWD	
Ooguchi	1	Aqua	Water	300	250	MR	This monster may attack your opp. LP directly
Ookazi	M	Magic	Norm. Magic			KSD	Inflict 800 points direct damage on your opp. LP
Oscillo Hero	3	War	Earth	1250	700	TpS	TP1-023
Oscillo Hero #2	3	Thndr	Light	1000	500	TpS	TP1-016
Painful Choice	M	Magic	Norm. Magic			MgRl	Select 5 cards from your Deck and show them to your opponent. Your opponent must select 1 card that will be added to your hand. Discard the remaining cards in the Graveyard
Pale Beast	4	Beast	Earth	1500	1200	MR	
Paralyzing Potion	M	Magic	Equip Magic			MR	A Non-Machine monster equipped with this card cannot attack
Patrol Robo	3	Mach	Earth	1100	900	TpS	TP1-004 If this card is face up during your stanby phase, you may look at one of your opp. Set cards

NAME	LEVEL	TYPE	ATTRIBUTE	ATK	DEF	DECK	DESCRIPTION
Peacock	5	Wng-B	Wind	1700	1500	MgRl	
Penguin Knight	3	Aqua	Water	900	800	MgRl	when this card is sent directly from your Deck to the Graveyard by an opponent's card effect, combine your Graveyard cards with your own Deck, shuffle them and form a new Deck
Performance of Sword	6	Ritual War	Earth	1950	1850	MgRl	This monster can only be Ritual Summoned with the Ritual Magic Card, "Commencement Dance".
Petit Angel	3	Fairy	Light	600	900	LoBEWD	
Petit Dragon	2	Drag	Wind	600	700	LoBEWD	
Petit Moth	1	Insct	Earth	300	200	MR	
Polymerization	M	Magic	Norm. Magic			LoBEWD	Fuses 2 or more Fusion-Material monsters to form a new Fused Monster
Pot of Greed	M	Magic	Norm. Magic			LoBEWD	Draw 2 Cards from your deck
Power of Kaishin	M	Magic	Equip Magic			LoBEWD	An Aqua-type monster with this card is +300/300
Prevent Rat	4	Beast	Earth	500	2000	MR	
Princess of Tsurugi	3	War	Wind	900	700	MR	FLIP: Inflicts 500 points direct damage for each Magic and Trap card your opp. has on the field
Protector of the Throne	4	War	Earth	800	1500	MR	
Psychic Kappa	2	Aqua	Water	400	1000	MgRl	
Pumpking the King of Ghosts	6	Zomb	Dark	1800	2000	MR	If "Castle of Dark Illusions" is face up on the field increase this monster by 100/100 on each standby phase. This effect continues until the 4th turn after this card is activated
Punished Eagle	6	W-Bst	Wind	2100	1800	MR	Blue-Winged Crown + Niwatori
Queen Bird	5	Wng-B	Wind	1200	2000	MgRl	
Queen's Double	1	War	Earth	350	300	MR	This monster may attack your opp. LP directly
Rabid Horseman	6	B-War	Earth	2000	1700	MR	Battle Ox + Mystic Horseman
Raigeki	M	Magic	Norm. Magic			LoBEWD	Destroys all your opp. Monsters on the field
Raimei	M	Magic	Norm. Magic			TpS	TP1-009 Decrease your opp. LP by 300
Rainbow Flower	2	Plant	Earth	400	500	MR	This monster may attack your opp. LP directly
Raise Body Heat	M	Magic	Equip Magic			LoBEWD	A Dinosaur-Type monster with this card is +300/300
Ray & Temperature	3	Fairy	Light	1000	1000	LoBEWD	
Reaper of the Cards	5	Fiend	Dark	1380	1930	LoBEWD	FLIP: Destroys 1 Trap card on the field – same rules as "De-Spell" except works on traps only
Red Archery Girl	4	Aqua	Water	1400	1500	MR	
Red Eyes Black Dragon	7	Drag	Dark	2400	2000	LoBEWD	
Red Medicine	M	Magic	Norm. Magic			LoBEWD	Increase your LP by 500 points
Reinforcements	T	Trap	Norm. Trap			SD(k,y)	Increase a selected monsters ATK power by 500 points in the turn this card is activated
Relinquished	1	Castr/Ritual	Dark	0000	0000	MR	Must be summoned by the [Black Illusion Ritual] Magic card.] Gain the attack and defense statistics of 1 of your opponent's monsters. While this monster has an absorbed monster, and a monster attacks it, the damage is also done to the attacking player. You can only use this effect once per turn, and the chosen monster becomes an Equipment card to [Relinquished]. Only 1 Monster can be absorbed at a time. WORDING MAY NOT BE EXACT
Remove Trap	M	Magic	Norm. Magic			LoBEWD	Destroys one face up trap on the field
Reverse Trap	T	Trap	Norm. Trap			SD(k,y)	All increases in ATK and DEF are reversed in the turn this card is activated
Right Arm of Exodia	1	Castr	Dark	200	300	LoBEWD	One of Exodia's arms
Right Leg of Exodia	1	Castr	Dark	200	300	LoBEWD	One of Exodia's legs
Ring of Magnetism	M	Magic	Equip Magic			MR	A monster equipped with this card is –500/500 but all opposing monsters must attack the monster equipped with this card

NAME	LEVEL	TYPE	ATTRIBUTE	ATK	DEF	DECK	DESCRIPTION
Rising Air Current	M	Magic	Field Magic			MgRl	Increases the ATK of all WIND monsters by 500 points and decreases their DEF by 400 points
Roaring Ocean Snake	6	Aqua	Water	2100	1800	MR	Mystic Lamp + Hyosube
Robbin' Goblin	T	Trap	Count. Trap			MR	Each time 1 of your monsters inflicts damage on your opp. LP, 1 card is randomly selected from your opp. Hand and send to the graveyard
Rock Ogre Grotto #1	3	Rock	Earth	800	1200	MR	
Rogue Doll	4	Castr	Light	1600	1000	KSD	
Root Water	3	Fish	Water	900	800	LoBEWD	
Rude Kaiser	5	B-War	Earth	1800	1600	KSD	
Rush Recklessly	M	Magic	Quick Magic			MgRl	Increase 1 monster's ATK by 700 points during the turn this card is activated
Ryu-Kishin	3	Fiend	Dark	1000	500	KSD	
Ryu-Kishin Powered	4	Fiend	Dark	1600	1200	MR	
Ryu-Ran	7	Dragon	Fire	2200	2600	MgRl	
Saggi the Dark Clown	3	Castr	Dark	600	1500	MR	
Salamandra	M	Magic	Equip Magic			DDSp	A Fire monster with this card gains 700 ATK points
Sand Stone	5	Rock	Earth	1300	1600	LoBEWD	
Sanga of the Thunder	7	Thndr	Light	2600	2200	MR	Reduce the ATK of an opp. Monster Atking this card to 0. This effect can only be used once, the card's owner chooses when to activate the effect.
Sangan	3	Fiend	Dark	1000	600	MR	When this card is moved from the Field to the Graveyard, move one monster with an ATK of 1500 or less to your hand. Your deck is then shuffled.
Seiyaryu	7	Drag	Light	2500	2300	DDSp	DDS-004
Senju of the Thousand Hands	4	Fairy	Light	1400	1000	MgRl	When this card is summoned to the field(excluding Special Summon), you may move 1 Ritual Monster Card from your Deck to your hand. The Deck is then shuffled
Serpent Night Dragon	7	Dragon	Dark	2350	2400	MgRl	
Seven Tools of the Bandit	T	Trap	Count. Trap			MR	Pay 1000 LP to negate the activation of a trap and destroy it
Shadow Ghoul	5	Zomb	Dark	1600	1300	MR	Increase the ATK of this monster by 100 points for every monster in your own graveyard
Share the Pain	M	Magic	Norm. Magic			MR	Offer 1 monster on your side of the field as a tribute. Your opp. must offer one monster on their side of the field and offer it as a tribute
Shield & Sword	M	Magic	Norm. Magic			MR	For 1 turn, each face-up monster's original ATK becomes their original DEF and vice-versa. Monsters summoned after this card's activation are excluded
Shining Angel	4	Fairy	Light	1400	800	MgRl	When this card is sent to the graveyard as a result of battle, you may select 1 LIGHT monster with an attack of 1500 or less from your deck and Special Summon it to the field in face-up Attack Position (no Tribute is required for monsters of Level 5 or more). The deck is then shuffled
Shining Friendship	4	Fairy	Light	1300	1100	TpS	TP1-024
Silver Bow and Arrow	M	Magic	Equip Magic			LoBEWD	A Fairy with this card is +300/300
Silver Fang	3	Beast	Earth	1200	800	LoBEWD	
Skull Knight	7	Castr	Dark	2650	2250	MR	Tainted Wisdom + Ancient Brain
Skull Red Bird	4	Wng-B	Wind	1550	1200	LoBEWD	
Skull Servant	1	Zomb	Dark	300	200	LoBEWD	
Slot Machine	7	Mach	Dark	2000	2300	MgRl	
Snake Fang	T	Trap	Norm. Trap			MgRl	Decrease 1 selected monster's DEF by 500 points during the turn this card is activated

NAME	LEVEL	TYPE	ATTRIBUTE	ATK	DEF	DECK	DESCRIPTION
Snatch Steal	M	Magic	Equip Magic			MgRl	Take control of one of your opponent's face-up monsters. Your opponent gains 1000 Life Points during each of his/her standby phases
Sogen	M	Magic	Field Magic			LoBEWD	Increases the ATK and DEF of Beast-Warrior and Warrior type monsters by 200
Solemn Judgment	T	Trap	Count. Trap			MR	Pay half of your LP as a tribute to negate the activation of a Magic, Trap or Summon (including Special Summon) and destroy all cards involved
Sonic Bird	4	Wng-B	Wind	1400	1000	MgRl	When this card is summoned (excluding special summon) you may move 1 Ritual Magic Card from your Deck to your Hand
Sorcerer of the Doomed	4	Castr	Dark	1450	1200	YS	
Soul Exchange	M	Magic	Norm. Magic			YS	Select an opp. monster and use it as a tribute in place of your own. You must skip your battle phase in the turn in which this card is activated
Soul Release	M	Magic	Norm. Magic			MR	Select up to 5 cards from either yours or your opp. graveyard and remove them from the game
Sparks	M	Magic	Norm. Magic			LoBEWD	Inflicts 200 points direct damage to your opp. LP
Spear Cretin	2	Fiend	Dark	500	500	MgRl	FLIP: After this card is flipped, when it is sent to the Graveyard, both you and your opponent select 1 monster from your respective Graveyards and special summon it on the field in face-up Attack Position or face down in Defense Position (no Tribute is required for monsters of Level 5 or more)
Spellbinding Circle	T	Trap	Perm. Trap			MgRl	Select 1 monster. As long this card remains face-up on the field, the selected monster cannot attack or change position except by the effect of a Magic, Trap, or Effect Monster Card. When the selected monster is destroyed, this card is also destroyed. If the selected monster is offered as a Tribute, this card is not destroyed
Spike Seadra	5	Srpnt	Water	1600	1300	LoBEWD	
Spirit of The Harp	4	Fairy	Light	800	2000	LoBEWD	
Star Boy	2	Aqua	Water	550	500	MR	As long as this card is face up on the field, increase the ATK of all water monsters by 500 points and decrease the ATK of all fire monsters by 400 points
Steel Ogre Grotto #1	5	Mach	Earth	1400	1800	LoBEWD	
Steel Scorpion	1	Mach	Earth	250	300	MR	A non-machine type monster atking steel scorpion is destroyed on the end phase of your opp. 3rd turn after the atk
Steel Shell	M	Magic	Equip Magic			TpS	TP1-007 A water monster equipped with this card is +400/0 and −0/200
Stim-Pack	M	Magic	Equip Magic			MR	A monster equipped with this card is +700/0 it then loses 200 ATK points on every Standby Phase afterwards
Stone Ogre Grotto	5	Rock	Earth	1600	1500	MgRl	
Stop Defense	M	Magic	Norm. Magic			LoBEWD	Select 1 of your opp. monsters and switch it to ATK position. If the card is face down, flip it face up. If the monster has a flip effect, it is activated immediately.
Succubus Knight	5	War	Dark	1650	1300	LoBEWD	
Suijin	7	Aqua	Water	2500	2400	MR	Reduce the ATK of an opp. Monster Atking this card to 0. This effect can only be used once, the card's owner chooses when to activate the effect.
Summoned Skull	6	Fiend	Dark	2500	1200	MR	
Swamp Battleguard	5	War	Earth	1800	1500	MR	Raise the ATK of this card by 500 for every face-up Lava Battleguard on your side of the field
Sword of Dark Destruction	M	Magic	Equip Magic			YS	A Dark monster with this card is +400/0 and −0/200

NAME	LEVEL	TYPE	ATTRIBUTE	ATK	DEF	DECK	DESCRIPTION
Sword of Deep-Seated	M	Magic	Equip Magic			MR	A monster with this card is +500/500. When this card is sent to the graveyard, place it on the top of your deck
Swords of Revealing Light	M	Magic	Norm. Magic			LoBEWD	Counting from your opp. turn, none of your opp. monsters can ATK for 3 turns after this card is played. When this card is activated, all face down monsters are flipped face up, but remain in DEF position. Flip effects are immediately activated
Swordstalker	6	War	Dark	2000	1600	KSD	
Tainted Wisdom	3	Fiend	Dark	1250	800	MR	When this card is changed from ATK to DEF position, shuffle your own deck
Terra the Terrible	4	Fiend	Dark	700	1300	LoBEWD	
The 13th Grave	3	Zomb	Dark	1200	900	LoBEWD	
The Bistro Butcher	4	Fiend	Dark	1800	1000	MR	When this card inflicts damage to your opp. LP, your opp. must draw 2 cards from their deck
The Cheerful Coffin	M	Magic	Norm Magic			MR	Discard up to 3 monsters from your hand to the graveyard
The Flute of Summon Dragon	M	Magic	Norm. Magic			KSD	If a Lord of D. is on the field when this card is played, you may special summon 2 dragon-type cards from your hand
The Forceful Sentry	M	Magic	Norm. Magic			MgRI	Look at your opponent's hand, then select 1 card and return it to his/her Deck. The Deck is then shuffled
The Furious Sea King	3	Aqua	Water	800	700	LoBEWD	
The Immortal of Thunder	4	Thndr	Light	1500	1300	MR	FLIP: You gain 3000 LP you lose 5000 LP when it is sent from the Field to the graveyard
The Inexperienced Spy	M	Magic	Norm. Magic			KSD	Select and see 1 card in your opp. hand
The Judgement Hand	3	War	Earth	1400	700	TpS	TP1-026
The Little Swordsman of Aile	3	War	Water	800	1300	MR	Offer one monster on your side of the field as a tribute to increase the ATK power of this monster by 700 until the end of the turn
The Reliable Guardian	M	Magic	Quick Magic			MgRI	Increase 1 monster's DEF by 700 points the turn that this card is activated
The Statue of Easter Island	4	Rock	Earth	1100	1400	TpS	TP1-019
The Stern Mystic	4	Castr	Light	1500	1200	YS	FLIP: All Face down cards are flipped face up and returned to their original positions. No effects are activated when cards are turned face up
The Unhappy Maiden	1	Castr	Light	0	100	MR	When this card is sent to the graveyard as a result of battle, the Battle Phase for that turn ends immediately
The Wicked Worm Beast	3	Beast	Earth	1400	700	KSD	This card is returned to your hand at the end of your turn
Thousand Dragon	7	Drag	Wind	2400	2000	MR	Time Wizard + Baby Dragon
Thunder Dragon	5	Thndr	Light	1600	1500	MR	Discard this card from your hand to add up to 2 Thunder Dragon cards from your deck to your hand. Your deck is then shuffled. This can only be done in your main phase
Tiger Axe	4	B-War	Earth	1300	1100	TpS	TP1-012
Time Wizard	2	Castr	Light	500	400	MR	Flip a coin and call it. If you call it right, your opp. monsters on the field are destroyed. If you call it wrong, all your monsters are destroyed and you lose LP equal to half the total ATK of the destroyed monsters. This card can only be used during your own turn, once per turn
Toll	M	Magic	Cont. Magic			MgRI	As long as this card remains face-up on the field, both you and your opponent must pay 500 Life Points per monster to attack
Tongyo	4	Fish	Water	1350	800	MR	

Card Game - List of Cards

NAME	LEVEL	TYPE	ATTRIBUTE	ATK	DEF	DECK	DESCRIPTION
Toon Mermaid	4	Aqua Toon	Water	1400	1500	MgRl	This card cannot be summoned unless "Toon World" is on the field. This card cannot attack in the same turn that it is summoned. Pay 500 life points each time this monster attacks. When "Toon World" is destroyed, this card is destroyed. If your opponent doesn't control a Toon monster on the field, this card may inflict direct damage to your opponents life points. If a Toon monster is on your opponents side of the field your attacks must target the toon monster
Toon Summoned Skull	6	Fiend Toon	Dark	2500	1200	MgRl	This card cannot be summoned unless "Toon World" is on the field. This card cannot attack in the same turn that it is summoned. Pay 500 life points each time this monster attacks. When "Toon World" is destroyed, this card is destroyed. If your opponent doesn't control a Toon monster on the field, this card may inflict direct damage to your opponents life points. If a Toon monster is on your opponents side of the field your attacks must target the toon monster
Toon World	M	Magic	Cont. Magic			MgRl	This card is activated by paying 1000 of your LP
Trap Hole	T	Trap	Norm. Trap			LoBEWD	If the ATK of a monster summoned by your opponent (excluding special summon) is 1000 points or more, the monster is destroyed
Trap Master	3	War	Earth	500	1100	SD(k,y)	FLIP: Destroys 1 Trap card on the field – same rules as "De-Spell" except works on traps only
Tremendous Fire	M	Magic	Norm Magic			MR	Inflicts 1000 points direct damage to your opp. LP and inflicts 500 points direct damage to your LP
Trent	5	Plant	Earth	1500	1800	MR	
Trial of Hell	4	Fiend	Dark	1300	900	LoBEWD	
Tribute to The Doomed	M	Magic	Norm. Magic			MR	Discard 1 card from your hand to destroy 1 Monster card on the field, regardless of position.
Tri-Horned Dragon	8	Drag	Dark	2850	2350	LoBEWD	
Tripwire Beast	4	Thndr	Earth	1200	1300	LoBEWD	
Turtle Oath	M	Magic	Ritual Magic			MgRl	This card is used to Ritual Summon "Crab Turtle". You must also offer monsters whose total Level Stars equal 8 or more as a tribute from the field or your hand
Turtle Tiger	4	Aqua	Water	1000	1500	LoBEWD	
Twin Long Rods #2	3	Aqua	Water	850	700	MgRl	
Twin-Headed Thunder Dragon	7	Drag	Light	2800	2100	MR	Thunder Dragon + Thunder Dragon
Two-Headed King Rex	4	Dino	Earth	1600	1200		
Two-Mouth Darkruler	3	Drag	Earth	900	700	LoBEWD	
Two-Pronged Attack	T	Trap	Norm. Trap			LoBEWD	Select and destroy two of your monsters and 1 of your opp. monsters
Tyhone	4	Wng-B	Wind	1200	1400	LoBEWD	
Tyhone #2	6	Drag	Fire	1700	1900	MgRl	
UFO Turtle	4	Mach	Fire	1400	1200	MgRl	When this card is sent to the graveyard as a result of battle, you may select 1 FIRE monster with an attack of 1500 or less from your deck and Special Summon it to the field in face-up Attack Position (no Tribute is required for monsters of Level 5 or more). The deck is then shuffled
Ultimate Offering	T	Trap	Perm. Trap			SD(k,y)	At the cost of 500 LP per monster, a player is allowed an extra normal summon or set
Umi	M	Magic	Field Magic			LoBEWD	All Fish, Sea, Serpent, Thunder and Aqua-type monsters are +200/200
Umiiruka	M	Magic	Field Magic			MR	Increases the ATK of all WATER monsters by 500 points and decreases their DEF by 400 points

NAME	LEVEL	TYPE	ATTRIBUTE	ATK	DEF	DECK	DESCRIPTION
Unknown Warrior of Fiend	3	War	Dark	1000	500	KSD	
Upstart Goblin	M	Magic	Norm. Magic			MgRI	Draw 1 card from your Deck. Your opponent gains 1000 Life Points
Uraby	4	Dino	Earth	1500	800	LoBEWD	
Versago the Destroyer	3	Fiend	Dark	1100	900	TpS	TP1-015 You can substitute this card for any 1 Fusion-Material Monster. You cannot substitute for any other Fusion-Material Monster in the current Fusion.
Vile Germs	M	Magic	Equip Magic			LoBEWD	A plant-type monster with this card is +300/300
Violet Crystal	M	Magic	Equip Magic			LoBEWD	A zombie-type monster with this card is +300/300
Waboku	T	Trap	Norm. Trap			YS	Any damage inflicted by an opp. monster is reduced to 0 during the turn this card is activated
Wall of Illusion	4	Fiend	Dark	1000	1850	YS	A monster atking this card is sent back to its owner's hand. Any damage is calculated normally
Wall Shadow	7	War	Dark	1600	3000	MgRI	You cannot normal summon this monster. This card can only be special summoned by offering "Labyrinth Wall" equipped with "Magical Labyrinth" as a tribute No other tribute monsters are necessary
Wasteland	M	Magic	Field Magic			LoBEWD	All Dinosaur, Zombie and Rock type monsters are +200/200
Water Omotics	4	Aqua	Water	1400	1200	MR	
Weather Report	4	Aqua	Water	950	1500	MgRI	FLIP: Destroys all opponents face-up "swords of Revealing Light" on the field. If "Swords of Revealing Light" is destroyed, you can perform your battle phase twice this turn (or your next turn, if activated during opponent's turn)
Whiptail Crow	4	Fiend	Dark	1650	1600	MgRI	
White Hole	T	Trap	Norm. Trap			TpS	TP1-005 If your opp. plays Dark Hole, the monsters on your side of the field are not destroyed
White Magical Hat	3	Castr	Light	1000	700	MR	When this card inflicts damage to your opp. LP, 1 card must be randomly discarded from your opp. hand to the graveyard
Winged Dragon, GOF #1	4	Drag	Wind	1400	1200	MR	
Winged Dragon, GOF #2	4	Wng-B	Wind	1200	1000	TpS	TP1-022
Witch of the Black Forest	4	Castr	Dark	1100	1200	MR	When this card is sent to the graveyard, move 1 monster with a DEF of 1500 or less from your deck to your hand. Your deck is then shuffled
Witch's Apprentice	2	Castr	Dark	550	500	MR	If this card is face up on the field, Dark monsters are +500/0 and Light monsters are -400/0
Witty Phantom	4	Fiend	Dark	1400	1300	LoBEWD	
Wodan the Resident of the Forest	3	War	Earth	900	1200	TpS	TP1-027 Increase this card's ATK points by 100 for every Plant-Type monster that is face-up on the field.
WOW Warrior	4	Fish	Water	1250	900	TpS	TP1-021
Yado Karu	4	Aqua	Water	900	1700	MR	When this card is switched from DEF to ATK position, you may place any number of cards from your hand to the bottom of your deck in any order you wish
Yami	M	Magic	Field Magic			LoBEWD	All Fiend and Spellcaster-type monster become +200/200. All fairy-type monsters become -200/200

A Trip to the Past: Yu-Gi-Oh! Forbidden Memories

— By Nick Moore (a.k.a. NickWhiz1)

In Ancient Egypt there existed a force so powerful, it had to be locked away for a millennia…

Ever wondered what happened in Ancient Egypt? What is this "powerful force?" Why did it have to be locked away? Who exactly is the spirit locked within the Millennium Puzzle? The answers to these and more can be found in Yu-Gi-Oh! Forbidden Memories for the Sony Playstation.

In this game, you are 5,000 years in the past, as a prince of the Egyptian royal family (notice the uncanny

resemblance to Yugi?). Sneaking out of the palace to play a game of Duel Monsters, you meet the ancestors of some familiar faces (such as Joey, Teá, and Seto Kaiba). When a high mage named Heishin attacks the palace with the power of the Millennium Rod, does the young prince have the strength to defeat this adversary?

Review
Play Control: 8/10 Star Chips

There aren't really any negatives to the play control of this game, since there is not really any fast-paced action. You need to be careful with your controls, however, because if you don't, you may make a move that you won't be able to reverse, and one missed move can be all the difference.

Graphics: 7/10 Star Chips

The graphics are very good for this game. The talking scenes have good artwork, and the actual dueling fields are a little plain, but they get the job done. My only gripe is with the 3-D models of the monsters. Some of the monsters, like Blue-Eyes White Dragon and Meteor Black Dragon, are very good, whereas monsters like Twin-Headed Thunder Dragon aren't quite up to par.

Sound: 9/10 Star Chips

The sound is very good for this game. There are different themes for each kind of talking scenes, there are diverse tunes for duels against differ-ent opponents, and the sound effects, when needed, aren't Hanna Barbara sound effects like in the anime.

Plot: 10/10 Star Chips

The plot is very well done here. The ancestors of popular characters fit in with the story line, and the overall sequence of events gives a good rep-resentation of the entire Yu-Gi-Oh! story line. Yes, they changed the modern-day section of the game from the anime/manga, but it makes more sense to the overall story.

Difficulty: 9/10 Star Chips

Not to scare you or anything, but this game has a very steep learning curve. Almost from the beginning, you will be thrown in head first with a relatively weak deck. I would suggest going into the "Free Duel" mode, and playing Duel Master K for a while. He uses the exact same deck as you, and can teach you how to use your deck (even if you lose to it a few times, it's worth it).

Game Play: 8/10 Star Chips

This game accurately represents the basics of the Yu-Gi-Oh! Trading Card Game system, but there are numerous differences:

- All matches are 1 duel only.
- You must have exactly 40 cards in your deck.
- You can only have a maximum of 5 cards in your hand. Believe me, there is no possible way to get more than 5 cards in your hand.
- Your can only play 1 card per turn, whether it is a Magic card, a Trap card, or a Monster card.
- Tributes are not required for Level 5 or higher monsters.
- No monster cards have effects
- All equip cards except Megamorph give a 500 point boost, Megamorph gives 1000
- All field cards give a 500 point boost/decrease
- You may play Fusion cards directly from your hand.

Fusion works differently in this game. Instead of having specific fusion cards and the Polymerization card, you can directly fuse monsters, and you can also fuse Monsters with Magic/Trap cards and Magic/Trap cards with Magic/Trap cards. This allows you to bypass the 1 card per turn rule in a sense, but you will still end up with one more card on the field at the end of your turn.

Your hand automatically replenishes to 5 cards at the beginning of your next turn.

You can only have a maximum of 8000 Life Points.

Many of the more popular cards in the Yu-Gi-Oh! Trading Card game, such as Change of Heart, Monster Reborn, and Pot of Greed are missing from this game. Due to the way the game is played, these cards would be impossible to use anyway.

You always go first. This makes it difficult to deck your opponent, if that is your strategy.

There is a "Guardian Star" feature. Each monster has two possible guardian stars. These stars allow for 500 point increases if your star has an advantage over your opponent's mon-ster's.

Overall: 51/60 Star Chips (85%)

This is definitely one of the better games I have played. It starts out slow and difficult, but once you learn how to play, it becomes a fun and excellent challenge.

Strategies

Unless you have played this game before, I suggest dueling Duel Master K first to get a feel for the game and to learn what fusions you can perform with your deck. Once you get the hang of it, you should be able to at least get a good start.

The Free Duel mode in general is your friend. If you are stuck in a cer-tain part of the game, you can duel the duelists you have already defeated to get stronger cards.

Learn the general fusion patterns. Most fusions can be performed by more than one set of cards.

Early game, try to get a lot of Dragon and Thunder cards. You will easily be able to make the "Twin-Headed Thunder Dragon" (2800/2100) by fusing a Dragon and a Thunder card, if one of them has an attack power of between 1600 and 2800.

Fusions can be performed with

more than 2 cards in succession.

Don't get too frustrated with this game. It helps to keep calm if you are stuck in a difficult situation.

Magic and Trap cards are your friends. You can't win this game with just sheer power.

Save at every opportunity you get. If you lose any duel in Campaign mode (except for the first duel with Heishin), you get a game over, and you will lose all your progress since the last time you saved. You can lose as many times as you want in Free Duel mode, however.

To get S and A-Pow ranks, defeat your opponent with an overwhelming offensive force as quick as possible. You will get stronger Monster cards this way.

To get S and A-Tec ranks, you must try to either deck your opponent or use defensive cards to stall as long as possible. You will get stronger Magic/Trap cards this way.

After you win a duel, you will win anywhere from 1 to 5 star chips, depending on your rank. Save these up, and you can buy cards using the codes on the lower-left corner of real playing cards. You won't be buying really powerful cards, as most of the powerful cards cost 999,999 starchips.

Confused about the Guardian Stars? Here's the weakness circles:

Sun (Light) defeats Moon (Dark) defeats Venus (Fairy) defeats Mercury (Shadow) defeats Sun (Light)

Mars (Fire) defeats Jupiter (Forest) defeats Saturn (Wind) defeats Uranus (Earth) defeats Pluto (Electric) defeats Neptune (Water) defeats Mars (Fire)

Remember, if you have the Guardian Star advantage, you get a 500 point attack/defense increase. Same goes for your opponent.

Some of the more powerful cards in the game, like Blue-Eyes Ultimate Dragon and Gate Guardian, can only be accessed by using ritual Magic cards. To complete the ritual, you must have 3 specific monster cards on the field and then play the Ritual card. Most of the required monster cards are

pretty weak, so you may need cards like Widespread Ruin to stall for time.

Walkthrough

When you get the first opportunity, select "Run away" to run from your "guardian", Simon Muran.

Go to the Dueling Field. You will meet Teana and three villagers. Duel them if you wish.

Leave the Dueling Field. Teana will take you to the Town Square and tell you about Heishin. You will also meet Jono and Seto for the first time. Seto vows to duel you in the near future.

(OPTIONAL) Go back to the palace and duel Simon Muran to get him in the Free Duel grid.

Go to the Dueling Field. You can duel Jono if you want. Seto will be your required opponent. He uses strong cards, but if you've mastered the art of fusion, you shouldn't have a problem.

Return to the palace. Simon Muran sends you to bed.

Heishin invades the palace. Seto tries to help you escape, but he takes you right to Heishin.

After receiving the Millennium Puzzle from Simon Muran, you must duel Heishin. You will be required to lose to proceed.

After the duel, choose to smash the Millennium Puzzle. Your soul will be sealed away in it.

You will wake up with a conversation between Joey and Yugi at the World Championship Tournament. Be prepared for some tourney dueling.

First opponent is Rex Raptor. Nothing to worry about here. He gives Dragons, so you may want to duel him in Free Duel.

Second opponent is Weevil Underwood. He has Jirai Gumo and Cocoon of Evolution, but other than that, he's a pushover.

Mai Valentine is third. I hope you can fuse Twin-Headed Thunder Dragon, because she can pull it out as well.

Bandit Keith is your final preliminary

opponent. He uses hard-hitting Machine monsters like Mechanicalchaser. He may also pull the Twin-Headed Thunder Dragon, as well as Zoa and Metalzoa. It's best to finish him off quickly.

Yugi and Joey meet up with Shadi, who helps Yugi meet the spirit in the Millennium Puzzle (i.e. you). The spirit gives you 6 blank cards, but he doesn't tell you what they are for.

The first opponent for the finals is, ironically, Shadi. He uses weak monster cards, but can make some pretty nasty fusions. If you win, the Millennium Key and Millennium Scales are absorbed into two of your blank cards. You must accumulate all 7 Millennium Items to go back to Ancient Egypt, I guess.

Next is Bakura, who is overtaken by the Millennium Ring to become Yami Bakura. I hope you are prepared for a long, grueling duel, as Bakura uses high defense monsters like Labyrinth Wall and Millennium Shield. Defeating him wins you the Millennium Ring.

The third opponent is Pegasus. He uses a lot of 2000+ attack monsters and Flying monsters. Finish him off quickly. If you give him the chance, he may have the deadly Meteor Black Dragon (3500/2000). Pegasus will relinquish (heh) the Millennium Eye when he loses.

Isis is your fellow semi-finalist. She uses a Umi deck, which is perfect for your Twin-Headed Thunder Dragon. Just watch out for the B. Skull Dragon (3200/2500). She will hand over the Millennium Necklace.

Kaiba is your final opponent. He uses a combination of high defense monsters and the deadly Blue-Eyes White Dragon (3000/2500). If you can outlast him, you will win the Millennium Rod. With all 7 Items, the prince can return to Ancient Egypt.

Simon Muran updates you on the current situation, then dies. You find yourself in a ruined temple.

Go left to the Valley of Kings. You will meet Sadin. When you get the chance, ask him to take you to the Forbidden Tomb. He doesn't know where it is. Figures. Leave the Valley.

Head towards the Metropolis. Go into the Metropolis, and go to the palace. Once in the palace, head to Simon Muran's room. You will have to face the Mage Soldier, the biggest joke duelist in the game. Finish him off effortlessly. Search the room, and you will find a map.

Return to the Valley of Kings. Sadin will take you to the Forbidden Tomb now. Check this place out. You will eventually run into Seto. He will tell you about the high mages guarding the Millennium Items. You must now set off to defeat them.

Go to the Dueling Field. Jono will meet you there. The Dueling Field was destroyed, so he shows you the new place. He and Teana then offer you duels. For now, leave.

Go into the Hiding Card Shop. Save your game here frequently.

Now it's time to face the high mages. There are 5 of them, each representing one kind of field (except for Dark). I would suggest approaching them in the following order: Sea, Desert, Mountain, Forest, and Meadow.

Before you start on the high mages, however, go to the Meadow Shrine. Defeat the lower mage, then leave. I suggest free dueling this guy to get strong cards like Meteor Black Dragon, Skull Knight, and Dark Magician.

High Mage Secmeton is easy to defeat using the Twin-Headed Thunder Dragon (who gets a boost with the Umi field).

High Mage Martis uses very few Desert cards, but uses some strong cards like Zoa and Dark Magician.

High Mage Atenza uses strong Dragon cards like B. Skull Dragon and Twin-Headed Thunder Dragon. If you win a Meteor Black Dragon or two from the low Meadow Mage, you shouldn't have a problem.

High Mage Anubisis uses the Perfectly Ultimate Great Moth (4000/3500 with field boost) and

Javelin Beetle (2950/3050 with field boost). Meteor Black Dragon is your only true chance here.

High Mage Kepura is the most difficult, as he has the Gate Guardian (4250/3900 with field boost). Before this duel, I suggest battling Pegasus and aiming for A or S-Tec rank (use defense until he has very few cards left). You will be able to get some strong Magic and Trap cards, like Widespread Ruin, Megamorph, and Bright Castle. You will need to use these in combination with a Meteor Black Dragon from the low Meadow Mage to stand a chance.

(OPTIONAL) After you have defeated two of the high mages, head back to the Dueling Field. Teana is missing, and you and Jono set off for the Vast Shrine to rescue her. Your first opponent is the Labyrinth Mage. He uses Labyrinth cards, like Gate Guardian, Labyrinth Wall, Wall Shadow, and Labyrinth Tank. To escape from the maze, follow the following order: right, right, left, right. If you mess up, you will face the Labyrinth Mage again, then have to start over. If you reach the end, you will face Seto again. He uses Labyrinth cards, as well as numerous 3000 attack monsters (Metalzoa, Blue-Eyes White Dragon, Black Luster Soldier). If you defeat him, you get Teana back.

After defeating all 5 High Mages, save one last time, then go to the Vast Shrine. Seto will lead you to a hidden entrance to the Dark Shrine.

You will run into two Guardians of the Dark Shrine. The first one you must duel is Guardian Sebek. He relies mostly on his Zoa and Metalzoa. Meteor Black Dragon or a boosted Twin-Headed Thunder Dragon will defeat him, as will Skull Knight.

Guardian Neku is next. Meteor Black Dragon works again here, but use him only in the Mars Guardian Star, because if you change him to Sun, he'll use Skull Knight in Mercury with a field boost to destroy you. Easier than Sebek.

At long last, you get to battle

Heishin again. He uses all the strongest monster cards in the game, as well as Megamorph to pump them up by 1000 points. Finish him off as quickly as possible.

Seto then reveals that his intention was to assemble all 7 Millennium Items at one place. He forces you to the Forbidden Tomb, where he reveals the tomb of an ancient evil that can only be revived with all 7 Items. You will then have to duel him. He uses basically the same deck as Heishin, except he has the most powerful card in the game, the Blue-Eyes Ultimate Dragon (4500/3800). The easiest way to defeat them is to use Widespread Ruin to get rid of them before he attacks with them. Otherwise, pump up a Meteor Black Dragon or any other 3000+ attack power monster, and pray.

Heishin then returns, holding a blade to Seto's throat (I didn't know they could show this in an E-rated game). Your only option is to give him the Millennium Items. He takes them, and summons DarkNite. DarkNite promptly finishes Heishin. He is about to finish you and Seto, but you reveal the cards that had the Millennium Items. He will then force you to duel him. DarkNite is a pushover. He uses very few cards over 3000 attack points. If you defeated Heishin and Seto, you can roll over this guy.

After being defeated, DarkNite will transform into his more powerful alterego, NiteMare. You must duel him one more time. NiteMare uses mostly the same deck as Seto, except he only has 1 Blue-Eyes Ultimate Dragon. Defeat NiteMare and you win the game!

Write down the code that appears before the credits. You can use this code to get a card in the upcoming Yu-Gi-Oh! Duelist of the Roses, the new Playstation 2. ✪

Be Your Own Hotshot Duelist: Oh! Dark Duel Stories

— By Nick Moore (a.k.a. NickWhiz1)

Ever wanted to duel against your favorite characters from the Yu-Gi-Oh! anime and manga? Don't like the modified rules in Forbidden Memories? Well, Yu-Gi-Oh! Dark Duel Stories for the Game Boy Color gives you this chance.

You can duel over 20 different opponents from the anime and manga, import cards from real life using the codes from Yu-Gi-Oh! Trading Card Game cards, and play using a variation of the Expert Rules (the Trading Card Game rules). You can even use the Card Construction system to make your own monsters!

Review
Play Control: 7/10 Star Chips

You have two buttons and the Control Pad. Between these, you have a lot of commands to use. This can get confusing at times. You have to get used to all the controls before you can fully enjoy this game. Honestly, the controls aren't that bad for only having 3 main buttons to use.

Graphics: 6/10 Star Chips

The graphics aren't really all that impressive, but they get the job done. For Game Boy Color, the graphics are pretty good, but they are very plain. The screen's color doesn't even change for each type of field, which would have been a big plus.

Sound: 8/10 Star Chips

For Game Boy Color, this game has very good music. The dueling themes are, for the most part, pleasant to listen to. There aren't many sound effects, for obvious reasons.

Plot: 4/10 Star Chips

There is not much plot here, to be honest. You're a beginning duelist, randomly taking on opponents to win access to the next level. Not too exciting.

Difficulty: 8/10 Star Chips

This game has a very good learning curve, as the early opponents are easy to beat. However, once you get near the end, the difficulty really picks up, as the opponents use 3 Change of Hearts, 3 Megamorphs, 3 Brain Controls, etc.

Game Play: 8/10 Star Chips

This game more accurately represents the basics of the Yu-Gi-Oh! Trading Card Game system than Forbidden Memories, but there are still numerous differences:

- All matches are 1 duel only.

- You must have exactly 40 cards in your deck.

- You can only have a maximum of 5 cards in your hand.

- You can only play one Trap card per turn, and they only last until the end of your opponent's next turn.

- Monster cards have effects, however they must be used while facedown. Using an effect will not allow you to touch that monster for the rest of the turn.

- Most cards have different effects than they do in the Trading Card Game.

- All equip cards give a 500 point boost

- All field cards give a 30% point increase/decrease.

- You may play Fusion cards directly from your hand.

- Fusion works differently in this game. Instead of having specific fusion cards and the Polymerization card, you can directly fuse monsters. You can only fuse a monster from your field with a card from your hand. If you perform a successful fusion, you will be able to play another normal monster card, but your fused monster can't attack.

- You can only have a maximum of 9999 Life Points.

- There is an elemental advantage system, similar to that in Pokémon. Whichever monster has the advantage instantly destroys the other monster. If the winning monster has a lower stat than the opponent's monster, no LP damage is done to either player. Otherwise, damage is dealt the same. Here's the element loop:

Light beats Fiend beats Dreams beats Shadow
Pyro beats Forest beats Wind beats Earth beats Electric beats Aqua beats Fire
Devine has no strengths or weaknesses.

- The Card Construction system allows you to create your own monsters using card parts you win from your opponents.

Overall: 41/60 Star Chips (68%)

You know what? Forget the rating. I still like this game, and you probably will too. Not to mention, you get 3 limited-edition promo cards with each copy of the game, so that's a plus over Forbidden Memories.

Strategies

- Don't forget that, although offense seems like the best way to win the game, defense can win you games too. Use the numerous Level 4 monsters with defense power of 2000 or more to protect yourself while you bring up your heavy hitters (Level 5 and above). Some of them also have useful effects. I'm sad to report that there is no Shield & Sword in this game =(

- You can use the password option at ANY time. The game does not require "star chips" or "points" or anything like that to buy cards.

- Every time you defeat an opponent, you win a card, a card part, 1-2 duelist levels and 5 deck points. The deck points are important because each card has a cost from 0-255, and you can only use that card if you have room in your deck and if you have a duelist level equal to or higher than the cost of the card. The highest duelist level is 255, and the highest deck capacity is 9999.

- The ideal way to build your deck is to build it so you have an advantage over most, if not all duelists. The easiest way to do this is to use a lot of Devine-type monsters. The problem is, all Devine-type monsters cost 255 deck points, so you can't use too many of them. Compensate by using high attack monsters (like Dark Elf and Jirai Gumo) and high defense monsters (like Big Shield Gardna and Cocoon of Evolution).

- The best way to use the Card Construction system is to make 1900+ attack power Level 4 monsters to make your deck superstrong.

- There are restrictions in the game. You can only have one of each of the following cards in your deck:

Right Leg of the Forbidden One, Left Leg of the Forbidden One, Right Arm of the Forbidden One, Left Arm of the Forbidden Arm, Exodia the Forbidden One, Dark Hole, Raigeki, Swords of Revealing Light, Megamorph, Brain Control, Change of Heart, Pot of Greed

- There are lots of little surprises in this game that you should try to discover for yourself. I don't want to ruin ALL of it for you.

Duelists

Level 1:

- From the upper-left, going clockwise, your opponents are Tristan, Joey, Mai, Mako, and Yugi.

- Tristan uses very weak monster cards. You shouldn't have a problem defeating him.

- Joey uses mid-power monster cards. Don't take him lightly, though, because if you give him the chance, he'll pull out the Red-Eyes Black Dragon (2400/2000).

- Mai has probably the strongest monsters in this level. She uses mostly female cards, including the Harpie Ladies.

- Mako uses mostly Aqua-type monsters. Finish them off, or Mako will summon the Devine-type Fortress Whale (2350/2400).

- Yugi uses mid-power monsters, and also uses Dark Magician (2500/2100) and Dark Magician Girl (2000/1700).

Level 2:

- The top row, from the left, are Esper Roba, Rex, and Weevil.

- Esper Roba uses mostly Machine-type monsters, similar to Bandit Keith.

- Rex uses mostly Dinosaur-type monsters (meaning they're mostly Earth).

- Weevil uses Insects, of course. He has some really hard hitters like Insect Queen and Great Moth, so pack plenty of Pyro monsters.

- The bottom row, from the right, are Seeker, Pandora, and Kaiba.

- Seeker uses high Defense monsters and Exodia. Use the hardest hitters you can to finish him.

- Pandora plays similarly to Yugi, focusing on the Dark Magician.

- Kaiba uses some of his cards from the anime, like Ryu-Kishin and Battle Ox. He also has Judge Man and the deadly Blue-Eyes White Dragon. Use Shadow monsters to counter the Blue-Eyes White Dragon.

Level 3:

- From the upper-left, going clockwise, are Paradox (Simon Muran), Priest Seto, Slysheen (Heishin), and Ishizu (Isis)

- Paradox uses mostly Light and Dreams-type monsters.

- Priest Seto uses mostly the same deck as Kaiba, except for a few stronger Magic cards.

- Slysheen uses mostly Dark cards, like Fiends and Shadow monsters.

- Ishizu uses an all-female deck. There aren't many strong female cards, except for Gemini Elf and Cosmo Queen.

Final? Level:

- Your final? opponent is DarkNite. He uses high-level monsters along with some nasty Magics. Finish him off before he can take control of all your monsters and summon his hard-hitters.

More Duelists:

- After you defeat DarkNite, you unlock Yami Yugi as an additional opponent. He uses mostly the same deck as Yugi, but he's a little smarter duelist.

- You can also unlock more duelists, but I'll leave that to you, as I don't want to ruin everything. ◐

ENOUGH TALK! DUEL!!

HOLD ON BONE BAG! WE'VE GOT SOME **3-D FIRST**!!!

Legend of Blue Eyes

Red-Eyes Black Dragon

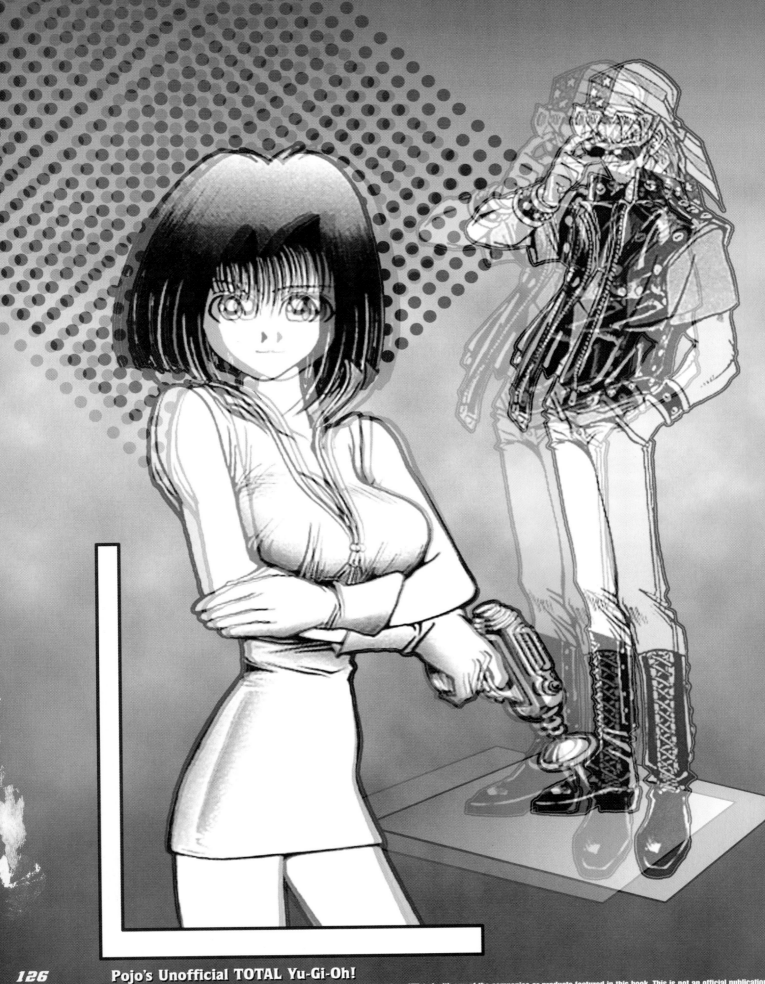